Author Note

I have a secret: Venice wasn't supposed to be Nolan's story. All through the planning of the miniseries, it was supposed to be Brennan's. But when the gentlemen arrived, it didn't work out that way. It didn't take long to see that Venice suited Nolan much better—the parties, the card games and the dark edge that haunts the periphery of *Carnevale*.

For the background to Nolan's story, I read John Ruskin's original journals on Venice from his visit in the 1840s. They are fascinating and eerily predictive of Venice's fate. I also consulted John Julius Norwich's *A History of Venice*, for those of you looking to do some reading on the city.

I was fortunate enough to stop in Venice the summer before writing Nolan's story to reacquaint myself with the beautiful city. Many of you write and tell me you like to "travel" in my stories when you can't get out and travel on your own, so this one's for you. Whether you've been to Venice in person or in your dreams, I hope you enjoy Nolan's Venetian vacation.

Stop by my blog at bronwynswriting.blogspot.com to share your own Venetian vacation stories.

Or visit my web page at bronwynnscott.com.

Bronwyn Scott

Rake Most Likely
to Seduce

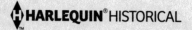

Recycling programs
for this product may
not exist in your area.

ISBN-13: 978-0-373-29866-2

Rake Most Likely to Seduce

HARLEQUIN®
www.Harlequin.com

Printed in U.S.A.

Bronwyn Scott is a communications instructor at Pierce College in the United States, and is the proud mother of three wonderful children (one boy and two girls). When she's not teaching or writing she enjoys playing the piano, traveling—especially to Florence, Italy—and studying history and foreign languages. Readers can stay in touch on Bronwyn's website, bronwynnscott.com, or at her blog, bronwynswriting.blogspot.com. She loves to hear from readers.

Books by Bronwyn Scott

Harlequin Historical
and Harlequin Historical Undone! ebooks

Rakes on Tour

Rake Most Likely to Rebel
Rake Most Likely to Thrill
Rake Most Likely to Seduce

Rakes of the Caribbean

Playing the Rake's Game
Breaking the Rake's Rules
Craving the Rake's Touch (Undone!)

Rakes Who Make Husbands Jealous

Secrets of a Gentleman Escort
London's Most Wanted Rake
An Officer But No Gentleman (Undone!)
A Most Indecent Gentleman (Undone!)

Ladies of Impropriety

A Lady Risks All
A Lady Dares
A Lady Seduces (Undone!)

Castonbury Park

Unbefitting a Lady

Visit the Author Profile page at Harlequin.com for more titles.

Chapter One

The Antwerp Hotel, Dover—March 1835

'You bastard! No one has that kind of luck!' The man across the table from Nolan Gray snarled in disbelief. 'If you lay down another ace, I'll…'

'What? You'll slice me from side to side? Shoot me where I sit?' Nolan Gray flipped the offending card on to the table—another ace indeed—with a nonchalance that suggested threats to his bodily well-being were a common occurrence when it came to cards and late nights.

The man half rose, a menacing hulk looming over the table. He was fully provoked by his evening's losses and Nolan's insouciance. 'When a fellow has the streak you've had, it isn't called luck any more. It's called something else.' He sneered, ready to leap the table for Nolan's throat.

'What *do* you call it?' Nolan leaned back in his chair, refusing to give the man the satisfaction of

standing. He took his opponent's measure through
alert eyes. The man outweighed him by two stone.
A fight wouldn't be fair, but it wouldn't come to that,
either because the man was nothing more than a bully
or because there'd be weapons drawn before fists.
Nolan had seen the type before, he just hadn't bargained on seeing that sort tonight. He should have
known better. This was Dover, not an elegant London gambling club where gentlemen had their codes.

The man growled. 'You know what I call it.' He
waved a hand at the other two men seated with them.
'You know what we all call it.'

Poor choice of allies, Nolan thought. The other
two at the table didn't look as committed to the con-
flict. Then again, they hadn't lost as much. 'No, I'm
afraid I don't. Care to spell it out for me?' Nolan
pushed, wanting to see how far the man would dare
to go. Further than Nolan had thought. He had just a
moment's warning.

The man leapt the table, but Nolan was faster.
A flick of his wrist and the slim handle of a blade
slipped into his hand from the hidden sheath in his
sleeve. He brought the blade up under the man's chin,
using the man's own momentum against him. If he
wanted to avert further trouble, now was the time
for a show of force. The others at the table discreetly
pushed back their chairs, making it clear they wanted
no part of this.

'Are you calling me a cheat?' Nolan asked coolly.
He didn't have time for this. Where was Archer? He'd
been right here a moment ago and goodness knew

Nolan could use some support right about now. Surely Archer hadn't left without him. They were supposed to meet Haviland and Brennan at the dock at an ungodly hour for their boat across the Channel.

It had hardly made sense to go to bed just to get back up, so he'd stayed awake. *All bloody night.* And look what it got him: the local Dover card sharp on the brink of calling him out; a duel his last night in England. Haviland would kill him if he was late and they missed the boat.

The man's chin went up a fraction either in defiance or an attempt to avoid the pricking of Nolan's blade. 'Damn right I'm calling you a cheat.'

'And I'm calling you a poor loser,' Nolan answered with equal vehemence. This wasn't the first time this had happened. Gambling had become tedious over the years: play, win a little, then win obscenely, duel, repeat. He hoped the French with their rumoured reputation for obsessive gambling proved to be better sports than his countrymen when it came to his flair with the cards. 'Shall we settle this like gentlemen somewhere or will you retract your comment?' He had to be at the docks in under an hour. Through the long windows of the hotel, he could see a coach draw up to the kerb—his coach. Perhaps he could squeeze in a duel if he was fast enough. Or maybe he should just make a run for it, although he hated the thought of letting this man get away with calling him names he didn't deserve. He'd counted those cards fair and square. Having a sharp mind was no crime.

They were starting to draw a crowd, even at four

o'clock in the morning. Workers who rose with the city were coming into the hotel for their early morning shifts and deliveries. Wasn't this what he wanted to avoid? Being conspicuous? Scandal had driven him out of London, his father finally appalled by his son's level of notoriety.

Nolan lowered the knife and gave the man a shove, sending him sprawling back over the table. He tossed him a look of disgust, scraping his winnings into his coat pocket. 'You aren't worth it.' The sooner he was out of England, the better, but this was hardly the note he wanted to leave on. At least it was unlikely rumour would get back to his father that his son had been involved in a near duel just moments before his ship left. The Antwerp Hotel was hardly his father's environs.

He'd nearly reached the door when a sixth sense alerted him. The bastard hadn't stayed down, hadn't recognised mercy when it was meted out. Nolan whirled with a shout, blade flashing. He caught the glint of a pistol barrel in the light of the hotel lobby's chandelier not yet doused for the oncoming day. Without hesitation, he let his knife fly, straight into the man's shoulder. The pistol clattered to the ground. The clerk behind the desk gasped in disbelief. 'Mr Gray, this is a decent establishment!'

'He started it!' Nolan retorted. 'He's not hurt too badly.' Nolan had been careful with his aim—too careful. There was no question of retrieving the knife. The man lurched forward, his adrenaline overriding his pain for the moment. Later there would be plenty of that. It was time for a getaway. The clerk would call the watch and there would be questions.

Nolan raced out into the dark courtyard, spotting Archer coming towards him in the darkness from the stables. That was to be expected. Archer loved horses more than humans. 'Archer, old chap! We've got to go!' Nolan seized his arm without stopping and dragged him towards the waiting coach, his words coming fast, well aware his pursuer had stumbled out of the hotel. 'Don't look now, but that angry man behind us thinks I cheated. He has a gun *and* my good knife. It's in his shoulder, but I think he shoots with both—hands, that is. It wouldn't make sense the other way.' Nolan pulled open the coach door and they tumbled in, the coach lurching to a start before the door was even shut.

'Ah! A clean getaway.' Nolan sank back against the seat, a satisfied grin on his face.

'It doesn't always have to be a "getaway". Sometimes we *can* exit a building like normal people.' Archer straightened the cuffs of his coat and gave Nolan a scolding look.

'It was *fairly* normal,' Nolan protested.

'You left a *knife* embedded in a man's shoulder, not exactly the most discreet of departures. You got away in the nick of time.'

Nolan merely grinned, unfazed by the scolding. If he had been discreet, he would have stopped playing two hours ago. The other players could have respectably quit the table, their pride and at least some money intact. 'Speaking of time, do you think Haviland is at the docks yet?' They were scheduled to meet two friends at the boat this morning to begin their Grand Tour. 'I'll wager you five pounds Haviland is there.'

Archer laughed. 'At this hour? He's not there. Everything was loaded last night. There's no reason for him to be early. Besides, he has to drag Brennan's sorry self out of bed. That will slow him down.' He and Haviland had known each other since Eton. Haviland was notoriously prompt, but he wouldn't be early and Brennan was always late.

'Easiest five pounds I'll ever make. I bet he's already there, pacing like a lion, and he's got his fencing case with him. He won't let it out of his sight.' Then, because he couldn't refuse the goad, 'Kind of like my knife.' But Archer hadn't heard. His friend had leaned back and closed his eyes.

Nolan was too alert to doze. He thought about his five pounds. They would indeed be easy winnings, but Archer could afford it. He looked out the window. Haviland was already there, he'd wager more than five pounds on that truth. Archer might be Haviland North's best friend, but Nolan knew *people* and Haviland was a warrior. He wouldn't be parted from his weapons of choice. Besides, Haviland was anxious to be off. Nolan wasn't sure what demons were driving Haviland, but they were driving hard and fast, as odd as the notion was.

To all appearances, Haviland North's life was perfect; he was rich, in line for a choice title and endowed with extraordinary good looks. Haviland had it all. And yet, he couldn't leave England fast enough. He would have been there an hour ago watching them load the carriages even if the trunks had all been stowed last night.

A movement outside the window grabbed his gaze. He squinted and rubbed a circle on the window for a better view. For a moment he thought they'd been followed. Was that his man outside? But, no, this was no man. He nudged Archer with a boot. 'Care to explain why a horse is following us?'

Archer mumbled, 'I sort of rescued him this morning.'

'You abandoned me for a horse? I could have been killed,' Nolan exclaimed.

'And yet it was your knife in his shoulder. You were doing fine on your own,' Archer replied drily, moving his gaze to the window.

The drive to the docks was short despite the foggy dawn, and the horse was still with them, running alongside the carriage. Nolan clambered down from the coach, letting Archer deal with the horse. He sighted a tall, lone figure on the docks and let out a whoop, calling to Archer, 'What did I tell you? There he is. I win! Look at that, he's even got his case with him.'

Haviland strode towards them and Nolan clasped him affectionately on the shoulder. 'Good morning, Old Man. Is everything loaded to your satisfaction? I told Archer you'd be here overseeing.'

Haviland laughed. 'You know me too well, the coaches went on an hour ago.' Nolan was glad Haviland was handling the details. If it had been up to him, he'd simply have packed a trunk, jumped on board a ship and left everything on the other side up to fate. He was far more spontaneous than Haviland and Archer. It was the one gift of having to live an imperfect life. He'd learned early to be one step ahead of the blow so that when it fell, he was miles away.

The other benefit in not having an ideal family life was that he had nothing to live up to, not like Haviland, who was going to inherit the Englishman's perception of Heaven on Earth, or Archer, whose family owned the most successful and expensive stud farm in Newmarket—for fun. Yes, they'd inherit perfection but they'd also have to spend their lives maintaining it for future generations. *That* was a lot of pressure.

He had no such pressure to conform to family tradition. The only perfection he'd inherited was his memory. He could count cards, three to four decks' worth if he had to, and he could calculate odds. *That* inheritance was quite portable. Of course, he'd inherited plenty of imperfections along with it. Those were in no short supply, starting with a puritanical father who firmly believed in beating excellence into his children at all costs and ended with the reality that choice created: his family hadn't seen each other in ten years. As soon as he and his brother had come of age, they'd scattered just as they had in the summers home from school—they'd never actually come home from school. They'd always arranged to spend the summers with friends. School might not have been intellectually edifying to him, but Nolan had found it freeing in other ways. He'd met Haviland, after all, and it had been the saving of him.

Archer was ribbing Haviland about keeping his case with him when Nolan's thoughts re-engaged the conversation. 'I told you that, too. I know these things, I'm a student of human nature.' He laughed.

'Too bad you couldn't study that at Oxford,' Archer joked. 'You might have got better marks.'

Nolan laughed. He and Archer had been sparring for years. They had each other's measure. When he hadn't been spending summers with Haviland, he'd been spending them with Archer. 'What can I say? It's true. You two were the scholars, not me and Brennan.' Nolan looked around, realising the absence of their fourth member. 'Is Brennan here yet?' Time was getting dear.

'No.' Haviland shook his head. 'Did you expect him to be? Scholar of human nature that you are.' He ribbed.

Nolan gave Haviland a playful shove. 'A scholar of human nature, yes, a psychic, no.' He grinned. He was looking forward to this trip more than he realised, the four of them back together again. It would be like old times. Indeed, they saw each other in London during the Season, but it wasn't the same. The four of them were never all together at once. Archer was always in Newmarket these days. It was either he and Brennan or he and Haviland. Even then it was usually just for drinks at the club or a quick greeting at a ball.

All of them were approaching thirty, that most important age for men of their birth, when they were expected to marry and settle down. This trip might very well be their last time together as bachelors unencumbered by the responsibility of wives and children. Haviland would marry—it had already been arranged. Archer would follow. A man who loved breeding horses would surely love to breed his own children. As for Brennan? It would depend on who would have him on a more permanent basis. He was probably with a woman right now.

The captain of the vessel approached and urged them to board, making it clear he would not wait for the rest of their party. Haviland blew out a breath after the captain left, blaming himself for Brennan's tardiness. 'I should have stayed with him.'

Nolan murmured something encouraging. Brennan would be here. He had to be. Brennan was always late, always on the verge of trouble. Not too unlike himself. He was just better prepared for it. Brennan never saw it coming until it was too late. Perhaps that was why he liked Brennan, they were kindred spirits of a sort. They both had messy, imperfect lives. They both lived in the moment. Brennan wasn't a planner and that was certainly working against him this morning. Nolan could imagine him oversleeping in some woman's bed only to wake too late and realise he'd missed the boat.

Waiting was a luxury they couldn't afford. It wasn't an issue of just catching another boat. Channel crossings didn't run on schedules, they ran on the weather. Nolan knew they were lucky their own crossing today was proceeding like clockwork. He opted to keep spirits up. He clapped a hand on Archer's back as the three of them moved towards the boat. 'I'll wager Brennan misses the boat,' he announced with forced joviality. 'Archer, are you in? If I'm wrong, you can win back your losses.' *Please let me be wrong.* He had every hope Brennan would come dashing up at the last minute.

They took up positions at the rail facing the dock. Nolan knew they were all hoping for a glimpse of their errant companion, but time was slipping away. He started at the sound of chains in motion. 'They're pulling the anchor. He's not going to make it,' Nolan said quietly, leaning on his arms. 'Dammit! I didn't want to win that bet.' He exchanged glances with Haviland and Archer as the boat slowly nudged away from the dock. The trip was off to an ominous start.

Then he saw it—commotion on the pier, a figure racing towards them, shirttails flapping. Suddenly, Haviland was shouting, 'It's him, it's Brennan!' And he wasn't alone. Nolan could make out two men behind him, one of them armed as they gave very hearty chase. Whoever they were, they meant business.

Haviland moved first, sprinting towards the back of the boat. Nolan stayed rooted where he was, his eyes focused on something else moving behind the men, something dark and swift. Next to him, Archer made it out first. 'My horse!'

Nolan and Archer thundered down the length of the boat behind Haviland who was waving his arms and shouting commands to Brennan. Impossible commands, really, such as 'jump' and 'don't jump here, it's too wide, jump at the back of the boat where it hasn't left the dock yet. Hurry!'

It was insanity, by the time they reached the stern, even that part of the boat had left a gap between the dock and the deck. Brennan would never make the jump. If Brennan missed... There was no time to contemplate the consequences. 'The horse, Archer, look!' Nolan shouted. The bay had come up alongside Brennan, matching his stride to the running man.

Archer took the idea from there, cupping his hands around his mouth. 'Get on the horse, Bren! Jump him!'

Nolan felt the moment suspend itself in time. He watched Brennan grab the mane and swing himself up bareback. It would be a mad jump even with stirrups and a saddle. But Brennan was an excellent rider, as good as Archer and far more reckless.

The horse leapt.

And landed. On its knees, on the deck.

Time sped up again. He and Archer grappled for the reins, trying to keep the horse calm. Haviland wrestled Brennan off the downed horse. Nolan glanced back at the shore. The two men in pursuit were forced to give up their efforts, having reached the edge of the pier. One of them raised his gun. Nolan hit the deck with Archer and the horse just as Brennan shoved Haviland to the ground. The bullet whined harmlessly overhead, but, dear lord, it had been a near thing. A second or two would have made a tragic difference. If Brennan hadn't pushed Haviland down...

Nolan's eyes narrowed in speculation. Deuce take it! Brennan had suspected they would fire. What kind of trouble had he got himself into this time? Haviland was already asking those questions as the group picked themselves up from the deck and brushed off their clothes. Archer marched the horse off to temporary stabling and Brennan was all smiles as he tucked in his shirttails despite Haviland's scolding. Definitely a woman, then. It was usually a woman with Brennan.

Clothing settled and greetings exchanged, Nolan drawled his question. 'So the real issue isn't where you've been, but was she worth it?'

Brennan's blue eyes were merry, his face splitting into a wide, satisfied grin as the wind ruffled his auburn hair. He laughed up at the sky and Nolan knew the answer before he even said it. 'Always, Nol, always.'

Nolan grinned, too. The crisis was past. The future lay spread out before them. It would be a while before he saw England again and that was fine with him. Deep down, he wondered if he'd ever see it again and was not surprised to discover he wouldn't mind if he didn't. Grand Tours took years and all he had was time.

Chapter Two

Venice, Italy—winter 1836

All gamblers are alike in luck. They know the exhilaration of dice rattling in boxes, the adrenaline fuelled by hot tables, the decadent thrill of hinging everything on the turn of a card and when that card favours them, they know a surge of elation so great they become immortal gods in the moment of victory. But no two gamblers are alike in their fall. From the moment the cards desert them, to the moment they should have walked away and didn't, gamblers are always unlucky alone.

Nolan Gray knew when a man was broke and Count Agostino Minotti was *very* close. Surrounded by the opulence of Palazzo Calergi where every whim was anticipated by the serving staff, where no one should have any worries, Count Agostino had worries aplenty. The signs were there in the desperate sweat on his brow, in the sharpness of his eyes as his brain rapidly inventoried his assets, searching for anything left worth bartering to cover the latest hand—the one in which he was sure his luck would turn.

Nolan knew it wouldn't. His own hand was too good, and if there was such a thing as luck, it favoured the intelligent. Surely, the count had to know the odds of drawing the queen of spades were nearly non-existent. The count would never complete his straight. He'd been rather obviously collecting high-end spades this hand and everyone at the table knew it. Nolan didn't suffer fools who couldn't count cards nor did he have much sympathy for men who overplayed their funds. The count should have walked away an hour ago. Nolan only hoped the man would be able to cover tonight's commitments. He had plans for that money.

The count pushed the rest of his money to the centre of the table, not nearly enough to cover the bet. What else would the count offer? The count's next words took Nolan alternately by surprise and then disgust. 'Two hundred lire and my daughter's maidenhead.'

That was certainly different than the items wagered at English tables. But it made the man no less of a bastard to offer it. The principle of the matter dug sharp claws into Nolan's sense of fair play. A gambler could risk anything he or she liked as long as it was theirs. But to risk what belonged singularly to another, to someone who was not directly involved in the play at the table and who had no say in the decision was beyond the pale of acceptability.

A quick glance around the table indicated he was the only one who apparently held any such scruples. There was a certain irony in that considering how jaded his palate had become over the years. He'd wagered and won numerous non-traditional items of interest in his career. But never a woman who hadn't first offered herself as barter. Even then, that particular woman had wanted to lose. To him. On purpose. This was entirely different, and Nolan wasn't sure he liked it.

The man to his left was greedily reassessing his hand. The man to his right made a crass comment about the girl in question and his own prowess that was better reserved for a cheap whorehouse than Palazzo Calergi's elegant interiors. The others at the table laughed and threw out their own crudities, each one worse than its predecessor. Nolan felt his temper rise on behalf of the unseen girl. He counselled himself with quiet caution. He did not need to get sucked into this. Logic reminded him there was much he didn't know about the situation. Logic also reminded him he was still the richest man at the table tonight and the one with the best hand. They were all playing against him. He was in charge. He would be the one to decide the girl's fate; take her away from this with him or leave her to one of the others unless he could head this disaster off.

His first line of attack was to dissuade the count, perhaps even to rouse some dissent on behalf of the girl once these men saw sense. 'Five thousand lire? That seems a bit expensive.' The table didn't seem to think so. These were born Venetians and this was Venice at Carnevale where virginity was a most elusive commodity. A city didn't acquire a reputation for having the most accommodating courtesans in Europe by hoarding virgins. The economics of supply and demand made the price believable. So did the count's desperation. Almost. This was a man who had been desperate before.

'What insurance do we have that she's actually a virgin? How do we know you haven't offered her before?' Nolan jested lightly, pushing his case as he watched the table, his body tensed for action should his comment meet with offence. The count was a desperate man and a reckless one if he was willing to sell his daughter to cover a bet. Assuming the woman in question *was* his daughter. The count didn't particularly impress Nolan as a fatherly figure for obvious reasons. Still, he wouldn't be the first man alive to be poorly suited for the occupation. Nolan's own father would rival him there.

Minotti's eyes narrowed dangerously. 'Are you saying my daughter is a whore?'

'Is she?' Nolan leaned back in his chair, the nonchalance belying the tension coiled within him. If Minotti came at him, he would be ready. He could feel the comforting press of his new blade inside the sleeve of his coat. It could be in his hand in under a second.

Minotti's eyes slid to the left, towards the long windows overlooking the Grand Canal, his voice smug with triumph. 'Judge for yourself. She's the one in pale blue, my Gianna.'

Nolan would have known her without the description. She was the one who looked out of place despite the blatant wealth exhibited in the expensive pearl-encrusted blue-damask gown. Good lord, the gown must weigh fifteen pounds on its own, adorning the *palazzo* as if it were an art piece designed for the room. Still, the richness of her costume couldn't disguise the fact that she didn't belong here. Palazzo Calergi might be a regal setting and this might be a private party for a few hundred of its owners' personal friends and their guests, but it was still a party in the middle of Carnevale, hardly the sort of venue one took a daughter to. Her head turned towards the table as if she sensed she'd become the topic of conversation, her eyes landing on Nolan. On second thought, five thousand might be a generous bargain indeed, virgin or not.

The girl was stunning in her own right once one got past the dress. Certainly not in the way the other women in the room were stunning with their cosmetics, low-cut silks, and elaborate *coiffures*, the products of hours and artifice. Her beauty was natural, clean, somehow apart from the cosmopolitan elegance surrounding her and yet her beauty was not the lesser for what could only be described as its plainness. It was her skin that did it; a smooth, pink-tinged alabaster and as translucent, framed by hair so dark it appeared black at this distance.

Her eyes might have helped the cause, too. He could not tell the colour from this distance, but it hardly mattered. Her eyes were shrewd and sharp as they held his; challenging, thinking. Nolan had the uncomfortable sensation he was being assessed. Did she feel the same with the eyes of the table riveted on her? Did she know her father had put her up for auction to the winning hand? If she didn't know, her fate would come as shock. If she did, however...

Cynicism flashed. Had father and daughter done this before? Was this some sort of scam they ran whenever the count was down on his luck? The whole offer smelled of trouble. Nolan's eyes dropped back to the cards in his hand. The tiny voice of caution that usually kept quiet in his head was barking loudly now, joined by a strong sense of self-preservation. He should throw the hand and win the money elsewhere.

This money came with strings—more precisely, it came with a virgin. That was the very last thing he needed. What would he ever do with a virgin? He certainly wasn't going to bed a woman against her will. Nolan's eyes went to the pile in the centre of the table. But the money was a temptation nonpareil. Only noblemen wagered sums like these. This would take several nights to acquire at lesser venues. It would be a shame to waste this rather golden opportunity. Tonight would put him at his goal. His hopes were within reach. One virgin wasn't going to stand in his way. Across the table, the count raised his hand and beckoned for the girl.

* * *

Gianna saw the summons, aware that the count and his table had been watching her. Worry pooled in her anxious pit of a stomach. What hell had he concocted for her now? Hadn't the hell he'd presented her with this afternoon been enough to satisfy his jaded palate? Dante's *Inferno* had nothing on Count Minotti when it came to exacting revenge or getting what he wanted.

She smoothed her hands over her elaborate skirts in a calming repetition of strokes and repeated her silent mantra: *the count would not stand in her way. She would not allow him to.* Whatever he did, she would be equal to the task. She would outthink him, outmanoeuvre him as she always had. She'd done it for five years. She could do it for four more weeks. *He cannot hurt you. He would not dare. The money will protect you.* But the usual comfort the words gave her was absent tonight. Her freedom was within reach, just a month away after years living under his so-called protection.

At the table, the count took her arm and she pulled away, not tolerating his touch. 'Still upset by this afternoon, my pet?' The count's tone was wry as if this afternoon had been a minor concern, a mere game. But it hadn't been, not to her and not to him. But she would not suffer him to touch her again.

'What have you done?' She kept her tones low, her eyes fixed on the count. The men at the table were eyeing her with something nearing avarice. Gianna's anxiety was rising steadily, although she dare not show it. The count would like to see her fear, like to know he had power over her.

The count gave a shrug of his shoulders as if to indicate it was nothing of significance. 'I am having a bit of bad luck tonight, I'm afraid. But that's about to change. I have a good hand. I am sure to win.'

Gianna knew where the conversation was going. It was a distasteful one, but one she could handle. She reached up to pull off the pearl earrings that had once belonged to her mother. The count had ordered her to wear them tonight. He'd probably planned on forcing her to surrender them. He knew how she treasured them. She had resisted giving them to him once. It had been a mistake. It had shown the count they had emotional value to her. She'd quickly learned not to make that mistake twice.

The count gave a slight shake of his dark head. Gianna's jaw tightened and her hands went to the clasp of her pearl choker. They were just things, she told herself. *Placate him, give him what he wants. These are nothing in the scope of the greater picture.* After their quarrel this afternoon, his demand could have been worse. She would be thankful for this small mercy. She only wanted to be done with him. She would do whatever it took to make it through the next four weeks. She would be twenty-two, old enough to claim her inheritance without him. Whatever her mother had seen in the man during her lifetime, Gianna could only guess.

The count shook his head again and Gianna froze. 'You are very generous, but I'm afraid your pearls won't be enough.' His mouth turned up in a cruel smile. 'Not those pearls anyway. There is one pearl these gentlemen seem to value, however.' He paused. 'I have wagered *you*, Gianna. More specifically, the pearl between your legs.'

Panic swamped her. He repeated himself, no doubt enjoying the perverse pleasure of saying the crude words out loud. On the surface, it was an appalling wager. Beneath that surface it was truly horrific in a way only the count would recognise. 'Does my mother mean so little to you that you would make her daughter a whore?'

'Your mother is dead. She holds no sway here,' he countered, his words bloodless. 'I offered you better this afternoon and you refused. You did this to yourself.'

Stay calm. Under no circumstances show him any emotion. She understood the men's stares now. They were undressing her, imagining what they would do with her, to her, all except one whose gaze was on the count. Her stomach turned. The grip on her 'calm' was slipping. It was a Herculean task to maintain her reserve. She wanted to grab up the carefully blown glass goblets on the table and smash them against the silk-clad walls, to rage out loud against the count's latest barbarism. She would show these men nothing, certainly not the count who thought he could pass her about, *wager* her as if she was nothing more than a bauble of mediocre value; as if he could wreck her plans with the turn of a card, as if she had no say in the matter. That last was a sticking point. Legally, she had no say, not until she turned twenty-two.

'This is revenge,' she accused, anger coursing through her, volcanic and explosive. If she was a man, she'd kill him. But if she were a man this would not have happened. She would have left the count years ago. 'You are blackmailing me.'

'This, my dear, is what happens when you leave me no choice,' the count hissed.

'Your offer was to marry the morally corrupt Romano Lippi, or to marry you,' Gianna spat. 'It was hardly a choice since either option turns a substantial portion of my inheritance over to you.' She knew a moment's triumph at the dark look stealing over his face. 'I'm not stupid. I know exactly what you and Lippi had arranged. The two of you decided to split the inheritance.'

'I must have something, Gianna. I'll have my five thousand pounds with or without you. I'm broke and you are all I have left. Don't worry. I will win and you can rethink your position on today's negotiations. This is nothing. You're only being wagered in theory.'

The count took his seat with a wide smile and a relaxed bonhomie at odds with their terse conversation. She was trapped. She would run if she could, but aside from the fact she had nowhere to run, she simply couldn't. The dratted dress was far too heavy for anything but a sedate walk. So Gianna stood, she waited, she watched and tried not to panic.

The count leaned forward, his face flushed with the fever of the wager and the surety that he couldn't possibly lose. 'All right, gentlemen, let's see your cards.' Gianna stilled. This was it, the moment of truth.

Chapter Three

Nolan knew the truth before the cards were laid down. The count's hand was good, good enough to understand why he'd had hope of winning. But the count, like many amateur gamblers, lacked the ability to see beyond his own hand. Nolan knew not only what he, himself, held, but what others at the table held as well. The count had not yet learned that a hand was 'good' only by comparison.

Nolan lay down his hand. There were a few humorous moans from the other players who hadn't bet more than they could afford to lose with some *élan*. But the count went pale. He'd lost everything, even his daughter. Ostensibly. Nolan still didn't quite believe she was his daughter or even a virgin, although the paleness of the count's face was starting to make it believable. Or perhaps it was only loser's remorse, the crash that came after the high of an extraordinary wager before it had gone bust. The girl beside him showed no reaction beyond the movement of her eyes locking on his, a sharp, hazel-green gaze.

In that moment he knew he'd been wrong. She was not a girl. This was a woman. It was hard to be sure of her age, of her experience. Certainly, she was not a first-Season débutante, but neither could she be more than a year or two over twenty. There were flashes of youth in her at odds with the shrewdness he'd seen in her gaze, but she was a woman. Girlhood had been left behind years ago. The question surfaced again: had she done this before? He could usually read people well, but she was blank to him.

'Perhaps another hand, Signor Gray?' The count's voice couldn't disguise the tremor. Nolan had expected it, the gambler's recourse; a second hand, a second try, anything to erase the sting of defeat.

'Do you have another daughter to lose?' Nolan queried in wry tones. He gave the man a rueful smile in the silence as he rose. The table had become deadly quiet. He needed to make a quick exit for everyone's sake. 'I didn't think so. You have nothing left to wager.' Nolan extended his hand to the daughter, her face still a blank canvas devoid of any emotion even as her fate clarified itself. There would be no quarter given to the count. He would be held to his brash wager. If she was frightened, angry, embarrassed or any of the thousand emotions one might feel after having been sold into a bargain not of their making, those emotions didn't show. But Nolan was not dense enough to assume those emotions didn't exist beneath her calm surface. Calm surfaces harboured all variety of dangers in his experience.

'*Signorina*, it seems we are to leave together.' Nolan took her arm. He would treat her respectfully until she gave him a reason not to. He did not envy her the situation. If she was innocent of all this, she must be in shock. If she was a knowing accomplice, she would be the one to directly endure the brunt of his anger when her duplicity was found out.

Nolan nodded once to the count. When he spoke, his words were for Minotti, but his manners were for her in the hopes of assuring her all would be well. '*Buonanotte*, your night ends here, I think, Minotti. Better luck another day. I shall return her to you.' It was generous of him. Returning had not explicitly been part of the arrangement. Neither had *not* returning her. The parameters of this arrangement were somewhat nebulous in regards to their permanence. Nolan wondered which choice offered her the better chance. Would going back to the count only lead to more of this? The idea of her staying with him was impossible, not part of his plans. Nolan could only imagine what Brennan would say—when he stopped laughing.

This was no laughing matter. Panic receded in the wake of her anger. She had been sold to a foreigner and now she was being carted off like chattel. Not literally, of course. She'd not been slung across his rather broad shoulders, but even the touch of his hand at her back, guiding her through the crush of the ballroom, was too much for her roiling temper. She stepped beyond his reach, her words cold and demanding. 'Take your hand off me. I am not your property.'

The Englishman chuckled, not the least put off by her cold tone, his voice was low and easy at her ear as he claimed her elbow, his arrogance unequalled. 'My four aces beg to differ with your assessment.'

'You don't own me.' Her words were vehement, but they were only words. There was no substance behind them and they both knew it. At the moment, she had nowhere to run, nowhere to go except with him. She needed a plan. She needed a way to see the silver lining. How could she turn this tragedy into an opportunity? If she could push past the panic that had consumed her at the table; the anger and disbelief that consumed her now, she could find a solution. But the Englishman's arrogant words made it difficult.

'Again, I must beg to differ. You're as much my property as five thousand lire, Signor Bellosi's gold watch and four diamond stickpins. The only difference is that you're not as useful. I can't convert you to cash.'

That did it. If there had been any lingering vestiges of shock, he'd effectively exorcised them. She would not be the pawn of any man again, not the count and certainly not this Englishman who acted as if this were a grand lark. At the bottom of the *palazzo*'s steep steps, gondolas bobbed on the waters of the canal. The Englishman handed her in and waited patiently for her to sit and arrange her art piece of a dress before joining her on the plush velvet seat. He had manners aplenty, even if he was arrogant, and that was something at least. She would take what she could get. It was starting to sink in just how much danger she was really in. If the money hadn't protected her, nothing would.

He called out directions to the gondolier. 'Hotel Danieli, *per favore*.' Gianna smiled to herself. He had good manners *and* good taste, part of his arrogance, she supposed. He was a man who liked the best and perhaps therein lay his flaw. A proud man was blind to his weaknesses. She would exploit them if she had to, as long as he let her stay.

It was the hotel that clinched her decision, that showed her the silver lining. Staying was the key. The count had attempted to frighten her into compliance tonight, but he'd made a grave mistake. When he'd lost his hand, he'd inadvertently set her free. For a few days or for as long as the Englishman was willing to keep her, she was beyond the count's control. Gianna didn't fool herself into believing it would be easy. If, after a few days, she didn't return, the count would come looking for her. She would have to act fast.

She couldn't go back, not after tonight. Gianna shuddered to think of what going back would entail. The count would be cruel, crueller than he'd ever been. If he was willing to sell her virginity in a card game, there was no telling what he'd do next in order to get what he wanted. His home was no longer safe for her, if it had ever been.

Safe was a relative term in this case. If it was

only herself to consider, she'd leave the city, but she couldn't leave the city, not yet. There were things she needed to retrieve from the count's home, she needed Giovanni and she needed her money. Otherwise there would be no way to support the two of them. Until those items were assured, she needed somewhere to live. She also needed a protector or at least the illusion of one.

Her mind began to work, a plan started to form, beginning with the premise that she'd catch more flies with sugar than vinegar. Perhaps the Englishman would play the role of protector for her if given the correct incentive. To do that, though, she'd have to change her current tack immediately. Everything hinged on the Englishman letting her stay beyond the night.

That conjured a host of other thoughts regarding what she might be required to do in order for her persuasion to be successful. Certainly, the Englishman was expecting to claim that which he'd won. A shiver took her. In her anger, her disbelief and panic over her plans being shredded, it had been easy to shove aside the more practical implication of what the wager involved: sex. With a stranger. With this man who sat beside her, a man about whom she knew nothing except his accommodations and that his manners, while nicely turned, bordered on arrogant. But perhaps she'd find a way to avoid that, too.

'The Hotel Danieli is the finest in the city...' she began, trying to make the stranger less strange. Perhaps if they talked, she could build some rapport. 'It used to be a private *palazzo*.' Gianna shivered again, this time from the breeze off the canal. She regretted not having had the Englishman stop for her cloak. Then again, if she had her cloak, she wouldn't have an excuse for what she did next.

'Are you cold?' He shifted in his seat, but before he could shrug out of his coat and play the gentleman, she inched close until there was no space between them on the seat and pressed against him.

'Just a little, I left my cloak behind. Would you mind if I...?' She put her hand in the pocket of his evening coat, letting her words trail off in a delicate fade. She tossed him a smile. 'Thank you, that's better, *much* better.'

It was also much more 'friendly'. The outside pocket of his evening coat proved to be a very intimate location indeed when one was seated. Her hand rested mere inches from a very private part of him that seemed compelled to stir at the proximity of her fingers. In a sense that was good. She wanted him attracted to her. But it was also a reminder of what might be surrendered in order to secure the larger goal.

They rode in silence after that, the Englishman not inclined towards conversation. The night spoke around them in the passing songs of the gondoliers and the laughter of revellers on the canals until the gondola bumped against the pier. The gondolier called out, 'Hotel Danieli, *signor*.'

The Englishman extracted her hand from his pocket rather reluctantly, and stepped out of the barque. He passed some coins to the boatman, his words catching her entirely by surprise. 'Take the lady wherever she'd like.'

Here! She wanted to be taken here, Gianna fought the urge to cry out. Surely he didn't mean to leave her? Is this what he'd been thinking in the gondola? How to get rid of her? In all of her imaginings it had never occurred to her that he might find the arrangement as distasteful as she did. He was a man, after all, and men were all alike, her mama had taught her. Men were governed by sex.

She'd tried to make herself agreeable. She'd made conversation, to which he hadn't responded. She'd put her hand in his pocket, to which he *had* responded. Sweet heaven, she'd almost touched his cock! He was not getting away this easy, not when she'd decided she had plans for him. Gianna bolted into action with a sharp cry. '*Aspetta!* Stop!' She climbed clumsily to her feet, her hasty efforts hampered by her heavy skirts. She stumbled and got back up, the gondola rocking. She should have stilled and waited for the boat to settle but her mind was fixated on the Englishman. Her plans were not going to be wrecked by two men in one night. He couldn't set her free. She had plans—admittedly, they were hastily concocted ones built in the silence of the boat ride, but plans none the less, to replace the ones the count had destroyed.

The Englishman stepped forward, holding up his hands in a placating gesture. '*Signorina*, I think you misunderstand. I am giving you your freedom. This is where you and I part ways.' He said it as if ending their association was a good thing. They were *not* parting ways, not until she decided it.

Gianna faced him, hands on hips, trying to look dignified in a dangerously rocking boat. She pushed back a strand of hair and tilted her chin in defiance, struggling to maintain her balance. 'No, *signor*, you misunderstand. This is the part where I—'

Stay.

The word never left her mouth. The gondolier gave a warning yelp and leapt for the pier. Gianna surged forward to the dock, hoping to escape the inevitable, but she was too slow. The boat tipped. She hit the water.

'Gianna!' The Englishman's voice was the last sound she heard before she went under.

Two sensations hit her simultaneously: the water was dark. No lantern light reached the depths— someone could fall in and simply disappear without being seen even if their fall had been noted. Second was that it was cold, so very cold. Gianna tried to push to the surface, arms and legs working to propel her upwards, but she had little momentum with nothing for her legs to push off from and an enormous amount of drag from her skirts. She needed more strength than she possessed.

She had no intentions of simply giving up. It would suit the count too well if she died. Everything she had would be his. He wouldn't have to wait out the next four weeks. It would certainly suit the Englishman who had been so eager to send her away. No one would care except Giovanni. Giovanni was counting on her. But her air was failing, her strength was failing. What would happen to Giovanni?

There was a splash in the water beside her, a hand about her waist, another arm pushing upwards with her now. She lent her own meagre efforts, hurrying them upwards out of the murk. Haste was important now. Spots danced behind the lids of her eyes. If she lost consciousness, her dead weight would drag them both down. The surface at last! Her head broke the water and she dragged in a great breath, the Englishman beside her, his voice filling the night with directions.

'We're over here! I've got her. Get her up! Someone bring a blanket.' It took two of them; the Englishman inelegantly pushing her up from behind, his hands on her bum, and the gondolier tugging her by the armpits to the pier. Task accomplished, the Englishman braced his hands on the dock and levered himself up with enviable, easy strength. He took the offered blanket and threw it about her shoulders. 'Let's get you inside.'

Gianna was shivering, unable to do anything but let him guide her into the opulent lobby of Hotel Danieli, his arm around her, holding her close to his side. She caught sight of herself in one of the long Venetian mirrors and groaned. She looked exactly like what she was—a soaking wet woman who'd just fallen into the canal. The Englishman, however, managed to look like a prince, all dripping six feet of him. Even wet and dressed in ruined clothing and barefoot. '*You* took time to remove your boots,' she accused testily. She'd

been panicking underwater, facing certain death, and
he'd taken time to pull off his boots.

The Englishman laughed, a warm, light chuckle.
She had the sensation again that everything was a
lark, even death. 'I assumed you didn't want us to
both drown? Your dress weighed enough without con-
tending with my boots.' He put his mouth close to her
ear the way he had in the ballroom. 'There's a reason,
Gianna, people swim naked.'

Her cold body went hot at the words, the sound of
her name on his lips, the tickle of his breath at her ear.
It was a most inappropriate comment made at a most
inappropriate time in a most inappropriate place. Not
surprising considering how the evening had gone. It
fit perfectly with everything else that had occurred:
she'd been wagered *and* lost in a card game by the
one man her mother had trusted to look out for her,
her plans for freedom from the count were now entirely undermined and her fate was in the hands of a
stranger. What else could go wrong? What else *was*
there to go wrong?

Chapter Four

The room was sumptuous. Perhaps it was safe to assume that the worst had happened. Perhaps her luck was starting to change. His rooms were of the finest quality: furniture upholstered in silk, long curtains with luxurious folds draped the windows like a woman's ball gown where the rooms looked out over the canal. From here, there was a view of the chamber beyond with its enormous bed strewn with pillows. Even at a distance, that room exuded decadence, a not-so-subtle reminder that what had started this night might still very well finish it. Sex was a powerful weapon when used correctly. Gianna hoped she knew enough to wield it. She shivered and drew the blanket tighter around her.

'Let's get you into a bath. Come with me.' He led her into the bedroom and through a door into the most incredible room she'd ever seen, a room entirely given over to the function of bathing. There was a porcelain tub rooted to the floor. He bent over the handles and turned them, water flowed. Steam rose.

'Oh.' She gasped. She'd heard of such features before, but they were non-existent at the count's house. This was positively divine. The Englishman moved about, laying out plush white towels and a thick bar of milled soap, so intricately carved she almost didn't want to use it and destroy its perfection.

His hands were at the back of her gown before she realised it. 'Let's get you out of this. What a mess.'

There was no sense protesting. She couldn't possibly take it off by herself. Gianna let his fingers work the long row of tiny pearl buttons at her back. His touch was swift, professional and yet beneath that layer of competence, there was a sensually compelling undertone that suggested his hands would feel good on her skin. Surely that boded well for the next level of her plan?

'It took my maid twenty minutes to do up the buttons. *You've* done this before.' Gianna tried for levity, anything to keep her mind off the fact that she was alone in a hotel room with a man she didn't know *and* she was there for the express purpose of being bedded by him. Never mind he'd tried to let her go. She'd refused. He would think that refusal was an acceptance of another sort…

He laughed, finishing the last of the buttons low on her spine. 'Let's just say you aren't the first woman I've undressed, wet or otherwise.'

She supposed she'd deserved that with her leading question. The gown fell open. She could feel his gaze on her back, a sensation that was provocatively possessive and not without its own thrill. 'Stand still,' he murmured at her ear. 'I'll have to use my knife.'

His knife? That galvanised her into action. Gianna spun away from him, clutching her dress to her, her eyes rapidly scanning the room for a possible weapon, all sense of flirting, of wanting to lure him with sugar evaporating in the wake of self-preservation. 'There is no need for knives, I assure you.' She tried her best calming tones, the tones she used to reason with the count when he was irrational—which was nearly always. Surely she could handle one Englishman.

Gianna snatched up a ewer, brandishing it in self-defence as she edged towards the door. A knife flashed in his hand from some secret place on his person and she knew she was right to have gone on the defensive. Good lord, he'd been armed all along! What sort of man carried a weapon to a party? She'd traded drowning in the canal for being stabbed by a madman in hotel room, who was *laughing*.

The Englishman held out his arms in a gesture of peace, apparently having found great humour in the situation. 'Put down the ewer, Gianna. The knife is for the laces. They're in knots. I'm afraid there's no saving them. Now, turn around and let me at them. Your bath is ready and you're shaking.'

Hot embarrassment crept up her cheeks. She'd completely overreacted. But what else was she to think? It was easier to turn around than to let him see her blush. She'd let herself look foolish. 'You find this funny?' she scolded. She felt the slice of a sure blade through the sodden laces of her corset, felt the tight garment slide away, felt her body breathe, set free.

His hands closed over the caps of her shoulders, warm and firm against her chilled skin. 'I think it's funny that you believe I would go to all the trouble of dragging you out of the canal just to stab you a half hour later in my room.' His fingers flexed gently against her skin, his mouth close to her ear. 'What holds no humour for me is why a beautiful woman would have reason to think a man would do that.'

His body was just inches from hers. She could feel the heat of him through his wet clothes, feel the strength of him—it was there in the low rumble of his words, in the remembrance of the arm that had brought her to the water's surface. This was a very different man than the count. She'd known it at the *palazzo*, but had not fully understood what it meant until now.

Where the count thrived on cruelty and force, this man did not. However, that mere discrepancy did not make him a saint. She had to be careful not to ascribe heroic attributes to him just because he'd dragged her out of the canal and hadn't ravished her *yet*. He was still a gambler and he was a still a rogue—a rogue who was growing more appealing by the moment.

A shiver of a different sort swept through Gianna. She knew danger when she encountered it and it was standing right behind her. It wasn't the knife in his hand that made him dangerous, it was his manners, his temptations.

He stepped back, releasing her. 'Take your bath.'

Gianna turned to face him. He'd saved her tonight. He'd looked after her. How long had it been since anyone had done that? He was a complete stranger, someone who didn't have to do any of those things and yet he had. She didn't even know his name. She stretched a hand out. 'You have my thanks, ah…?' She waited for him to fill in the space left by her words.

A small smile twitched on his lips as he took her hand. 'Are you asking me my name? It's Nolan Gray.'

'I'm trying to thank you, Mr Gray.' She couldn't resist a smile of her own, something warm unfurling in her stomach. She imagined he rather regularly had that effect on women. Once more she counselled caution. She didn't want to like him. She just needed him to get through the next four weeks.

He just had to get through the night. He had a naked woman in his tub and no idea what to do with her, a most novel situation to be sure. Usually he knew *exactly* what to do with a naked woman in the tub, out of the tub, on the bed, off the bed, against the wall, out on the balcony with the moon overhead. He had to stop, this was starting to sound like an erotic prepositional exercise or bad poetry. Too bad his tutors had not aspired to such creative lengths—he might have done better in school.

Nolan stripped out of his clothes at last, glad to be rid of the damp and stench of the canal. He towelled dry his hair and slipped into his banyan, feeling warmer, cleaner already, but that raised another point of concern. What was *she* going to wear? Her gown was beyond use, wet and ruined. It was past mid-night. There were no shops open and he didn't know any shopkeepers to rouse. But he did know a friend... Brennan. Nolan grinned and hurried next door.

Brennan answered, half-dressed and less than half-sober. 'Do you still have that nightgown, Bren? The one you just ordered.'

'The one I ordered for my special lady,' Brennan drawled his correction.

'I need it, Bren.' Nolan leaned against the door-jamb, his voice low. If Brennan was home this time of night he wasn't alone and he didn't want his busi-ness broadcast to all and sundry. 'I have a situation.'

'I have a *situation*, too, as it were.' Brennan di-rected his eyes downward meaningfully where his robe gaped.

'Please, she fell in the canal and has nothing to sleep in.'

Brennan raised a brow. 'And that's a problem how? I thought you screwed naked.'

'Normally I do.' Nolan stopped. What was he doing? He did not have to justify *that* to Brennan. Nolan rolled his eyes. One of the consequences of living in his friends' pockets was that they knew ev-erything about him, personal habits and all. He had no privacy left even when he had separate rooms. Nolan pushed a hand through his hair, striving for clarity. 'It's complicated, Bren. I won her in a card game, she fell out of the gondola, she's in the tub right now.' Striving and failing. Nolan blew out a breath. He could see the explanation didn't help. He was flubbing this up miserably in his haste to get back to the room.

Brennan waved him off with a hand. 'Enough, you're making my head hurt. You can have the damn nightgown if you'll just stop with all these details.' Brennan retreated into the dark of his room and came back, a silky white item in one hand. 'Just to be clear, I won't want it back when you're done.'

'Thanks, I owe you one.'

Brennan laughed. 'One *nightgown*, to be precise. I will want it replaced. Now, *go to bed*.'

Bed was an interesting proposition indeed given there was only the one in his suite and he'd not planned on sharing it with the lovely, mercurial Gianna. He'd also not planned on having her *in* his room, let alone his bed. Nolan stepped into the steamy bathing room, calling out his approach from the dressing screen that shielded the tub from any intruders. 'Are you decent? I found you something to wear.'

He heard the water slosh, her voice momentarily flustered. 'Toss it over the screen, I'll be out in a minute.'

'There's no need to rush,' Nolan called back, trying to sound cheerful. No need at all. He was still trying to figure out what to do with her, but before he could do that, he had to figure out what to *make* of her.

He draped the silky material over the screen. The evening hadn't gone quite as anticipated. He was supposed to have won money, not a woman. But he'd had a plan for that, too. That woman was supposed to have embraced her freedom and left him at the pier. It was a nice, expedient option that should have satisfied them both. In the main room, Nolan poured himself a drink and went out on the balcony to think and to wait. He'd had one plan, but apparently, she'd had another, and *that* was cause for wonder.

Nolan leaned on the railing, his gaze going out across the dark waters as he sipped at the brandy, letting his thoughts come fast and logical: Was Gianna Minotti a fraud? Was she for real? Was she a little of both, part fact, part fiction? Perhaps of more immediate concern, what did she want badly enough to turn down her freedom and accompany an unknown man to a hotel room, an act that had obviously inspired at least a little fear in her?

There was a delicate cough behind him. He turned, preparing himself for the sight of Gianna Minotti in whatever passed for Brennan's taste in nightwear. There would be no reason to overreact. This wasn't his first woman in a nightgown or his first woman anything—he was way beyond firsts when it came to what happened in a bedroom.

His preparation was not enough. Thankfully, years of rote response came to his aid. 'Will it suffice?' The words came out of his mouth with little effort from him because the rest of him seemed tongue-tied. The pale-blue dress with its heavy adornments had not done her justice. It had, in fact, distracted the viewer with its opulence from the full onslaught of her beauty. But there was no distraction now.

Nolan's eyes were riveted on her face, helped there

by the simple classic lines of the gown, the thin unobtrusive straps at her shoulders that demanded no attention and the dark cloud of her hair hanging loose and damp at her shoulders, framing her face and those striking hazel eyes. Her face itself was ultimately feminine, at once managing to be compassionate without being soft or delicate, intelligent without being hard. A smart man, a man who wanted to understand her, would study that face for hours and recognise its layers, the complexities of her expressions. Only when that was mastered would he move on to study the rest of her body, shown to perfection in the simplicity of the white gown. Tonight he could not be that man.

Nolan felt his body, typically well trained to reserve its judgement until his mind was made up, stir with arousal. The gown flowed over her curves at the behest of her body, not of fashions. Where the blue gown had forced her to conform, this silk conformed to the wearer, flowing over the swell of her breast, the nip and flare of waist and hip. No wonder Brennan had been reluctant to part with it. The gown had been made by a magician.

'It suffices, I'd say.' She took a few steps forward to the cluster of furniture around the fireplace, the silk emphasising the sway of her hips, her mouth quirked in a wry smile that said she'd noted his interest. Damn. He hated being the transparent one. Usually, those roles were reversed. Usually... How many times had he thought of such contrasts tonight? The 'usual' held no power here. Nothing that had happened tonight had gone according to plan or prediction.

'I see the tea has come.' She sat on the curved sofa and prepared to pour, presiding over the porcelain like a naughty angel in her white gown, her hazel eyes looking preternaturally green against the paleness of her surroundings. 'Perhaps you'd prefer something stronger?' She gestured to the decanter on the sideboard, noting the half-empty glass in his hand. 'I think I'd prefer a little of both after all the excitement tonight.'

Nolan brought the decanter over and sat down, one leg crossed over the other, and let her serve him. If women served tea in nightgowns like this more often, men might actually enjoy the event. He admired the way in which she had manoeuvred things. It was neatly done indeed, masterful even. Of course, he recognised her strategy. It was a trick he used often. To take charge of a situation, one merely had to find a task to perform and then incorporate others into the scheme by asking them questions. Suddenly, you were giving orders and people were looking to you for direction.

She refilled his glass and passed it to him before splashing a healthy amount into her teacup, slightly self-conscious for the first time now that there was no task to perform; no wager to watch, no canal to be hauled out of, no bath to take, no tea to serve. Their action-packed evening had come to a screeching halt and now it was just them and the original reason they were together to start with.

'So, here we are." Nolan drawled with lazy nonchalance, settling back deep in his chair. Despite his misgivings over her authenticity, he was starting to enjoy this. The next move was hers. What would his bold lady do next?

Chapter Five

Here they were. In their nightclothes. Together. Gianna took a slow sip of the hot tea. There was a reason polite society didn't encourage conversation in dishabille and this was it. Without the trappings of one's wardrobe, one was entirely exposed in more than the obvious ways, although just the obvious exposure alone was enough to leave her feeling flustered and hot at a time when she need to be completely in control.

'Here we are.' She smiled, trying to give away none of her nerves. 'I must thank you again for all you've done for me tonight.' No, that was all wrong, it was too bland. She had to say something more than that if she meant to hold his attention. 'The gown is lovely. I'm amazed you were able to find anything on such short notice.' No, that was wrong, too. A man like him must have access to all types of female venues and females. She wondered where the gown had come from, which woman had sacrificed it for her, in return for what? What had the intriguing Nolan Gray promised in exchange?

'I'm only sorry it didn't come with a robe.' Nolan Gray said easily, casually, from his chair, as if he talked with barely clad women over tea all the time. And he might. He'd made it clear in the bathing room undressing women was not a rare occurrence in his life.

'Liar.' Gianna caressed the word, a knowing half-smile on her lips. Women were easy for him. This was a man who would want to be flirted with, a man who would want a sensual challenge, something that differed from the norm of his usual experience. She let her eyes hold his over the rim of her tea cup. They were mesmerising eyes, not hard at all to look at with their quicksilver flecks, but hard to look away from. A woman could get lost in them and the decadent promises they held. 'You're not sorry at all.' They were bold words from a bold woman, the sort of woman this man would find appealing.

Nolan Gray wasn't the sort of man who *had* to win a woman in a card game. An expanse of well-muscled chest showed in the open vee of his robe, reminding her of the powerful body that had propelled her out of the water, reminding her, too, that she played with a certain intimate fire here. She'd initiated an assertive flirtation and he was very willing to respond in kind.

His eyes drifted over her in a deliberate slide of quicksilver on silk, his gaze making his unspoken thoughts evident: he wanted her. It was to be expected given the circumstances. She was his to want, won

fair and square according to the rules of men. But
there was more in that gaze than sheer male cov-
etousness and *that* was what made her pulse race.
Those thoughts conveyed possibilities, *promises*, of
pleasure. 'No, you've caught me out. I'm not sorry.
You're a beautiful woman. The blue dress hid you.'

'The blue dress was worth a fortune,' she countered, encouraging the flirtation. Flirting was a
means to an end, part of her arsenal. If he wanted
her, he would let her stay. She *had* to view that as
progress. On the docks he'd been ready to let her go
and that did not suit her purposes. But to get what she
wanted from him, she'd have to tempt him beyond coy
flirtation and who knew where that would end? Well,
she *knew* where that would end—in his bed, with
her taking one step closer to becoming her mother,
one step closer to being dependent on men, the very
thing she'd fought so hard against the count to avoid.

'It's too bad the count didn't wager the dress instead, then.' Nolan took a swallow of brandy. She
followed that swallow down the strong length of his
throat. Did she really have a choice in the short term
if her long-term goals were to be met?

Gianna stopped her line of thought. How often had
her mother said the same? She'd married the count
based on that exact logic. She'd wanted respectability for her children, the kind that came cloaked in a
title. And yet, despite that cautionary tale, Gianna
couldn't help but think that if she did have to sacrifice herself to the Englishman, then so be it. Was it

wrong that part of her didn't think it would be a *terrible* sacrifice if it came to that?

The man across from her was attractive with his grey eyes accented by the sweeping upper curve of his cheekbones. It made for an appealing combination of strength and approachability, drawing the eye up to the spill of water-dark hair pushed back from his forehead. His hair would be lighter once it dried, although right now it was the shade of walnuts. His hair had been the colour of sweet pralines in the ballroom. He was a finely made man, too. She'd already noticed how tall and lean-muscled he was and with the manners to go with the looks. To dance with him in a ballroom would be a dream…a dream she should not be entertaining given her circumstances. It would certainly have helped lessen his appeal if he'd been a boor.

'Why do you suppose he chose to wager you and not the dress?' Nolan was musing out loud, and she needed to pay attention. Listening was one of a courtesan's most powerful weapons—the source of information.

'He was angry with me,' Gianna replied, not wanting to go into the details. If she was too messy, too complicated, or if he sensed an association with her could be potentially dangerous, he would be rid of her. Nolan raised a brow as if to suggest 'angry' didn't quite explain why a man would wager his daughter in a card game.

She didn't want to explain. She didn't want his pity just yet and certainly not his rejection. That was what she'd have if she told him the whole sordid story. She'd tell him later perhaps if she was desperate. Pity could be a tool, too. Besides, telling the story exposed her hand more than she wanted. They might be drinking tea in their nightwear and he might have saved her from drowning but he was still a stranger. So much lay unknown between them. At the moment, she was operating off nothing more than her assumptions about his character.

'More brandy?' she offered. She rose with the decanter in hand to cross the short distance between them, but Nolan waved it away.

'More answers.' He set his glass down on the low table, pushing it away from him with a sense of finality. Gianna swallowed hard. Small talk was over.

It was time to be bold. She needed a distraction or he'd drag the entire story out of her. She would tell him when she was ready, when she knew she had him and he wouldn't send her back. Until then, she needed to give him a reason to let her stay. Gianna put down the decanter and pulled off the stopper. She gave it a long, slow lick of her tongue, her eyes on Nolan, watching his reaction. 'Perhaps we can think of something else to do with the brandy besides drink it.' Her voice was husky and provocative, the implication clear.

His grey eyes went black at the fantasy she conjured. 'What are you suggesting?' His voice had become a husky growl. It was now or never. Gianna seized her courage. She could do this. She knew in theory what men wanted and how to deliver it, if not in practice. But truly, how hard could it be?

Gianna knelt at his knees in the small place between him and the tea table, careful to keep her eyes on his, never letting him guess the boldness was an act. 'We can find something better to entertain ourselves with besides talk. After all, you didn't win my conversation in a card game.' She ran her hands up the insides of his thighs beneath his banyan, over the rough hair of his legs, and she knew the heady sensation of success.

Already his body was shifting, opening to accommodate her touch, his robe falling away to reveal all of him, his phallus starting its journey to arousal as her thumb met with its head, his tip rubbery and tender. She'd not thought it would feel so…*vulnerable*… when the rest of his body was so very hard. She closed her hand over the length of his shaft, feeling its heat, its pulsing life as it grew harder. She started to stroke.

His hand came down quick and fierce, shackling her wrist. 'What the hell do you think you're doing?'

'Do you prefer something else?' Gianna fired back, defensive in her doubt. *Was* she doing it wrong?

'I'd *prefer* the truth.' His grip was hard as he brought both of them to their feet. Standing nose to nose or rather nose to chest, she felt the whole force and strength of his presence. Had she misjudged him? Was there cruelty in him yet? Gianna tensed and waited.

'You haven't the faintest idea of what you're doing, of what you're playing with,' he accused, and she felt her cheeks burn with shame. He had roused to her touch, her efforts couldn't have been that far off the mark. Gianna willed herself not to look away from him as he continued his scold. She would not give him or any man the satisfaction of victory. Nolan's eyes were hard, near-obsidian shards as he made his case. 'At the *palazzo* you were not the least interested in sleeping with me. I believe your words were "take your hand off me". That seems to have changed in a rather short time. Frankly, I find your about-face unbelievable. Perhaps we should try your resolve before this goes any further.'

It was all the warning she had. He seized her mouth in a bruising kiss that left her breathless and reeling from its onslaught, but there was no mistaking this kiss for anything other than what it was—a punishment, a proving ground.

Nolan dragged his mouth away, his eyes narrowed in flinty speculation. 'That's what I thought.' He ran his hand across his mouth, and Gianna knew whatever test he had put to her she had failed. 'A woman always kisses her truth. Now, why don't you tell me how it is that a woman who didn't want to be wagered turns down her freedom when it's offered to her, especially when she's not particularly interested in sleeping with me?'

Gianna gathered her dignity and looked him in the eye. She was losing him, not because she lacked competence in the arts of seduction, but because he saw through her, he knew her game and it dulled her one weapon. 'I'm sure I don't know what you mean.'

'Before you oh, so conveniently fell into the canal you were about to say "this is where I stay",' he prompted, not believing her feint of ignorance. 'Somewhere between the ballroom and the canal incident, you decided you didn't want to be free of me.'

His meaning was evident. Anger surged. 'You think I planned this? You think I *wanted* to fall into the canal?'

Her own accusation didn't appear to stoke his temper. His gaze remained steady. He let go of her wrist and crossed his arms over his chest, entrenching. She recognised the signs. 'There are those who would say you've done well for yourself tonight. You're here, after all, in this sumptuous room. The question is why?' His voice was a sensuous caution, reminding her that she toyed with a dangerous man in spite of the kindnesses he'd shown her. 'What do you want so badly, Gianna, you're willing to put your hand and no doubt eventually your mouth on a stranger's cock?'

It would have been better to have simply called her a whore. His crass description of her efforts to bribe him into compliance put her over the edge. Whatever restraint she had left fled in the wake of her temper at full boil. She raised her hand and struck him hard across the face, across that beautifully curved sweeping cheekbone.

'How dare you!' But she knew how he dared. He dared because it was true. She'd been willing to do that much and more if need be and it shamed her. In those moments she'd become like her mother, the very life she was trying so hard to avoid—a life dependent on a man's reactions to her charms.

Nolan stepped away from her, his body coiled but controlled. He didn't even raise a hand to touch the red stain she'd left on his face. She envied him that reserve he could conjure at will. 'I'm sorry if the truth stings, *signorina*,' he said coldly. 'Please excuse me. I find I'm not good company this evening. I'm going to find a nice stiff drink or two. Make free of the room. I will not be back tonight.'

He couldn't leave! She was already regretting her actions. Didn't she know by now violence solved nothing, it only made things worse? How quickly she'd sunk to the very depths she despised in the count. 'You're not dressed,' she asserted hastily. In her anger she might have ruined everything. She couldn't let him go with things like this. What had she been thinking to strike him? What if he sent for the count? She couldn't go back.

Nolan's hand stalled on the doorknob, and he gave her a wry smile. 'For what I pay here, princess, they'd let me drink naked.' Then he was gone, leaving her alone with a bed and a half-full decanter of brandy. It should be enough to numb the pain. Things would look brighter in the morning. They had to, because they looked impossibly dark right now.

curtains the staff knew to keep drawn until noon and his miracle remedy against all nature of hangovers on his bedside table.

Nolan shifted, his body conflicted in its priorities. Did it stay still, to dull the ache in his head, or give in to the urge to stretch and relieve the stiffness of having passed out in a club chair hours ago? His body opted to move. That was a mistake. He regretted moving instantly, then regretted having drunk so much brandy. Well, it hadn't entirely been brandy. There'd been some wine, too. This was all her fault, every aching, throbbing body part of it. The evening in its entirety flooded back in head-splitting flashes; the card game, the gondola, the canal—oh, Lord, the canal—he still carried a faint whiff of it on his skin— and the girl who had ruined everything, even his solution to save them both from further complication.

He'd offered her freedom from the agreement. She was supposed to have taken it and left him at the pier—dry and ready to move forward with the next step of his plans. It was a nice expedient option that should have satisfied them both. Apparently she had a different option in mind—one that involved falling into the canal. Even now, he wasn't sure if she'd done it on purpose. It had been an enormous chance to take on her part in a dress weighted down by pearls.

That wasn't the only thing he wasn't sure about. Was she really a virgin or had the count lied about that, too? It *was* rather hard to believe and yet he couldn't rule it out as truth. Nolan groaned again, this time from the realisation of what he'd done based on accepting the count's word at face value. What if he'd been wrong to trust her? If she had manipulated everything, it meant he'd just left a very experienced con artist alone in his room with all of his winnings. Nolan forced himself into an upright position, fighting hard to ignore the spinning room and the stab of pain. He had to get upstairs.

It was an absolute labour of Hercules to pull himself up the grand staircase in his dressing gown in front of bright-eyed tourists heading out to see the sights. It wasn't the dressing gown that bothered him. If he'd been in better spirits, he'd have made a game out of it, bowing and nodding to the ladies as if he were fully clothed. But he was in no mood for games. His head ached, his stomach roiled on the verge of nausea and it was suitable punishment for what he'd done. Had he let her manipulate him or was she simply that good and he hadn't seen it coming, he who prided himself on being a student of human nature?

Nolan ran through the progression of events. She'd been trying to seduce him, which had been an obvious if enjoyable ploy. He recalled with clarity the feel of her warm hand on his very responsive cock. If she'd been a different sort of woman in different circumstances, he would have taken her generous offer. But he'd been wary of her motives. When seduction had failed, she'd opted for a quarrel. In hindsight, he could see how that would work to her advantage. Perhaps she had intended to blind him with anger, knowing he'd storm out, maybe knowing, too, that a man who had bothered to drag her out of the canal, run her a hot bath and find her a nightgown wasn't going to throw her out after all that trouble.

Nolan fumbled for the key in his dressing-robe pocket and fitted it to the lock. He held his breath. This was the moment of truth. He opened the door to his room. The front room was empty except for the abandoned tea set and his stomach dropped. He strode into the bedroom, fearing the worst—that she was gone and his money with her. He stopped in the doorway and smiled, a big, wide smile that hurt his head. Right now, he didn't care. The pain was worth it.

Gianna Minotti lay sprawled face down on his bed, the silk nightgown bunched up high on her thighs, revealing long, slim legs and a glimpse of rounded buttock. Her hair was a glorious tangled mop over her face. Was that a small trail of drool at her mouth? One hand trailed limply over the bed. Nolan followed it down to the empty glass on the floor just beyond her fingertips.

His eyes darted to the nightstand and the nearly empty decanter. She'd had the same idea as he. Chances were, she'd get the same results. His magic morning was still at the bedside, too. He grabbed up the glass and drank, making sure to save some for her. She was going to need it. Nolan fought back the urge to laugh as he headed for the bath. It was true. Misery loved company. He was feeling better already.

There was a man singing in the bathroom and she just wanted him to stop! Gianna moaned and rolled over. It was a bad idea, but obviously just one of many, the brandy having been the first bad idea. What had possessed her to imbibe like that? Then she remembered. *Him*. This was all his fault. Sort of. At the moment, she couldn't remember exactly *why* it was his fault. Oh, yes, he'd *won* her in a card game. Not her specifically, but her maidenhead. Which he hadn't claimed, *yet*, proving the brandy hadn't accomplished anything except for giving her a monstrous headache.

The door to the bathing room opened, and she cracked one eye, then two. If she had to wake up with a pounding head there were worse sights to wake up to. Nolan Gray emerged from the steam, wrapping a white towel around his waist, water dripping from his hair. His singing stopped when he saw her but he didn't stop smiling. '*Buongiorno, signorina*. How is your head?'

The smiling, singing bastard knew exactly how her head felt—she could see the mischief in his eyes. Gianna reached for a pillow, intending to throw it at him. The effort was too much for her body. Her stomach rebelled, the world swam and spun in front of her abruptly upright head. She went hot, then cold, entirely out of control of her body. Oh, no! She couldn't stop it. Her throat made a panicked sound. Nolan was there, kneeling beside her, a chamber pot at the ready, his hand sweeping back her hair just in time.

She retched most thoroughly not once but twice, her stomach spilling its contents into the chamber pot. It was humiliating and healing all at once. Realising that somehow made it even more mortifying because, when the wave of nausea passed, she was *glad* she'd done it. Casting up accounts had been exactly what she'd needed.

'Better?' Nolan brought a wet washcloth and helped her with her face. The cold water felt refreshing on her skin. She lay back against the bed pillows, feeling drained, but immensely improved. 'If I could get rid of the pounding in my head, I would be at a hundred per cent.' She managed a smile, but it was hard considering she'd just thrown up in front of a man dressed in a towel—a man who had already fished her out of the canal and tried to save her from the count's reckless wager.

He had an answer for that, too. 'Drink this. It will help your head.' He passed her a half-filled glass filled with a greenish liquid.

She sniffed and wrinkled her brow. 'What is it?'

'My secret recipe for mornings like these.' He chuckled at her reticence. 'You can live with the headache or you can try it. I've already had mine and look at me.' He held his arms wide. Look at him indeed. It was hard not to. He was as well made as the glimpses last night had purported. Lean muscles defined his arms and chest beneath the lingering tan of his skin. It was not a deep tan, of course, they were too far into the winter for that, but he *had been* tan at one point. It made her wonder what he'd been doing. Cards were usually an indoor pursuit, in her experience. It was nice to think he might be more than a gambler.

Gianna gave him a dubious look and downed the

glass. She cringed at the taste and swallowed. 'This had better work.'

'It will work. It tastes too awful not to.' He laughed and rummaged in the drawers of the bureau and tossed her a shirt. 'You can put this on until we can find you something better to wear. I'll dress in the other room. Come out when you're decent. Breakfast will be here soon. I have it delivered every day at noon.'

Breakfast? Decent? She was sceptical of both ideas, but Nolan merely laughed at her frown as he gathered up clothes. 'Nothing fancy, just toast and coffee,' he assured her. 'It will help, too, you'll see.'

Gianna held the shirt against her. She was sceptical of more than breakfast. They had not parted on good terms last night. He'd accused her of deliberately falling into the canal, and she had slapped him. 'Why are you doing this? Why are you being so nice?'

Nolan shrugged. 'Does there have to be a reason? Maybe I'm feeling grateful that my hangover is behind me. It is a glorious feeling to be restored to health, don't you agree?' The last was added rather pointedly.

Gianna blushed, but she was not diverted. 'Maybe it's more than that.'

'Maybe,' Nolan drawled, letting his eyes roam over her. 'I'm just glad to find you're still here and that you haven't robbed me blind. You knew exactly how much I'd won and where it was at.'

'You insult me.' She must be feeling better. Her temper stirred a little, a sure sign she was recovering her spirit. It stung that he still didn't believe she was innocent in all this, that she'd had no part in the wager, no designs to steal from him and return to the count.

'No,' Nolan corrected, tossing the words over his shoulder as he exited to the other room. 'I *honour* you with the truth. In cases like this, I find it's best to know where we stand with one another.'

Ah, they were not so dissimilar. They both believed one caught more flies with sugar than vinegar. He was flattering her. Not with words, necessarily. In fact, he was purposely using his words to do the exact opposite in the hopes that she wouldn't notice. But she'd been in the world of men too long. She knew better. He was flattering her with actions, luring her trust with nightgowns and shirts; hot baths and tea trays; miracle headache cures and timely placement of chamber pots. *Do not like him*, she admonished, slipping out of the nightgown and folding it carefully before placing it in a drawer.

Gianna slipped her arms into the sleeves of the shirt. The garment was too big, of course. The sleeves had to be rolled up and it fell nearly to her knees. But it was clean and soft against her skin the way only expensive linen could be. She breathed deeply. The shirt smelled good, like him, she realised. It matched the scent that had trailed out of the bathing room with him; sandalwood with the faintest hints of patchouli. She drew another deep breath and knew she had to be careful.

He was a worthy opponent at a time when she

needed a more naïve one. Nolan Gray did nothing without a motive. Even this act of dressing her in his shirt was an act of intimacy designed to draw her closer, designed to create the illusion of a bond between them. *He wants you to like him*, came the thought. She played a question-and-answer game with herself as she fastened the shirt.

Why? Last night he'd wanted to be rid of her.

Because friends tell one another their secrets.

In his eyes, what was her secret?

Answer: he wanted to know why she didn't want to leave when she hadn't wanted to come in the first place.

Gianna paused, hesitating before picking up the brush laid out on the dresser. He wouldn't mind. He'd want her to use it, one more act of kindness to bind her to him. She dragged the brush through her tangles, feeling more in charge with each brushstroke, more like herself. Regardless of what anyone said, appearances mattered, even when one was only wearing a shirt, or perhaps especially when one was wearing only a shirt. It was already noon and the clock was ticking. How much time did she have before her freedom ran out?

There were voices in the other room and the clatter of dishes. Breakfast was here. She couldn't hide in the bedroom any longer. It was time to go out and beard the proverbial lion in his den. For that she needed a strategy, or, better yet, she'd just borrow his tactics. He wanted her to like him. Was that such a bad idea? Wouldn't she, too, be served by the concept of liking?

Maybe being friends was the preferred strategy here. After all, friends did things for one another and there were things she needed doing before she could leave Venice, before she could truly be free. Who better to do them for her than her new friend, Nolan Gray?

Be careful, her conscience whispered, *that you don't do this because it's easy. You want to like him and this gives you an excuse. This was your mother's downfall, she liked attractive men and they all failed her in the end. Nolan Gray might have fished you out of the canal, but he also won you in a card game. How good could a man be who'd entertain such a wager?* That was the problem. She didn't know. But at the moment he was all she had. She *did* feel a twinge of guilt over what she meant to do. But if he was a gambler, he'd understand. A girl had to use her resources and take her chances where she found them.

The smell of coffee greeted her as she stepped into the other room, feeling conspicuous in Nolan's shirt when he was fully attired in shirt and waistcoat, breeches and boots. In truth, the shirt covered far more of her than the nightgown had, but then, the playing field had been more equitable when they'd both been in nightwear. But Nolan rose, playing the gentleman, only his eyes betraying his appreciation of her apparel. He was good at hiding his emotions.

'Coffee?' He poured her a cup and passed it to her with a smile. 'There's toast and butter, a pot of jam, if you like. Help yourself.' He'd left the sofa empty for her, perhaps anticipating the difficulties of sitting in a shirt. She ended curled up on that sofa, her legs tucked under her, the shirttails tucked modestly about her, and a plate of toast balanced on her lap.

It was a cosy position and she was struck by the domestic tranquillity of their breakfast. Nearby, flames popped occasionally in the fireplace. Nolan sat easy in his chair, one booted leg crossed over the other, his own plate balanced on a knee. Beyond him the light of the grey day filtered through the windows. It was a perfect day for staying inside. If they'd been lovers, perhaps they would have. But Nolan's attire suggested he at least had other plans.

She took a bite of toast smothered in jam, aware of him studying her. She readied herself. He was going to launch his next salvo. But when it came it wasn't the question she'd expected.

Nolan took a swallow of coffee and said with all the casualness of someone who was asking about the weather, 'So, what kind of man sells his daughter's virginity? And don't say a desperate one because I already know that.'

Chapter Seven

'What kind of man buys it?' she countered, fixing him with her brave hazel gaze. This woman backed down from nothing. She was as confident sitting on the sofa in his borrowed shirt as she was in Venice's finest ballrooms in a gown worth a fortune. It might be said that clothes made the man. In this case, it was confidence that made the woman. She wore it well, but Nolan was hardly about to come undone over a direct gaze and one uncomfortable question. He was far too experienced for that.

'Oh, no, you don't.' Nolan set aside his plate and took the offensive. Part of him was glad to see she was willing to put up a fight. Still, she would find he was not as easily played as all that. 'You do not get to answer a question with a question and you *absolutely* do not get to make me the villain in this scenario.'

'There can be more than one villain,' she replied coolly.

'There may be, but they are not me. I was your best choice at that table.'

'Were you? That's an arrogant statement.'

'I did not ravish you. You are still in possession of your virginity,' Nolan pointed out, enumerating his evidence on his fingers. 'I doubt the other men at the table would have allowed you to keep it. Secondly, and more importantly, you are still in possession of the choice regarding who to give that particular feminine jewel to. Thirdly, I offered to set you free of the wager.' He was well aware she had artfully manoeuvred him into defending himself. This was not what he wanted to discuss. He wanted to discuss the count and whatever arrangement she had with that blackguard.

She arched a dark eyebrow over her coffee, unimpressed with his accomplishments. 'You are a veritable saint.'

'Does that make you the martyr in this scenario, then? We're quite the pair, the martyr and the saint.' In all likelihood they were both liars, hardly candidates for such religious monikers. She wasn't forced to play the suffering victim. He'd given her the choice and heaven knew he wasn't anywhere near a saint when it came to her. She'd been stunning in his white shirt when she'd entered the room, the tails skimming the tops of her knees, leaving her long, slim legs bare to his gaze, urging a man to run up their length until they disappeared beneath the fabric and the eye was drawn to the curve of hip visible only to the discerning eye beneath the fine linen, and above that, the slope and swell of her breasts, provocative reminders that every inch of her was naked beneath *his* shirt.

He had to get this conversation back on track before his mind and body decided he didn't need to play the gentleman. He could have her, he could seduce a 'yes' right out of her, right now, an hour at most and they could both be enjoying that big bed in the other room. But in the long run, that wasn't what he wanted. There would be no thrill in conning her into sex. He wasn't sixteen any more, cajoling a lonely widow into bed just to see if he could do it. These days, the more sophisticated thrill was in the choice, in being chosen.

Nolan recrossed his legs and tried a different tack. 'You are only protecting him with your refusal to answer. I confess to finding that a rather odd strategy to adopt on behalf of someone who sold you against your will.' Nolan feigned nonchalance and reached for another piece of toast.

'If I were in your position, I'd be furious. I'd want revenge.' He looked up from buttering the bread and knew a moment of sweet victory. He had shocked her. She was trying to hide it, but it was there in the stillness of her body. It was funny how people found the truth shocking, their own truths even more so when repeated back to them. 'Is that why you want to stay? Do you think I will help you with your revenge?' He took a self-satisfied crunch of his toast. He'd hit the target.

'It's not revenge, exactly. I just want what is mine.' Sweet Heavens, the man was a mind reader. If she'd been a target, he'd have hit the bullseye and she didn't like it one bit. He would be so much harder to manipulate if he knew what she was up to. She knew now that she'd been naïve last night when she'd thought her luck might be changing. But, no, she'd managed to be won by the only mind-reading card player in Venice, a man who could see right through her, linen shirt and all. And he *was* looking. He had been since she'd entered the room. He might not have ravished her, but that didn't mean he wasn't interested. A smart woman would use that to her advantage. He might be a mind reader, but he was still a man.

'I couldn't possibly consider leaving Venice without that which is mine.' She dropped her eyes at the last moment, a gesture that was demure and well practised from hours in front of the mirror, designed for precisely this sort of situation. She didn't want this disclosure to be a challenge, she wanted it to be… compelling. She counted silently in her head. One, two, three, four…come on, bite.

'Why would you leave Venice?' Nolan said at last.

That was the wrong bite. She wanted to scream. Why couldn't he be curious the way a normal man was curious? Anyone else would have asked what the count had that was hers, which was precisely the question she wanted him to ask. Only in retrospect did she see how she'd overplayed her hand. She should have said nothing about leaving Venice. It gave away too much, it invited too many questions, questions Nolan Gray was well on his way to asking and she didn't want to answer.

She speared him with a disdainful look that said the answer was obvious. 'I can't possibly stay in a city where everyone knows my guardian wagered me in a card game.'

'Where will you go? Do you have plans?' he asked, calmly unfazed by her attempt cut him down to size. He was trying to test her truth and her resolve, wondering how much of this was made up. He folded his hands over the flat of his stomach with long slender fingers that gave his gestures a touch of elegance. Those hands had undressed her last night, those fingers had worked the buttons of her gown. They'd been competent and swift, reminders that he knew his way around a woman.

She infused her tone with a touch of hidden despair. 'I don't know where I'll go. I can hardly think of such things before I have my resources to hand.' She tried again to lure him into asking the question she wanted. She wanted him to offer, wanted his assistance to be his idea. Men worked better that way and she had no intentions of owing any man anything ever again. She wasn't going to beg him to help her— then she would owe him. There would be a debt between them.

'I could loan you the funds, gift them to you, if that would help,' Nolan offered. He was so very eager to get rid of her. That was interesting in itself. She needed to remember that. Last night he'd offered her freedom and now he was offering her money. Therein lay her leverage. She could bargain with her absence. She would leave as soon as she had what she needed. He would quickly see that his help would expedite that.

Outwardly, she opted for genteel chagrin. 'I am

not asking you for money!' She flung an arm towards the bedroom. 'I have enough pearls on that ruined gown in there to see me on my way and then some.' And that pride went before her fall. She could almost hear proverbial fabric ripping as she metaphorically tripped. Nolan wasted no time calling her out.

'Yes, you most certainly do, not to mention the necklace and earbobs. A resourceful woman could turn those into a comfortable living if she were frugal.' A wide smile took his face, mischief lit his silver eyes. He crossed his arms over his chest, looking quite satisfied with himself. 'It seems we've established you could indeed leave Venice tonight, despite your earlier claim to the contrary. Now, why don't you tell me what your father has that you so desperately need?'

'He is not my father.' If she had to give up some truth, it might as well be this one. 'He's my stepfather and not a very good one. That's the sort of man who would sell his daughter's virginity to cover a bet.' The same sort of man who would propose to his stepdaughter and then threaten her when she refused such an unholy alliance. But she was not about to tell Nolan Gray that. She didn't have to. No doubt he already surmised there was more to it than the count's random whim to wager her. Cataclysmic events didn't happen in isolation. They occurred as end results of a sequence of events that led up to them.

An honest shadow of sadness passed through his eyes. 'I am sorry.' For a moment, they were no longer embattled opponents; she trying to hold on to her secrets, he trying to pry them loose. They were allies of a sort and in that moment. She sensed his compassion transcending their agendas, as if he *knew* what it had meant to live with the count. The compassion was there, just as it had been when he'd dragged her out of the canal, helped her out of her gown, saw to her bath, asking nothing for himself in exchange, not even that to which he was entitled on the base of the wager.

Those three words, *I am sorry*, were more compelling than any argument he could have made, and, oh, how they tempted her to spill every last secret. Which of course was what he wanted. Logic waved its red flag. *That's what he wanted you to believe last night, just as he wants that now. He is using it to sneak past your defences.* Trust like love was a very dangerous thing to give.

'I won't send you back,' he said in even tones that matched the firm set of his jaw. There was a steel in him that had not been there before and it did things to her stomach she couldn't blame on the brandy. 'But perhaps I won't have to. Perhaps he will come looking for you?' He asked it casually, but she was not fooled. There was a feral tension uncoiling in him. 'Tell me, Gianna, is the count dangerous?'

She thought of Nolan's knife. He would be better able to protect her, maybe even more willing to assist her if she told him the truth about this as well. She gave him her second truth. 'Yes.'

Nolan grinned. 'Well, so am I.'

In more ways than one. Her mind-reading, knife-wielding, card-gambling, virgin-winning Englishman might protect her from the count, but who would protect her from him? She wasn't naïve enough to think he'd offered out of altruism. He would expect to get paid.

Gianna wet her lips in a quick motion and untucked her legs, hoping to guide his response with the movements of her body. 'What do you want in return?' Her voice was low and throaty, a temptress's tone.

'What I've wanted all along, Princess.' He let the words hang in the air long enough to make her pulse race, to steer her thoughts down a dark, seductive path, only to yank them ruthlessly back to reality. 'I want you to leave.' He rose and strode towards the door. 'I have plans of my own and you do not figure into them. But since you won't take my money or my offer of freedom, perhaps you will take my help.'

He opened the door as if he'd heard a silent knock. On cue, a porter stood there with two women and their trunks, their arms draped with the frills and lace that denoted feminine garments. 'Thank you, Antonio. Ladies, do come in. You are just in time.' In time for what? Gianna wondered. Nolan turned to her. 'You'll need clothes if we're to do this. You can't wear my shirt for ever.' He fished a folded sheet of paper out of his coat pocket. '*Signora*, here is a list of the things we'll need, perhaps you will also have some ready-made items to leave today.'

The dressmaker smiled knowingly. Gianna knew what the woman was thinking: here was a rich Englishman outfitting his Italian mistress, and she bristled at the implication. It was hard to hold on to one's dignity dressed in a man's shirt, no matter how good it smelled. '*Signor*, I know exactly what to do,' she assured Nolan.

'I know you do.' He swept her a bow and then made one to Gianna. 'I leave you in Signora Montefiori's capable hands. If I have left anything off the list, please order it. I will see you tonight for supper.'

It took Gianna a moment to register what was happening. He was *leaving* her here, in this room, to be fitted for clothes while he went off and did who knew what with who knew whom. She was in no position to protest. What woman turned down new clothes? Certainly not the woman who literally hadn't a thing to wear.

Besides, she had no claim on him. She could not make him stay nor, in reality, would she want him to stay. Right? On a practical level, being fitted for clothing was a rather intimate experience. Did she want him to be present while she stood in nothing but undergarments—assuming the dressmaker had brought some temporary ones—to be measured and draped, those grey eyes fixed on her for hours?

The thought made her hot. She was a wicked girl not rejecting the notion out of hand. But she needn't worry about that particular event coming to pass. Nolan was gone, the door shutting behind him and his promises to return for dinner.

'*Signorina*, if you will stand here?' Signora Montefiori brought forward a small dais. '*Allora!* We will get started. We have a lot to accomplish this afternoon. We have a man to please, no?' She clapped her hands, and her two assistants sprang into action; taking out measuring tapes and notepads from their baskets, opening the trunks and pulling out bolts of cloth. In a matter of minutes, the room could have passed for a dressmaker's shop.

Signora Montefiori walked the perimeter of the dais, a finger tapping against her lips, murmuring indistinct sounds every so often. 'Mmm-hmm, mmm... Ah, *sì*.' Then, she stepped back and went to work, issuing commands to Gianna this time. 'Raise your arms, straighten your shoulders...'

Gianna followed the instructions automatically, her mind disengaging from the process. Her mind was more interested in contemplating what had just happened with Nolan than it was in pins and fabric. Apparently, an accord had been reached: his help in exchange for her promise to leave so they could both get on with their lives. It was precisely what she wanted, except for one small catch. She wondered how he would feel once he discovered there wasn't just one thing she needed to retrieve from the count, there were three.

She would have felt guilty about not fully disclosing that titbit if not for the fact that he'd done a little misleading of his own in an attempt to bilk information from her. He'd made his mind up to help her *before* they'd sat down to breakfast, *before* he'd been asking questions about the count. She'd not needed to persuade him. He'd already decided, yet he'd opted to play with her, to see what she would give up, what she would be willing to bargain with in order to get what he'd already decided to give.

The dressmaker was proof of it. He'd known down to the minute when she'd be outside his door, evidence that he'd arranged for her in advance; some time between getting drunk last night and getting dressed this morning. She'd got what she wanted. She should be ecstatic.

Gianna turned on the dais and held out her arms for another measurement. But the victory was hollow. He'd decided to help her and yet he'd still left, turning her over to strangers; proof that the help he offered was offered begrudgingly. His departure this afternoon made it clear assisting her wasn't a priority, merely a means to an end. When that end was achieved, he'd wash his hands of her. Unless…unless she could entice him to keep her longer. He would have to want her more than he wanted his plans, whatever those might be.

That should be for the good. She didn't want a lingering attachment any more than he did. When she had her things, she would pack up her new clothes, her pearls, and she would move on to a new life just as he would move on with his. It was what had been decided. *By him*. Maybe that was what galled her. She'd got what she wanted, because he'd decided to give it to her. Somehow, in spite of her best efforts to maintain control of the situation, the decision hadn't been hers.

Chapter Eight

He'd made the decision to help her when he'd seen the little puddle of drool drying on her cheek that morning. It was the best conclusion Nolan could come up with as he lingered over coffee in Piazza San Marco, reviewing the last fourteen hours and his rather surprising capitulation this morning. It was slightly past four o'clock and the piazza was busy with late-afternoon strollers taking in the day before winter darkness fell.

In Venice, this had become his favourite time of day. He'd made a habit of sitting in the piazza, bundled up in his greatcoat and muffler, watching people, guessing their stories. He'd helped one young man a few weeks ago find the right words to mend a quarrel with his sweetheart. Words were simple enough things when you knew which ones you needed. Unfortunately, most people didn't.

Usually, he had company; one of the many friends he'd made in Venice—novelists and artists, people like himself who made a living from understanding others, or the Austrian Countess Louisa von Haas, who was wintering here for Carnevale. She was an elegant, worldly woman who understood the physical pleasures available in such a setting. Nolan had availed himself of those pleasures on occasion. He was by no means the only man in Venice who had. But today, he sat alone—no artists, no writers, no temporary mistresses—and preferably so. Today, he wasn't watching people as much as listening to his own thoughts.

Common sense dictated that if he'd truly wanted to be rid of her, he should have taken Gianna back to the count, returned her immediately to the security of her home. Only, there was no security to return to, something her reaction to his knife in the bathing room had confirmed long before she more explicitly confirmed it over breakfast. Of course, he hadn't needed such confirmation. He'd known from the start. A man who wagered his stepdaughter was no protector at all.

Such a situation had found purchase with him. There'd been no security in his own home life growing up. Once he'd decided to leave his family, he'd had no desire to be returned there either. He certainly wasn't going to inflict on her a fate he would not have wished for himself. He knew what it was like to be alone in the world, entirely reliant on one's own resources. Frankly, it was scary, but the thought of going back was even more frightening.

He took comfort in knowing there was a basic explanation behind his motives for helping Gianna: his decision had merely been influenced by the experiences of his own past. Those experiences had been helped along by emotions such as the elation he'd felt when he'd realised she hadn't stolen from him. The drool had been the *pièce de résistance*. She'd looked vulnerable and young asleep on his bed, hardly a femme fatale to be feared and thrown out into the world to fend for herself, but a person in need of some luck.

He'd decided he could be her luck as long as that luck didn't extend beyond giving her a place to stay for a few days, buying her some clothes and offering her some money. Those items wouldn't interrupt his plans and at present he had the funds to spare. Venice at Carnevale had proven very lucrative. That was as far as he was willing to go and that was the plan he'd had in place before breakfast. Anything more would have to be refused. But that's not what had happened.

At breakfast, everything had changed. She'd refused his initial position, turned down his money, and then had the audacity to renegotiate with him. Somewhere between his third and fourth piece of toast, he'd found himself straying from his original offer to an offer of actual physical assistance. In return, she would leave after he helped her retrieve something from the count. Goodness knew what that might be and what it might involve. Certainly, it would involve covert action and that meant it would involve risk. He would be ready for it. To that end, he had two more stops to make before dinner. The sooner they could expedite their association the better.

Nolan braced his packages under one arm, pushed open the door and stared in amazement. This was his room? For a moment he thought perhaps he'd gone to the wrong place. In all the weeks he'd lived here, it had never looked like this: candles flickering, the curtains pulled back to reveal the lanterns on the canal, the long, highly polished but little-used dining table set with white cloth, silver and crystal. This was a setting fit for a prince. It carried an elegance far beyond that of an itinerant gambler who had money but not much else in life. If he'd known what was waiting for him, he might have come back sooner. Or, he might be highly suspicious.

Nolan chose to be the latter. This was the same woman, after all, who had tried to suck him and then slapped *him* for a kiss moments later. This was a woman who was with him because he was her only alternative for the moment, a rather lowering thought for a man who prided himself on the ability to seduce anyone.

Gianna moved from the shadows. Her entrance was masterfully staged. She only drew his attention after he'd had a chance to absorb the scene. And rightly so. Nolan thought he might have missed the table and all its finery if he'd seen her first. She was a queen in the candlelight, dressed in a silver-grey silk gown banded at the waist and trimmed at the hem in bands of black velvet. Her dark hair was piled high, exposing the slender column of her neck, a few curls left loose to tempt a man's hand. 'Welcome home.' She moved forward, a glass in her hand, its cut facets catching the light of the candles. 'There is chilled champagne and dinner will be here shortly.' She handed him the glass and took his packages to set aside. Now, he was officially suspicious. She played the hostess far too well. A less-cautious man would be drawn in before he even knew the net had been cast.

'What is all of this?' Nolan kept his tone casual.

'This is thank you and I'm sorry.' Her hands were at the shoulders of his coat, helping him out of it. 'I should not have slapped you last night. You have been kind to me none the less.' She folded his coat and draped it over the sofa. She gave him a sly smile. 'Don't worry, it's all on your bill if that makes you feel better. I can hardly seduce you on your own money.'

'Is that how it works? Perhaps that explains why my other mistresses failed,' Nolan said coolly. He was finding her premise fairly debatable. The candlelit suite, the cold champagne and the woman herself were doing a fine job seducing his senses and his body, although his mind was holding out for something more rational before he was entirely persuaded there was no other agenda.

A knock sounded at the door, and Gianna moved to answer it, favouring him with a chance to watch the grey silk move over her curves. Apparently, the session with Signora Montefiori had gone well.

The *facchini* stepped in with trays and laid the rest of the table with quick efficiency. Covers were removed, a second round of champagne was poured, bread was sliced in advance. Gianna dismissed the porters and stepped towards the table, holding a hand out to him in invitation, her voice husky. 'Will you come and dine with me?' She might as well have said, *Come to bed with me.*

Her eyes were on him. He felt his body start to fire with arousal. Direct eye contact with a woman who knew her own mind had always turned him on. Tonight was proving to be no exception. She was all Eve with the apple, tempting him to believe in the mirage she'd created—this elegant domesticity mixed with sophisticated intimacy. He found her intoxicating, this beautiful woman in grey, who had so effortlessly taken charge of the setting. It conjured up thoughts of other settings in which she might take charge; what would it be like to take such a woman to bed? Would she take charge of her own pleasure? Would she take charge of *his*? It was certainly probable. His cock recalled the feel of her hand on him and his body raced at the prospect of such possibility.

He joined her at the table, holding out a chair for her, thankful for the shadows that disguised his response to the fantasy she'd created. 'Everything looks delicious.' The compliment was designed to encompass more than the food, although everything on the table was in fact his favourites—the *trota al burro*, the thin strands of angel-hair pasta, the careful geometric piles of white polenta and at the centre of it all was the bowl of steaming *go* risotto.

Of course, the kitchen had all of his favourites on file. All one had to do was ask the kitchen what Signor Gray liked to eat. He was known throughout the markets of Venice for his love of Venetian seafood. It wasn't the resourcefulness that touched him, it was her thoughtfulness. *She'd* gone to the trouble of asking. If she even guessed how compelling he found that little courtesy, he'd be entirely vulnerable despite his rather healthy layer of cynicism. Oh, it would be very prudent indeed to expedite their association as quickly as possible if this was her effect on him. Randy, well-fed men didn't always think with their brains. He was on the verge of becoming both, a very dangerous fate considering he lived by his wits.

'More champagne?' She poured him the rest of the bottle and then opened another. 'You have fallen in love with our seafood, it would seem. The lagoon is a fisherman's paradise. But the risotto dish is hardly rich man's fare.'

'Perhaps that's why I like it.' Nolan sat back in his chair, letting his food settle. 'Or perhaps it's the risk in it that appeals to me. I'm a gambler by trade, I thrive on it. Once, on Burano, I saw someone make the *go* risotto. I saw the chefs carefully prepare the *go* fish so that they didn't ruin the broth, I saw the risotto flipped in the air for aeration. There were so many variables needed to make perfection.'

He watched her take in his words, unravel their meaning. Her hand stilled on the stem of her flute. Did she know she did that? Whenever she felt caught, her body stilled while she gathered her mental resources. It was her tell. Everyone had them. Some just hid them better than others. He pitched his voice low, caressing each word deliberately. 'One false move, one missed step, and the dish becomes disaster.'

Her hand came up and played with the pearl drop that lay just below her throat. Nolan's hand itched to take its place. Perhaps she'd made the gesture on purpose to distract him, to redirect his thoughts. He could almost feel the pearl in his hand. It would be warm from the heat of her body. It would be a natural progression of movement to draw a finger down the column of her throat to the shadow between her breasts. As lovely as this interlude was, he needed to end it before he was entirely at her mercy.

'Is that what we're doing tonight, Gianna? Making perfection? If so, a man has to wonder why?'

Everything had been going perfectly until now. She'd known from the outset Nolan would have to be massaged into compliance, but she'd not guessed it would be over this. These—the dinner, the dress, the direct looks—were all designed to ensure his compliance, not to rouse his suspicions. They were supposed to help her avoid suspicion and now, her efforts had accomplished the very opposite of her intentions.

She'd left nothing to chance: not the foods for dinner, not the temperature of the champagne, nor any aspect of her appearance seen or unseen from the elegant fall of the grey evening gown Signora Montefiori had left to the silky undergarments beneath, compliments of an unclaimed wedding trousseau. And it still wasn't enough.

Nolan leaned across the table, his eyes on her, dark and serious, his sharp mind already a step ahead of her. 'Is this about the count, Gianna? If so, it's wasted effort. I've already pledged my assistance.' He paused. 'Unless there is something you haven't told me? Does this have to do with the item we need to retrieve?'

The truth was her only option. This was not a question she could answer with a pretty dress or champagne or silky undergarments. 'Retrieving it will be a delicate task, one that will require some stealth…' Gianna began, watching Nolan raise an eyebrow. At least he hadn't thrown her out for what she implied.

'Is there any chance in this discussion that you have substituted the words "retrieving" and "stealth" for "stealing"?' Nolan swallowed the last of his champagne, giving every appearance of a man who was making usual conversation over dinner.

'No.' She was on definite ground here. 'It is mine, legally.' More legally in four weeks, but it had been willed to her and that made it hers no matter what her age. 'But the count will be reluctant to give it up.' The count's reluctance stemmed from a different reason than hers. He wanted the item for its overtly displayed contents and what money they could bring. She wanted it for what it hid, for what it protected. Those secrets were still safe. The count would not have proposed otherwise—there would have been no reason to.

'May I infer that we will not be able to simply ask him for it?' Nolan pushed back from the table to give himself room to cross one long leg over another. 'We

will have to *take* it? Will the sight of my knife be
suitable enough force for him to concede the object?'

Gianna set her jaw. He knew very well it wouldn't
be. There were just two of them. They could not lay
siege in broad daylight to the count's *palazzo* simply
by walking in. His footmen, all burly, highly trained
brutes, would evict them in short order, or at least
evict Nolan. They might not let her go. The thought
of being trapped in that house again made her shudder. 'It is important that he not know we have it.'
The longer her 'retrieval' of the item went unnoticed
the better. She would not hesitate to use it as leverage later. But without it, she would have nothing to
bargain with.

'You're asking me to burgle the count's house?'
Nolan's tone registered a certain amount of incredulity.

'I'm not asking you to do it alone,' Gianna answered swiftly. 'I'll be there with you.' She'd meant
it as encouragement, but, yes, she was asking him to
break into the count's house. 'I have a plan.' As if that
made it better. She rose from the table. 'We need to
go tonight, while the count is out. His staff will have
the evening off.'

Nolan's hand closed about her wrist, the steel of
his voice matching the steel of his grip, his answer
firm. 'No.'

For the first time, Gianna began to panic. He
couldn't refuse. He simply couldn't. She'd not allowed

herself to contemplate what to do if he said no. She'd been so sure. Everything hinged on going back. She would lose Giovanni if she didn't.

Chapter Nine

'We have to. You said you would help and I need your help tonight.' She tried to stay calm. Too much panic and he'd suspect there was more she hadn't revealed.

Nolan did not yield. 'I also said the perfection of *go* risotto was ruined by the smallest of missteps. You cannot simply go breaking into someone's house without careful planning, no matter how prettily you sulk.'

Perhaps if she *argued* prettily enough, then. 'What is there to plan? I know the house, I know the schedule of the servants. I know the location of the item. I am your plan and I assure you, I have no desire to be caught.' No one would be more careful than she when it came to that.

Nolan dragged her over to his packages and let go of her wrist. 'I have a better plan. We go tomorrow night. Open these.'

The packages were soft and pliable. Gianna undid

the string and tackled the brown wrapping. Inside one package was a heavy, red-damask gown trimmed in velvet and done in the medieval style. Beneath it lay a matching, fur-trimmed cloak and a final paper-wrapped package, this one hard and contoured. A mask, beautifully painted in red and white and sequined. She turned the mask over in her hand with a dubious scowl. 'This is for a masquerade, not a break in.' No doubt the second package, similar in shape, contained a male costume to match.

Nolan gave her a smug smile and fished out a heavy white square of paper from his coat pocket. 'I believe Count Minotti's annual masquerade ball is tomorrow night.' He passed her the invitation.

'Are you crazy? There will be people crawling all over the *palazzo*,' Gianna argued. Was he suggesting they try and remove the item during the masquerade? It was madness.

'The more the merrier.' Nolan grinned. 'No one will even know we're there. We'll go, we'll drink a little wine, we'll dance, we'll make free of the count's hospitality, we'll help ourselves to this item of yours, and be off. We won't even have to skulk around.'

His plan was starting to sound plausible, safe even, when Nolan said it. There was only one thing. Did they dare wait one more day? How long would the count wait before he demanded she come back to him? If confronted, would Nolan make good on his word not to send her back? Above all, how long would it be before the count could get to Giovanni and hold him for ransom against her return? Against her secrets? She knew already she'd give those secrets up to protect Giovanni, but then how would she support them?

Gianna did quick calculations in her head: How long would it take a message from the count to travel? When would he send it? Surely, not until tomorrow at the earliest and only then if he felt sure she was not coming back. Perhaps she could afford to wait twenty-four more hours, especially if waiting ensured her success and reduced her risk. With Nolan's plan, they wouldn't have to break in, only retrieve the item in question.

'Now that's settled...' Nolan smiled, sensing her acquiescence before she gave it '...I must thank you for the delicious meal and make my excuses. I need to change and be off.'

'You're leaving?' Gianna trailed behind him into the bedroom. This was not going as planned, but why did that surprise her? Nothing had gone as planned.

Nolan pulled off his coat and undid his cravat, quick hands undoing the buttons on his waistcoat and pulling out the tails of his shirt. 'Yes. I am committed to a card game this evening and I cannot be late. Can you pass me my evening jacket?'

'No, I cannot pass you your jacket.' Gianna fumed. This was not where she'd imagined the evening headed. They were supposed to be in a gondola by now, headed towards the count's house. Since they weren't burgling him tonight, she didn't have a back-up plan for the evening—perhaps do a bit of planning with the masquerade? Go over the layout of the count's *palazzo*? Whatever it was, it wasn't this.

Her temper started to rise. 'I've been stuck in this room all day, I've been pricked with needles and pins, draped with bolts of fabric and discussed as if I was nothing but a doll. On top of that, I planned you an excellent meal and all you have to say is "I'm going out"?'

Nolan tossed his old shirt on to the bed, obviously less concerned than she that he was undressing in front of her. He faced her, hands on hips, chest gloriously bare, his arms and torso an exhibition in lean, muscled strength. 'Yes, I am going out. I am committed to a card game this evening and I cannot be late, not if your penchant for spending my money is any indication of what it will cost me to keep you for the interim. You, my dear, have proven to be a very expensive acquisition. You have me buying wardrobes, eating silver-plated candlelight meals, drinking French champagne and burgling the homes of nobility.' He reached for a clean shirt and slid his arms into the sleeves. 'Now, I am going to change my trousers. You are welcome to stay and watch.'

Gianna fought the childish urge to stomp her foot. His arrogance was insufferable! He knew he was an attractive man in *and* out of his clothing. Two could play this game. 'I am not that desperate for entertainment. Perhaps, I shall go out as well. There was a concert at San Giorgio I wanted to take in.' It was true, a quartet of some talent was performing Vivaldi tonight. She moved with brisk efficiency towards the wardrobe where she'd stored some of the items Signora Montefiori was able to leave behind this afternoon. There was a gorgeous, fur-collared cloak she was eager to try.

Nolan's hand came over her shoulder and slammed shut the wardrobe door, his voice a growl in her ear, 'Don't be a fool, Gianna. You can't possibly go out, not if the count is as dangerous as you say.'

'Let go of the door, Nolan. You're being ridiculous. I'll be perfectly anonymous. It's dark out, there are revellers everywhere. No one will notice me.' She flashed him a coy smile over her shoulder, trying to ignore the fact that his half-dressed body was mere inches from hers. 'The more the merrier, isn't that right? Why is it that we can hide in plain sight at the masquerade tomorrow, but I can't hide in plain sight tonight?' There. Hoisted by his own petard, she thought smugly.

'Because there's no "we" tonight. You cannot go out in the dark *alone.*'

He had a point. Secretly, she was starting to rethink her hasty decision. Hardly anyone would notice her, that much was true, but that also meant no one would notice if anything untoward happened to her. Carnevale was a fun time, a free time, but it could also be a frightening time if one wasn't careful. She wouldn't be the first to go missing during Carnevale and never be heard from again. 'Come with me, then,' she challenged.

That was the last thing he wanted to do. The longer he was with Gianna, the further from sanity he slipped, and admittedly, he didn't have the world's tightest grasp on it to begin with. He needed distance and the card game would provide it. Just being in close proximity with her as he was now, breathing in the herbal scents of her toilet, rosemary and sage with a hint of lavender beneath, was enough to throw caution to the proverbial winds. Having already sat through a dinner, staring at her expressive face, watching her caress the pearl pendant at her throat, he thought caution might as well pack up and leave. It didn't stand a chance.

Ignoring caution was by no means a rare occurrence for him, he was a risk-taker by nature and by trade, after all. Caution spelled doom. The moment a gambler started being cautious was the moment he lost. But his risks were calculated. Most of the time. He'd gone a little berserk at the Palio in Siena for a good cause, but that could not be the case tonight. He needed his wits. An idea started to form, his mind ran the calculations. His hand released the wardrobe door. 'All right, we'll go to the concert.'

He stepped back, distancing himself from the smell of her, the heat of her, watching her as she gathered her things. Gianna flirted and enticed for all the wrong reasons. He wasn't about to take her to bed under those auspices no matter how tempting she was. As long as she used sex as a weapon, he had to be vigilant for both of them even if his body would prefer otherwise. Before that could happen, he needed her to recognise the power of the weapon she wielded. What would she do if he actually took her up on her offers? There might be a lesson for her in that. The sooner she learned it the better.

Still, Nolan was honest enough to admit that in the past twenty-four hours, Gianna had managed to get him to act not out of logic but out of emotion, not once, but three times. He was helping her because he empathised with her, not because there was any logical reason to do so. There was nothing logical about compassion. As long as he could recognise that, perhaps he wasn't as far gone as he feared.

Tonight, he would convince her she didn't want to be anywhere near him and that would buy him all the freedom he needed to keep his distance. He'd invest his time now for freedom tomorrow. If his plan went well, he wouldn't need to see her at all tomorrow, except for the masquerade. And if *that* went well, she'd be gone the day after, out of his life, just another adventure that had come and gone. He merely needed to survive the next forty-eight hours. But he was good at surviving. He'd been doing it for years.

Downstairs in the lobby, Nolan hired a gondola to take them across the canal to San Giorgio Maggiore and whisked Gianna outside into the dark. The fewer people who saw her the better. There was a wide hood on her cloak, but Nolan encouraged her to leave it down. Hiding her face only sent the message that they didn't want anyone to recognise her. Mystery bred attention.

'Get in and sit down. No rocking the boat this time,' he scolded her teasingly as he handed her in.

'I have no desire for a swim tonight.' He gave the gondolier their direction and ducked under the *felze*, taking his seat beside her as the boat pushed away from the pier.

'Thank you.' Gianna's gloved hand squeezed his in friendly appreciation where it lay on his leg. It was an honest and spontaneous gesture devoid of her more sensual flirtations.

Nolan chuckled. 'Oh, no, you're thanking me again. That means you want something.'

'It does not,' she protested with a small bit of outrage and a large bit of defensiveness.

'Yes, it does,' Nolan insisted with a laugh, enjoying this particular argument. He covered her hand with his. 'The first time you thanked me, you wanted to know why I was being nice to you. The second time you thanked me was followed up with a request to have me burgle your father's home. So, you'll have to excuse me if I'm a little suspicious.'

'Stepfather,' she interjected firmly. 'I don't know who my real father is, but it's not the count.'

Touchy subject, that. But the count was also a subject about which Nolan needed, *wanted*, to know more. He was going to burgle the man's house, he wanted to know what he was up against. And of course, there was the issue of knowing her. If he wanted to truly know Gianna, he had to know her past. Who was Gianna Minotti? That was the question that concerned him most as the gondola glided over the canal.

Nolan moved his thumb the length of her hand in a

slow caress through the leather of their gloves. 'And your mother? Where is she in all this?' A low, quiet voice, the soothing motion of his thumb, the privacy of the gondola all made for a most intimate atmosphere conducive to sharing secrets, and he would take advantage.

She looked down at their hands, her voice quiet. 'My mother has been dead these last five years.'

She'd been alone with only the count to guide her into adulthood. She'd been seventeen? Sixteen, maybe? On the verge of being presented to society. What sort of effort or commitment would the count have made on her behalf? Nolan had no sisters, but he had cousins and he'd watched them prepare for their débuts. Mothers were essential. What did fathers know of gowns and parties and navigating society when one was a young girl? Boys simply threw themselves on society, their wildness, their wilfulness, their mistakes tolerated as the sowing of oats. But girls had no such luxury. One mistake was fatal, like *go* risotto.

'Do you have any aunts nearby?' He knew before she answered that she did not. She would not have stayed with the count otherwise. But he was unprepared for the leashed vehemence in her response.

'My mother had no friends, not females friends at any rate. She was a high-class courtesan who managed to marry a nobleman before her looks went. So, no, I don't have any aunts, or any of the extended family Italians pride themselves on. The count does, of course, but there is no use in me accessing any of them even if they would acknowledge me.'

'There is just you?' Nolan traced circles on the back of her hand, feeling some of the tension go out of her. That gave rise to innumerable scenarios. A young woman alone, under the care of a guardian who had no compelling reason to look out for her best interests. The situation was ripe for all nature of scandal and the abuse of power. But it wouldn't last for ever, would it? Nolan thought about majorities and coming of age. 'At some point, you will outgrow the count's power. Is that what the other night was about?'

'He didn't think he'd lose. He meant only to use the wager as leverage to blackmail me into marriage.' Her voice was quiet.

'With whom?' A suspicion started to lay down roots in his mind. If she came of age the count would no longer have control over her. To some that would be a boon, a welcomed burden removed. Nolan would have thought the count would be overjoyed to be free of the obligation. Unless the count didn't want to lose control of her.

'Preferably with him,' she said matter-of-factly. 'You do see why I can't go back to him now. Going back would be a rather permanent arrangement.' Of course it would be. She had something the count wanted and every man and legal system in Europe knew the best way to control a woman and her property was through marriage.

'What is the item we're going to get tomorrow night?' It must be of great value if she'd risk walking back into the count's house. He'd seen her shudder earlier. Now he better understood what going back meant to her. It must also be the item the count wished to control through her.

'My mother's jewel case,' she said simply. Too simply. Nolan stopped caressing her hand. He didn't quite believe her. She'd told him more in this boat ride across the canal than she'd told him all day and while the atmosphere certainly prompted confidences, he had to wonder about the last. He didn't doubt that it wasn't true, only that the truth wasn't quite complete. She was still hiding something.

The gondola bumped against the pier at San Giorgio Maggiore and Nolan handed her out, keeping a hand at her back as they made their way into the church. The crowd was negligible. There were grander festivities all over Venice tonight. A few folding chairs had been set out and they found two on the far side of the aisle where they'd be out of the direct light. All the better for the lesson he wanted to teach.

He'd learned a great deal about this woman tonight, but he wasn't certain it had advanced his plan of convincing her how much distance she needed to keep from him. If anything, it had done the opposite and drawn him closer. A woman's physical beauty was something he'd disciplined himself to understand as a superficial characteristic and if need be to resist. But physical attractiveness coupled with a sharp intelligence that sparred with his wit, that defended her secrets—well, that was nigh on irresistible. It didn't help that his body was so keen on remembering the way her hands had felt and less keen on remembering why she'd done it. She'd wanted him distracted. Her gamble had been one-part genius and two-parts desperation. As such, it had and hadn't worked. He might have stopped her from seducing him, but her strategy had also succeeded in stopping the conversation.

The musicians took the small stage and the quartet settled into their chairs, giving their instruments a final tune-up. The audience went collectively still in anticipation. Silence filled the church and the music began, the plaintive strains of a lone violin announcing Vivaldi's 'Adagio in D'.

This was why he didn't go to concerts. The music was too damn beautiful, too damn soulful. It made him feel, it eroded his edge. It was why he pushed music away, but not Gianna. The music drew her. Beside him, Gianna was enrapt, the willingness to give herself over to the music evident in her eyes, in the soft smile that lingered on her lips over the familiar tune.

She looked over at him and that soft smile became his. He knew a moment's victory in that smile. He'd managed to steal it from the music. Her mouth began to move, to form words of gratitude. 'No,' he stopped her with a whisper and private smile. 'Don't even think about saying it, because I can't imagine what you might want next.'

He had no trouble imagining what *he* wanted next, though. He wanted to make love to her, wanted to show her sex was so much more than a weapon. But not yet. First, he had to show her how dangerous it was to wield, especially for a purported novice in the arts. Was the count's claim true? If so, it was all the more reason to protect her from herself and from him. Nolan nearly laughed out loud. There was a certain irony to the situation. In London, he was the man most likely to seduce, well, anything. Now, he'd become a protector of virgins.

The adagio ended and the quartet launched their full assault on his senses with their main presentation, the classic *Four Seasons*: forty-three minutes of mental lovemaking. Nolan did not try to fight it. He gave his imagination free rein. He wanted to pull the pins out of her hair to the languorous melodies of summer, wanted to watch her hair fall in slow accord to the violins' indolent, lazy strains.

The quartet moved into the rousing melodies of autumn and he imagined dancing her up against the wall of the church, running playful kisses down her neck, over her breasts, kneeling before her and skimming her navel with his lips in a celebration of passion and life before he took her with hard thrusts, to the sharp, icy rhythms of winter, letting passion break over them with the force of an avalanche. He let his eyes slide in her direction. Did she have any idea of the thoughts running through his mind as she sat there? This was why he was dangerous to her, why she should have let him play cards tonight instead. She thought he was her assistant, that she had somehow manoeuvred him, when really he was winter's wolf and he would ravish her with the slightest of invitations.

Chapter Ten

The music faded in a single, quivering note, followed by the applause of the modest audience. 'Did you enjoy it?' Gianna reached for her cloak where it draped over her chair, but Nolan was faster. He held it out for her, letting his hands linger firmly at her shoulders in a gesture that left no room for misinterpretation. This was no subtle brushing of hands that might be dismissed as accidental. This was a man issuing an invitation, and it made her mouth go dry. This particular man didn't have to 'invite', he could have simply announced his intentions. She was technically his and she hadn't forgotten. Yet, he'd given her the choice.

His voice hovered warm and private at her ear. 'I did. However, I enjoyed watching *you* far more.' She'd known that. She'd felt his gaze on her throughout the concert, hot and intense but she'd not found it repellent or frightening. Just the opposite. Heat had pooled low in her belly as if he were the flame to her match and her pulse had raced at the thought of attracting the attentions of a man like Nolan Gray; a man who was powerful, handsome, skilled in the art of seduction.

She should not be excited by him. What did that say about her? Did such an attraction make her wanton? Did the blood of a courtesan run in her veins, too? Perhaps there truly was no escaping her destiny. The strategist in her whispered the tempting thought: *If it is inevitable, why not embrace it, embrace your power? He desires you. Use it to your benefit.*

Gianna turned in his grasp, a coy smile on her lips as she raised her eyes to his, her voice pitched husky and low. 'Was I a worthy subject for your ruminations?' Her hands rested on the lapels of his coat, against the strength of his chest.

His hands reached behind her neck, drawing the pins from her hair. She could feel the *coiffure* loosen, a few curls fall. His fingers combed through them, his touch brushing against her neck, sending a shiver of delight down her spine. She suddenly wanted his touch on her everywhere. 'You were more than worthy.'

Those words had her making rapid justifications in her mind now. If she chose this course, there would be no going back, but Giovanni needed her even if he didn't know it yet and she feared she would not be able to reach him alone. The greater good would be worth it. She would not be the first woman to use that most feminine of powers for gain.

Even as she bargained with herself, she knew the

real fear was that Nolan would not be the only one swept away if she committed to this path. The race of her pulse when he touched her, when he looked at her, was indication enough that she could very well become caught in her own web. That had been her mother's downfall—not that she was a courtesan. Gianna had never faulted her mother for that, only for falling in love or what passed for it.

Nolan's voice was low for her alone. He gave a half-smile, his fingers tracing a lingering trail at her neck. 'You inspire a man to wickedness, Gianna. Shall I show you?'

Around them, the church had emptied quickly. There was only the two of them and the light of the votive candles in the prayer racks. Her back hit the smooth wall beside the little flames. She hadn't realised they'd moved. 'I thought of taking down your hair and watching it fall through my fingers.'

The pins disappeared out of her hair with alarming swiftness, the length of it pooling in the hood of her cloak. Nolan's hands were at her temples, smoothing away her hair, his eyes dropping to her mouth. 'After your hair was loose, my hands tangled in its length, I would put my mouth on you.' His lips hovered above hers, her body on fire at his words, her head tilted up to his, all of her eager for his touch.

'Where, Nolan? Where would you put your mouth?' She breathed the question in the merest of whispers.

'Here.' His mouth covered hers, and she opened for him, ready for him as she'd not been quite ready last night. There was no hesitancy tonight. Tonight, she was his partner, coaxing and encouraging him to give free rein to his fantasies. His tongue teased her mouth, running over lips, teeth, even her own tongue in slow, exploratory strokes. She leaned into him, into the kiss, answering his exploration with one of her own, and it stoked the fire in her higher.

'And here.' Nolan's mouth moved to her throat, pressing a kiss to the pulse point that beat at the base. His hand reached beneath the folds of her cloak to push back the shoulders of her gown, his mouth finding her skin above the lace trim of her chemise, his lips skimming the hint of bare breast that rose above the lace. She arched against the wall, arched into him, her body begging, inviting more as his hand slipped beneath the fabric. This was torture, to have his touch, but not enough of it. His mouth, his hands, it was not nearly enough. She wanted to be naked beneath him, wanted him to strip away the garments that kept his mouth from devouring all of her.

His mouth returned to hers, leaving her breast to the warm competence of his hand and the wicked caress of his thumb over the peak of her nipple. She kissed him with abandon this time, her hands in his hair, her body pressing recklessly against his. But she was not the only reckless one, his body was hard against hers, his own heart beating strong and fast in rhythm with the madness. Somewhere in the distance, bells chimed.

Midnight! The thought registered vaguely in Nolan's heated brain, but it was enough to sound the alarm. He'd been in Catholic Italy long enough to know what midnight meant. Nolan broke from her, his voice hoarse with need unfulfilled. 'Right yourself, we must go. The monks will be here for matins soon.'

Nolan stepped back, giving her a chance to arrange her bodice. What had he been thinking? He'd nearly ravished her in a church! If it hadn't been for the risk of monks discovering them *in flagrante delicto*, he would have. He raked a hand through his hair. His father would have had a fine time with that—Oliver Gray's son tupping women in churches would be a sin beyond imagining, worse than anything Nolan had done to date in his father's eyes.

He'd begun this interlude with a plan in mind: Let her see that she played a dangerous game. If she wanted to flirt with him, there would be consequences and he would show her what they were. He'd not expected it to go as far as it had. He'd expected to feel the reticence of last night when her hands had slid up his thighs, not entirely certain. He'd expected to feel the hesitation of her mouth when he'd kissed her. Instead, she'd answered him with her tongue, with her body, her hands, and it had left his plan in shreds.

She'd not been frightened off by his bold sensuality. She'd embraced it and it had ratcheted up his desire to the point that he would have taken her against the wall if not for the bells. And it shamed him. Tonight, she had bested him. She'd taken his game and turned it against him. He should have been more astute.

Nolan ushered her out of the church, his steps brisk, his hand at her back propelling her towards the pier, his words coming in terse businesslike sentences. 'The gondolier will take you to the hotel. He will see to it that you're safe. Go directly up to the room, just in case the count has bothered to discover where you are. If there is any emergency, you can go next door and ask for Brennan Carr, my travelling companion.'

They reached the edge of the pier before Gianna staged her rebellion. She crossed her arms and faced him. 'Where might you be going to in such a hurry? You practically dragged me out of the church.'

'For which you should be glad. If we had stayed we might have been discovered in a most indecent position. I told you earlier, I had a card game. I *still* have a card game.'

'When will you be back?' She was furious. 'You are always leaving me.'

Nolan took a step closer to her, keeping their conversation private, his voice a growl. 'Do you want me to stay? After what happened in the church, there can be no doubt about where our evening is headed if I do.' Dammit all, he didn't want to have to spell it out for her. 'You tempt me to sin and yet I don't think those are sins you are ready to commit.' The knuckles of his hand grazed her cheek in a slow stroke. He watched her eyes meet his at the contact and then drift away. He had his confirmation. 'I do not think you understand how powerful sex can be. Men have gone to war over it.'

She would be a sensual partner in bed, when she

was ready, but not yet. He did not want to *take* her like a battle prize, something he'd conquered.

'Let me know when you make up your mind.' He wanted her to come to him, and then—oh, then the things he could show her. There was nothing more seductive than choice. In the meantime, if sex was what he wanted, he knew where to find it. Louisa von Haas would be more than accommodating. He took her hand and kissed the gloved knuckles. 'Now you see why it is best that we part ways for the evening. Get in the gondola and go.'

She'd not seen the dismissal coming! What a fool she'd been to be taken so unaware. She'd thought they were making progress in the church—well, perhaps not 'they', but certainly she was in her attempt to draw him close.

Gianna drew off her gloves and threw them on the small table next to the door. Apparently kissing a woman up against a church wall was all in a night's work for Nolan Gray. Which might explain why he was capable of walking away from it without as much as a backward glance. There was another explanation, too. He had simply seen her coming, strategy and all. He'd been wary of her motives from the start.

Gianna trailed her cloak over the back of a chair, its haphazard drape ruining the perfection of the room. Someone had been here after they'd left to clear the dinner things, to turn down the lamps. In the bedroom, someone had turned down the bed and laid out the silky nightgown. Nolan Gray must indeed be paying them a fortune for the flawless service he received, proof enough that she wasn't beggaring him with her dinner and dresses. Proof enough, too, that he didn't *need* the card game in the way he suggested. But he had needed it in other ways. He'd needed the distance. If he had walked away, it hadn't been without some effort. There was consolation in that.

She should be glad for his restraint—if that's what it could be called. There'd been nothing restrained about the encounter until the end. What had happened in the church had affected them both. Gianna changed into the nightgown, the slide of silk against her body reminding her of other touches, of his hand on her breast, his mouth on her neck, on her mouth, and how her body had thrilled to his touch wherever it had been, she had thrilled to him in other places, too, that had gone untouched by his hands but not untouched by his words. *I want to put my mouth on you, here and here and here...* Even now those words could recall the thrill they had raised.

She faced herself in the mirror, her hands moving to cup her breasts, through the silk of the nightgown, lifting them, running her thumbs over the peaks, feeling them rouse a little like they had for him, but it was only a mere facsimile of the truth he'd wrung from them, from her.

That truth still seared her. She'd not wanted him to stay for the sake of her game—the game didn't need him to stay. She already had his consent. He'd burgle the count's house without it. He'd pledged his help in return for her leaving, not for sex, not for pleasure, not for the liberties he could take against a church wall. Staying was something she wanted for herself alone. She wanted more of what had happened against the church wall, more of his mouth, more of his hands, more of his body pressed indecently against her, his need for her evident in the bold erection he'd made no attempt to hide.

Perhaps it was her curiosity that had driven her wild as much as his mouth. Maybe she was her own worst enemy in her efforts to resist his lures or were those lures really cautions? Tonight had been meant to warn her away, but it had only served to heighten the complex pull she felt when she was with him.

He had cautioned her to make up her mind, to lay down her weapon and seek pleasure instead, and yet she felt those words suited him as well. He was not without his own conundrum. He wanted her *and* he wanted her to leave. He could not have both. It made her wonder what sort of plans he had? Did a real mistress await him? Was he looking forward to her leaving? She hoped he'd regret the thought of her leaving a little, otherwise her next revelation might come as an unpleasant surprise.

Gianna slid beneath the covers of the big bed. She didn't dare think beyond tomorrow night and the masquerade. She would focus on the jewel box. Once she had it, then, and only then, would she think about the next item. She'd seen too many people tripped up by looking too far ahead. It was better to focus on the immediate future. Somewhere in the distance, a clock chimed the hour. She blew out the lamp beside the bed, leaned back against the pillows and said her prayers. They were very simple ones, ones she'd prayed every night since her mother passed away. *Please let Giovanni be safe. Please let me be enough.*

The clock chimed two in the morning and Count Agostino Minotto ran a hand across the chessboard, scattering the pieces in play on the floor. '*Basta!* Enough!' He could hardly concentrate on the game, so distracted was he by Gianna's absence. What was she doing? Was she still in the city? Had she enticed the Englishman to help her? Had she slept with the English bastard? If she'd done any of it, it was all his fault. He'd let her slip through his fingers with that wager.

His opponent, the decadently handsome, dark-haired Romano Lippi, merely laughed. 'She'll be back.' Romano bent down to pick up the pieces. He set the queen back on her square. 'The Englishman will return her when he is done with her. It's only been a day.'

The count grunted and said nothing. It had seemed like a good idea at the time. He'd thought to frighten her into accepting his proposal. He'd imagined putting the wager to her and watching her beg him not to do it, watching her bargain anything not to be sent away, even marriage to him, which would give him everything he wanted. He was well aware she didn't like him, didn't trust him. But better the devil you know. Or so he'd thought. But Gianna hadn't quivered, not once. She'd merely marched off with the Englishman.

'You're just upset she preferred a stranger over you.' Romano poured each of them another drink.

Hell, yes, he was upset. He took a long swallow. He'd misjudged her. She'd called his bluff and allowed him to wager her instead of crying and begging. Even then, he hadn't worried. He had had a good hand, one that should win. He wouldn't really lose her. He'd only meant to scare her. Then that Englishman had laid down an unbeatable hand. Now she was gone.

He didn't regret what he might have doomed her to. He was hardly bothered about the fact that he might have sent his ward to lie with a stranger. He *was* bothered that she'd slipped out of his control. For all intents and purposes, she was loose in Venice, able to cultivate an ally in the Englishman if she wished to, able to strike back at him if he didn't strike out at her first. To be honest, it did make him nervous. There was a small fortune and jewels at stake that would see him through for some years.

If she remained free for four weeks, all of her money would be hers. He would lose every last bit of control, everything he'd worked for in the past five years. That would set a domino effect in motion. He would lose the *palazzo*, he would become a *barnabotti*—a nobleman with no funds—as he had been before Gianna's mother had presented with him with an opportunity he couldn't refuse.

The count fingered a pawn and set it down. She might have her freedom, but it would cost her. He'd given Gianna twenty-four hours to decide her fate: return to him or run. She had chosen to remain at large. What happened next would be on her head. Tomorrow, he would send the letter that would decide Giovanni's fate. As long as he controlled her brother, he could still force her hand. He gave Romano a long, lingering look that Romano returned before rising and coming to massage his shoulders. Agostino sighed and let the tension go. He understood Romano, Romano was easy to please: money and attention were all he required. But women were damnably frustrating creatures.

Nolan sipped the coffee and watched the Piazza San Marco come alive in slow, predictable rhythm. First would come the carters and vendors bound for the markets, then the shopkeepers and the restaurant owners who depended on the vendors to supply their businesses. Finally, long after he'd drunk his coffee, would come the daily shoppers and the tourists.

After six weeks in Venice, he still hadn't tired of the rhythm. Venice felt good. The city suited him, as if they were made for one another. In a way, he supposed they were. Like him, Venice was a city that had accrued its power through wealth instead of landownership. He owned nothing, not yet.

Of course, that was the old Venice, the Venice of the sixteenth and seventeenth centuries, a Venice that was long gone now. But modern Venice was like him, too. Modern Venice preferred pleasure. Venice had refashioned herself around that pleasure, lifted herself from the ashes of Napoleon much as he had lifted himself from the ashes of his family and his father's unyielding dominance.

The city was a subdued phoenix, certainly not the pleasure capital she'd once been, but a phoenix none the less. The city and himself had decided not to tolerate their dismal situations and had taken efforts to change them. There was a saying he was quite fond of: if you do what you've always done, you'll get what you've always got. In other words, change was only possible when one changed his circumstances. The Grand Tour had been his chance to do that in the most literal of ways.

Why aren't you doing that with Gianna, then? You know it works. The thought hit him forcefully. He was *waiting* for her to convince herself sex didn't have to be only a weapon, a means to an end. But her convincing might need some help. What if she didn't know how to convince herself? What if he changed her mind for her? The whole day lay before them, with nothing to do but wait for the masquerade. Until now. Nolan rose. He was going to seduce Gianna for her own good and what better place to do it than Venice, a city made for pleasure.

'Get dressed, we're going out, sleepyhead!'

Gianna threw an arm over her face against the invading light. She'd slept poorly and it seemed patently unfair that Nolan should be so freakishly cheerful. She had not pegged him as morning person. Gianna rolled over and hid her face in the pillow with a mumbled protest. 'Whatever happened to breakfast at noon?'

'We've got a lot to do today.' She could hear Nolan moving about the room, opening drawers and wardrobes. Something soft and filmy hit her face.

'Please stop going through my undergarments.' She nudged the chemise aside.

'Then get up and get them yourself.' Nolan dropped a pile of clothes on the bed and pressed on the mattress with the full force of his hands, bouncing it.

'You're obnoxious, just like…' She stopped herself. She'd nearly said *my little brother*. She didn't want that to slip out, not yet. She'd tell Nolan about

Giovanni when the time was right, or if the time was ever right. Perhaps, once she had the jewel case, she would be able to go after Giovanni on her own. Nolan need never know the count had her brother locked away on the mainland. Tonight was the first step in getting him back. Gianna swallowed back the lump in her throat.

'Just like what?' Nolan stopped jiggling the bed and moved away. She could hear him pouring something. Then the aroma hit her.

'Ahhhh.' Gianna sat up, eyes open. 'You brought coffee. I love you.'

Nolan passed her the cup. 'Twenty minutes, that's all you get. It's already half past ten. The day's a-wasting.'

Gianna took a long, fortifying swallow of coffee. 'Where are we going? You haven't forgotten we've got the count's house to burgle.' She said it lightly but she did fear for a moment that perhaps this was a strategy to get out of his promise.

Nolan leaned down so she could see those amazing grey eyes and that infectious smile up close. 'We are going to the fish market and, second, I have not forgotten about the count's house, but that is hours away, a whole day away and we must do something to pass the time.'

'The fish market?' Gianna wrinkled her nose. 'Whatever for?'

'You'll see.' Nolan grinned and pulled out his pocket watch, snapping it open. 'Eighteen minutes, Gianna. Tick-tock.'

She dressed quickly in the deep-raspberry walking gown because she was curious and because the dress was exquisite. At least that was what she told herself as she tucked a final pin into her hair. She told herself her quickness had nothing to do with the excitement of being out with Nolan, or the anticipation of what might happen next between them. She knew there was a sexual game between them. How could there not be under the circumstances that had thrown them together? And yet, even knowing that game was there, he constantly took her by surprise.

The church last night had been enlightening. It had stripped her bare in all ways; her wanting exposed by his hands, his lips; her strategy exposed by his words. He'd spiked her guns most effectively. He *knew* she meant sex to be her weapon against him, the tool by which she would manoeuvre him into compliance. He'd called her bluff against that hard wall at San Giorgio Maggiore and then given her the choice— to explore the pleasures of sex instead of the politics of it…with *him*.

Gianna flung her cloak about her shoulders. If that was what today was about, she'd best be on her game. *Or off it*, a wicked little voice tempted. The thought gave her pause. Perhaps today wasn't meant to be so much about being on her guard as it was about letting her guard down. Did she trust him enough for that? Did she trust herself? The part of her that remembered his mouth on her in the church, his hands in her hair, wanted to. The cynic in her launched a violent protest.

What would happen if she let him in? It was frightening to contemplate. Letting him in risked much. Her world was a dark mess full of the count's betrayals and cruelties. If Nolan truly knew the darkness that surrounded her, he might rethink all of it—the burglary tonight, even his association with her. Giovanni needed her to act circumspectly. She'd failed her brother once. It had led to him being sent away, an act the count had meant to punish her and it had. For four years now, it had been the driving force behind everything she'd done, everything she'd endured at the count's hand: *save Giovanni; make a new life for the two them where he could not be made to suffer for her rash actions.* She had cost him four years of freedom already, she would not cost him any more. She would make it up to him somehow, even if it meant resisting the temptations Nolan offered.

Nolan was waiting for her in the lobby, offering her his arm, sweeping her out to the piazza and into the throng of sightseers who'd come to enjoy the city for Carnevale. Apparently, along with rooting out her clothes, he'd grabbed some for himself as well and had taken time to freshen up somewhere else, perhaps the club room, while she'd changed. He'd traded his evening clothes for walking attire and tall boots. He'd even managed to shave. No one looking at him would guess he'd been up the entire night.

'Isn't this a little backwards?' Gianna asked as they headed towards the Rialto. 'Shouldn't *I* be showing *you* around the city? Technically, you're the visitor.'

Nolan merely grinned. 'No, today, you are the tourist. I am going to show you Venice my way.' When he smiled at her that way, making her the sum of his world in that gaze, she had the feeling resistance would be pointless no matter what vows she'd made herself.

North of the Rialto Bridge was the fish market, the *pescheria*, the largest and arguably the oldest in the city…and it was exciting. With Nolan's hand at her back, they navigated the stalls, taking in the fish, all fresh caught that morning in the lagoon or farther out in the Adriatic: shrimps, scallops, lobsters, crabs, cod, sole. The rows of stalls piled with fish on display were mesmerising in their diversity—fish of all shapes and colours stared back at her.

The market was bustling with customers. Fishmongers called out their wares, people haggled over prices, loud voices rose and fell in hearty competition. 'It doesn't smell, not really,' Gianna commented as they stopped beside a booth that served bowls of fish stew.

'Fresh fish doesn't usually smell.' Nolan gave her a curious smile and turned to the vendor, ordering two bowls and a half loaf of fresh-baked bread. He handed one to her. 'I believe you are in need of breakfast. Let's sit.' He motioned to a set of rough benches and plank tables set to the side of the market.

Gianna couldn't imagine a better breakfast. She followed Nolan's lead and dipped her bread into the stew broth, laughing when she dribbled. Nolan whipped out a handkerchief and dabbed at her chin. 'It's delicious.'

'I think simple food is often the best food.' Nolan tore off another chunk of bread and offered it to her. 'Tell me, have you been here?'

The question caught her off guard. Gianna looked up from her stew. 'I've lived in Venice my whole life.'

'That's not what I asked. Have you ever come here?'

'Not since I was a little girl. Even then only once or twice. My mother's…' She paused, hesitated. 'Er… *protectors* always arranged for servants, at least a cook and a lady's maid.'

Nolan nodded, not put off by the reminder of her mother's profession. 'And the count?'

'He had servants, too. There was no need.' Her voice trailed off and she concentrated on her stew. But she'd already given too much away.

'You didn't come here on your own just to walk around by choice? Or the count didn't permit it?' Nolan probed. His eyes were on her. 'You don't have to lie for him, Gianna.'

She met his gaze. 'Perhaps I have to lie for myself,' Gianna answered softly, 'so we can enjoy this lovely winter morning you've planned for us. There is no need to burden you with my life.'

'Maybe I want to be burdened.' Nolan dipped a piece of bread into the hot broth and held it to her lips. 'Or shall I make it easy for you and guess? The count did not allow you to leave his *palazzo*?'

Gianna summoned her courage. Would he offer

pity and then politely distance himself? Perhaps it was better to know now what sort of man he was than to know later when perhaps it was too late to save herself. 'After my mother died, the count did not allow us to leave the *palazzo*. He said that was what servants were for, but we knew better. If we left, we might never come back and he knew that.'

'We? Who is we?' Nolan asked softly, lifting another piece of broth-dipped bread to her lips.

It was all or nothing now. 'My brother and I.' She watched his grey eyes take in the news. It seemed that the bustle of the fish market had receded, leaving them in a cocoon apart from the world. There was only the two of them and her story if she was willing.

Nolan's voice was quiet and prompting. 'Where is your brother now?'

She didn't answer immediately. The shame was too great. Where he was, was all her fault. 'The count sent him away when he was thirteen.' She'd not meant to say even that much, but it had come spilling out of her.

'Why?' Nolan divided the last of the bread between them and offered her a section. 'You can tell me, Gianna. You needn't worry you'll shock me.' It was what a lot of people said. Few of them meant it or even knew *how* to mean it. But Nolan's next words convinced her that perhaps he might be different. 'I have a brother, too, Gianna.' He lifted his eyes to hers. 'I know what it means to want to save them... and to fail.'

'I was stubborn. I had stood up to the count one too many times in the months after my mother died.

I was furious that he had managed to be named our guardian. He was furious that I wouldn't sign over complete control of the money my mother had left me.' Gianna broke the bread into little pieces, trying to tell the story with some detachment. That day was still so vivid although it had been four years ago. In his anger, the count had swung his fist at her. It wouldn't have been the first time the count had hit her or tried physical force to gain her compliance, but it was the first time Giovanni had been present.

'My brother stepped between us, trying to defend me.' It happened in slow motion again in her mind. 'The count grabbed him and flung him against the wall. He hit his head.' She had been the one to call the doctor. She had stayed beside him for endless days, fearing that if she left him, the count wouldn't let her back. She loved Giovanni on his own merits, but she'd also promised her mother they would be together always. It was a promise she hadn't been able to keep.

'When he was well enough to travel, the count sent him away to punish me. I haven't seen him in four years. But not a day goes by I don't think about him, about what I should have done differently.'

'I know. Sometimes our best isn't enough.' Nolan's reply was solemn. Nolan was always so confident, always in charge. She was hard-pressed to think he'd ever fail. They'd finished their bread and stew and it was time to move on. Around them, the fish market came to life again.

Nolan tucked her arm through his as they strolled into the *erberia* that abutted the *pescheria*. Another time, she would have been captivated by the fragrant rows of sage and rosemary, and the bright vibrant colours of the vegetables, but her attention was for the man beside her who confided in quiet tones the secrets of his childhood. His voice was at her ear, low and private, his words surprising. 'My father is a staunchly religious man who believes evil is best handled at it root.' Nolan struggled at first, searching for words. She had the sensation perhaps he was putting words to this story for the first time. She was patient, letting him fill the silence on his own.

'The moment he sees evil, it is to be stamped out. In his opinion, the best way to do that is with a swift and sure whip hand. I am two years older than my brother. When I was at home, it was easy enough to protect him. I would just take the blame for whatever my father accused my brother of.'

'And the whipping for it, too?' Gianna asked, feeling Nolan's eyes on her, hard and flinty. To his credit he did not pursue that to its logical conclusion. Perhaps he didn't have to.

'Yes,' was all he said. 'My brother is a kind soul, a soft soul, even if he is a bit rambunctious at times. I'd rather have been whipped than see his spirit crushed. It was my choice. He never asked it of me.' Nolan's jaw tightened. 'Then I was sent away to school and there was no one left to protect him. I did what I could to buy him some time before he could go away to school, too. I managed to get sent down from Harrow right away and a couple of other schools followed in short order. After a boy gets a certain reputation, it gets easier to be sent down.'

Nolan shrugged. 'My strategy worked for the first year, but it wasn't enough. My grandfather is an earl, my father, viscount. Between them, they called in some favours and got me sent to Eton, the best of the best. They called in more favours to ensure I could not be sent down for the sake of the family name. There was nothing I could do.'

Gianna felt his grip on her arm tighten, sensed the helplessness in his tone, the blame, too. She covered his hand with hers, implicitly giving him strength, recognising, for the first time, he needed her in this moment. How many times had she felt the same? How many times had she protected Giovanni in the same way only to fail him at the end? 'There's more, isn't there, Nolan?' Gianna whispered, her eyes locked on him, willing him to stay with her, to not pull away. 'What happened?'

'Only Archer knows. I've never told anyone else. Not Haviland, not Bren.' Nolan's voice was barely a whisper. He looked down at her hand where it rested on his arm, gathering himself. 'That year, my father shoved my brother down the stairs. The fall shattered his leg. He'll walk with a limp for the rest of his life. He is lucky it wasn't worse.'

'Nolan, how horrible!' His story threatened to undo her. It was as if his words echoed the fears of her own heart. If she had simply done something differently, Giovanni would still be with her. She had no illusions the count had sent him anywhere edifying. She feared what she would find when she finally reached him.

Then came the confession. 'To this day, I feel like it's my fault. If I had been there, I could have stopped it.'

What could she say to that? She knew words of denial were inadequate. There'd been no comfort in such words when she'd faced them with Giovanni. All she could do was hold Nolan's gaze and let him see her eyes fill with tears on his behalf.

It wasn't only the story itself that brought tears to her eyes. It was the man telling it. There were depths to this man, impressive depths of honour and courage. She'd been wrong to think life was a lark to him, everything a game. *Do not like him,* came the warning, followed swiftly by another: *What will he want in exchange for his story?* But the admonition came too late. In that moment when he brought his eyes to hers, his soul was naked for the briefest of seconds and Gianna knew she was lost. She was going to fall for him—the only question was how far?

Chapter Twelve

Nolan steered them out of the *erberia* away from the crowd. They both needed space and silence in which to appreciate and dissect what they'd shared. He had not meant to tell her so much, but once the words came he'd not wanted to stop. He'd heard the pain in her voice when she'd spoken of her brother and he'd wanted her to know he understood. Simply saying the words 'I understand' wasn't enough. She wouldn't believe them. He'd wanted to prove it to her, wanted to prove to her that she wasn't alone. He gave her his story; the secret story of his home. He'd given her a glimpse of the depths of his family's dysfunction in exchange for her tale, for a peek into her world, into what drove her.

As difficult as it had been to summon that story, it had been worth it. He was horrified to hear about her life with the count, but it helped him understand her—why she was so wary, why she viewed sex as a weapon, why she was so desperate: she was planning her escape from imprisonment, from isolation.

The very thought of it raised Nolan's anger. The count needed to be served justice for what he'd done. But justice could wait until tonight. Today was for more than sad memories and regrets. Today was for trust and for pleasure. He had made inroads on the trust— they'd given each other their secrets. Now it was time for the pleasure.

They passed quiet shops selling groceries and Nolan ducked inside one shop, coming out with a modest basket of bread and cheese. At another shop, he added a bottle of wine. The wine made Gianna smile. 'What is all this?'

'This…' Nolan swung the basket '…is for the next part of our afternoon,' Nolan said mysteriously. He found them a gondola with its *felze* up for privacy and handed her in, giving instructions to the gondolier to row them through the quiet canals where they wouldn't be disturbed.

Gianna reclined on the plush cushions beneath the *felze*, shrewd eyes watching him as he settled beside her, his basket between them. Nolan reached for the bottle, pulling the cork with practised ease. 'Is this the part where you get me drunk on wine?' she said, part-wariness and part-flirtation as he handed her a glass.

Nolan clinked his goblet against hers, offering a wicked grin. 'You misunderstand my motives, my dear. Consider this fair warning. This is the part where I seduce you.'

He already had. The lightest of touches would topple the fortress of her restraint, or what remained of it. The fish market, the most unlikely of venues, had wiped out her resistance entirely. Gianna sipped at the rich red wine, contemplating the man beside her. Who would have thought a trip to the fish market, a most innocuous site entirely devoid of any romantic connotation, would have undone her so completely? And yet it had.

The remnants of her resistance gathered themselves into a final defence. Gianna held his gaze steady over the rim of her goblet. 'Did you know I had not been out of the Minotti *palazzo* under my own power for over four years?' When she had, it had been with the count as a guard to functions like the Calergi *palazzo*. The simple pleasure of attending the concert last night and walking through the market, eating fish stew this morning had been intoxicating almost beyond measure, second only to the glimpse of pleasures found in his arms.

'No, I did not realise it until this morning when you told me.' Nolan met her gaze evenly, eyes full of sincerity and heat.

'Are you sure?' Her tone was full of cynicism for himself as well as for her. It was a masterful plan if that was what it was and she had fallen for it. 'Take the pitiful girl to the fish market and she'll tell you everything.' She could add to that, *Buy her new clothes and make her feel cherished. Slam her up against a church wall, kiss her a few times and make her feel desired.*

Nolan merely laughed. 'Do you know how ridiculous that logic is? A man that manipulative wouldn't be invested in your cause anyway, he wouldn't be planning to burgle the count's house on your behalf.'

Gianna's eyes narrowed. 'My logic is not "ridiculous", as you put it. A man would do those things if there was something in it for him.'

'Like what?' Nolan's elegant hand lifted his goblet to his lips. 'A stay in an Italian jail? I believe stealing is still a crime in Venice. I doubt anything in the jewel case is worth the risk. At any rate, it's not a gamble I would take simply on merits of profit.'

'Then why are you?' The words were out of her mouth before she could stop them, the question a natural evolution of the conversation, but not a wise one. What would she do if he realised the rashness of his commitment and backed out now? Did she dare storm the *palazzo* alone? It was sobering to acknowledge how much she'd come to depend on him in such a short time. She, who'd sworn to never be dependent on a man, was relying quite heavily on a stranger she'd met two days ago. He had been generous and she'd been cruel. She offered a hasty apology. 'I'm sorry, I don't know why I said that.'

'I do. You've been fighting for so long you don't know how to do anything else.' He took the goblet from her, a hand cradling her jaw as the gondola rocked gently beneath them. 'Stop fighting, Gianna. Just for the afternoon. Let me show you the possibilities of pleasure.' He didn't wait for an answer, for permission. But he'd already given fair warning, hadn't he? He moved into her, covering her mouth with his, wooing her with the subtlety of his kiss. She tasted the rich flavour of wine on his tongue as it made a slow tour of her mouth, her lips.

She opened to him, her own tongue wanting to explore, too, wanting to tangle lazily with his. Nolan made it sound so simple. *Just for the afternoon.* It was a temporary indulgence after years of loneliness. As such, what harm could come of one afternoon? She couldn't summon an answer. There was no reason to resist when she felt his arm slide around her, his hand drawing her close against the length of his body as they reclined on the velvet cushions. This was their world, here beneath the privacy of the *felze* where there was no one to see, no one who would ever know. The fantasy would end with the boat ride.

His hips moved against hers, inviting, luring, his lips whispering temptation with his words. 'Let me show you pleasure.' He made it sound as if she had a choice, but that choice had already been made. Perhaps she'd made it long before this.

Gianna placed his hand on her breast, her mouth at his ear with words of her own in answer. 'Touch me, Nolan, show me how it can be.' She knew, of course, how it could be, in part. Last night in the church had offered her a taste. But this was different. He wasn't trying to teach her a lesson, wasn't trying to scare her off as he had been last night, although that lesson had been quickly forgotten by both parties by the time it was done. This was something altogether different, in some ways gentler but no less in its intensity. His hands worked her bodice loose, the cool air brushing

over bare skin to be replaced by the slide of his warm
hands over her breasts, the contrast of heat and cold a
decadence all its own, heightening the sensitivity of
her skin to even the lightest of touches. The palm of
his hand ran reverently over the slope of her breast,
her body tightening, priming itself in anticipation of
his touch in other places.

'I want to touch you, too,' Gianna murmured, her
hand dropping to the fastenings of his trousers, working them free before he could protest. He was hot beneath her hand, ready and entirely alive in a way he
had not been that first night when she'd knelt before
him. He had roused, certainly, as would have any
healthy young male. But this was not limited to the
perfunctory provision of physical release in exchange
for something in return.

She slid her hand along his length, her thumb running over his tender head, eliciting a gasp. She did it
again and he sucked in his breath. '*You* are a temptress,' he growled with a chuckle, his teeth nipping
at her earlobe in playful retaliation. But he was not
without his own temptations, his own sensual retali-
ations. His hand slid beneath her skirts to the damp-
ness between her thighs. Her breath caught at the
intimate contact. She knew with a certainty of instinct, this was where they would have gone in the
church if they'd allowed themselves to continue; to
an intimacy far greater than any they had shared yet,
to a pleasure greater than any he'd given her.

'Look at me, Gianna.' His voice was a soft com-

mand, his gaze steady as she held it. 'I want to see
the pleasure in your eyes when it comes.' He stroked
her then, his hand pressing on her mons with intimate force, his thumb running up the narrow furrow
to find the nub inside.

She gasped against the sensation: startling, pleasing, addicting. 'Again, Nolan, please,' she whispered,
watching a smile take his mouth in response to what
he saw in her eyes. He took her then in full force, his
mouth on hers, his hand at the core of her pleasure,
his thumb mirroring the caress of his tongue until she
arched against his hand in a desperate need to accommodate the release sweeping her. She was torn. She
wanted nothing more than to be swept away by this
pleasure, yet she wanted nothing more than to linger
on this new shore a while longer, suffering the pleasure to lap in waves against her body.

'Let go now, Gianna, no more fighting. Let it carry
you away, you won't be sorry,' Nolan coaxed, his own
words coming breathlessly, he, too, caught up in her
pleasure. 'Trust me.'

She let go then, like someone giving up a life rope
amid tossing waves. There, in the intimate privacy
of the gondola, she let herself be swept out to sea,
clinging to Nolan as the pleasure took her, testing her
passion and her resolve. The former soared in those
moments, the latter shattered.

She had misjudged pleasure. It was her first
thought when she'd recovered the ability to think.
Her second thought, lying against the curve of Nolan's body, was that he had not made that error. He

was far too experienced for that. He'd known from the start pleasure was far more powerful when it wasn't wielded as a weapon. No wonder he had been so eager to show it to her, so eager to disarm her. Perhaps he'd known, too, that there was no way to limit pleasure's power to the span of one afternoon, no way to cage its effects.

She had yet to determine how detrimental those effects might be, it was all too new, too wondrous. She wanted to wallow in that wonder a while longer before she had to dissect it, understand it. What she *could* do now was even the playing field. 'I have had my pleasure, but you have not had yours.' She moved into the curve of Nolan's body and reached for his phallus.

His hand covered hers. 'There is more pleasure to be had,' he promised, 'but I have to ask, Gianna, are you a virgin?'

She was feeling reckless and bold in the wake of her climax. 'Does it matter?'

Nolan's gaze was solemn. 'It does. It determines the sort of pleasure we can have. Tell me the truth, Gianna. Did the count lie about that, too?'

The count's lie or hers? Nolan would know if she lied. There would be no hiding it. 'He did not lie.' She opted for the truth even though she knew what it meant. Nolan would not make love to her here in this gondola. He was waiting for something, some sign from her she had not given yet. The admission left her feeling bereft. Now that she'd sampled pleasure, she wanted all of it.

'Well then, that settles it.' Nolan released her hand, but took no action to remove it from his phallus. He lay back on the pillows and gave her a wicked smile, his eyes dark with unfulfilled desire. 'Take me in hand, Gianna.'

It was another lesson in pleasure, she realised; that there was pleasure for the giver as well as the receiver, that she could take joy in his joy, another reminder of how potent pleasure could be beyond weaponry; this was mutual pleasure, *not* a double-edged sword. She revelled in the swell of him beneath her strokes, in the milky bead that formed at his tip, in the moans from his lips. This, too, was addicting, to know she could provide this man of experience with experiences of his own.

She reached for the tender sac beneath his phallus and felt the balls within tighten, contracting with their own reaction to the pleasure as Nolan's body built towards its release. His head was thrown back against the pillows, his phallus pumping into the cylinder of her hand, warm and pulsing as it came. It was beautiful, *he* was beautiful in those moments, utterly male and wholly hers.

Gianna lay down beside him, her hand pressed to his heart, feeling the rhythm race and slow. Nolan lay a hand over hers, his voice cracking a little as he spoke. 'I don't think I could stand much more. It's a good thing we have a house to burgle.'

The reminder of business was the perfect segue to move out of the idyll of the afternoon and back to reality, but Gianna wondered if there really was any going back. Only forward. They'd shared secrets and they'd shared pleasure. Both of which might or might not have been part of this game they played. Nothing would be the same.

Chapter Thirteen

The count knew how to give a party, Nolan had to concede that much. Under other circumstances, he would have enjoyed the masquerade immensely. There was just the right sort of women, the right sort of wine, and food; champagne, snails, oysters, chocolates and cheeses abounded along with an abundance of private alcoves in which to take advantage.

As it was, Nolan only appreciated the crowd for its camouflage and even that enjoyment was tempered. Where was Gianna? It was almost impossible to find anyone in the crush. They had come together, but decided to separate in the hopes of drawing as little attention to themselves as possible. He'd managed to keep her in sight most of the evening, for safety's sake, he told himself. Nothing more. It certainly *wasn't* a twinge of envy that tugged at him as he watched her dance. She had to dance, after all. Not to dance would have been noted as odd. He had danced as well. His partners were sophisticated women who had promised to do sophisticated things with him, to him, in those elegantly curtained alcoves the count seemed so fond of. Brennan would have loved this party.

Three months ago, three weeks ago, even three days ago, he would have loved this party, too, would have taken the sophisticated ladies up on their decadent offers of physical pleasure. He and Brennan had come to Venice for precisely nights like this. Everyone could prose on about coming to Venice for the art and the history of the Serene Republic, but he and Bren had come for the sex. Art be damned. Napoleon had taken most of it anyway.

Now that he had the night of nights ahead of him when it came to free pleasures, Nolan wanted no part of it. The ladies and their offers seemed unexciting, nothing more than empty activities to while away the time, certainly nothing that competed with the thrill of Gianna finding her pleasure against the plush pillows of a gondola and knowing he'd been responsible for it, had been the *first* responsible for it.

He could argue that perhaps it was the mission that diverted his attention from the entertainments tonight, but Nolan was honest enough to admit it might be Gianna who had him distracted. The problem with being first was that it implied there would be a next and a last. Normally, those concepts didn't bother him if he thought of them at all. He'd been the next man, well, always, and it was understood there would be a next man after him. That was the kind of woman he associated with.

Not so with Gianna. He could be her first, but that was it. There was no future for them. They were thrown together by circumstance, neither of them looking for a long-standing affair. Nolan craned his neck to catch sight of her red queen-of-hearts costume. He thought he saw a flutter of red among the crowd and then lost it again. Perhaps it hadn't been her, after all.

In truth, tonight marked the beginning of the end. Once she had her jewel case, she would be free to leave Venice. Her need for him was satisfied even if his need for her wasn't. *It's for the best. She's nothing but a piece of lovely trouble.* But knowing it didn't make it any easier. He might have let her go before today, before the fish market, before the exchange of confidences over fish stew. But now he knew the danger she would be in. She would be a woman alone without his protection, facing an evil adversary if the count ever decided to hunt her down. It was almost a surety the count would after tonight.

Nolan flipped open his pocket watch. Ten minutes remained before they were supposed to rendezvous. He was starting to worry. Gianna was still out of sight. That made him extremely nervous. She wasn't to leave the room—that had been their agreement. Had she been recognised? Was she in danger even now? Had she decided to retrieve the jewel case on her own?

Nolan began to quarter the crowded ballroom with his eyes in earnest now. Another flash of red caught his eye on the ballroom perimeter close to the terrace doors. There she was. Nolan knew relief and then anger. She wasn't alone. A man had a hand on her arm, tugging, but it was hard to tell with the distance and the crowd. Nolan began to make his way to her side, carving a path through the crowd with his body.

His instincts were correct. The closer he got the more clear it was the man's attentions were unwanted. Nolan flexed his arm, taking comfort in the feel of his knife hidden in the secret sheath in his sleeve.

'Whomever you're meeting, darling, he isn't coming,' the man holding her arm slurred drunkenly. 'Besides, we're all in masks, how would you know anyway? Maybe it's me you're supposed to meet. Come outside with me and let's find out.' The man was drunk enough to be dangerous. He would need to move quickly and not let the confrontation turn into a protracted scene.

Nolan stepped between them, his body a shield for Gianna. 'What's going on here?' His knife flashed in his hand, coming up under the other man's chin.

Usually the cold prick of steel against one's soft vulnerable skin was enough to create instant sobriety. Not in this case. 'The Queen of Hearts and I are just talking,' the drunk man drawled. 'Who the hell are you anyway?'

Nolan pressed the blade into the chin, drawing a tiny bead of blood. 'The King of Hearts. Now bugger off.' He gave the man a shove, sending him stumbling through the terrace doors outside, to all appearances just another drunk taking the air. Nolan grabbed Gianna's hand and disappeared into the crowd, making his way towards a darker exit that gave out into the depths of the house. Once in a less-populated hallway, Nolan made use of a vacant alcove. He pulled the curtain around them.

'Are you all right?' He untied his mask.

'I'm fine.' Gianna took her mask off, too, but her hands trembled. 'Nolan, thank you.' She held up a hand when he would have protested. 'No, let me say it. *Thank you*. I could have managed him—' her voice softened '—but it was nice not to have to.' He had the sense that she'd had to handle too many men on her own. Something protective fired in him. Not on his watch. Even the strong needed champions.

She reached up and kissed his cheek. It was sweetly done, the innocence of the gesture seductive even. His blood fired at the brush of her lips. The alcove, the tight-fitting bodice of her costume, the kiss, his own imagination were conspiring against him. But they had work to do and a limited amount of time in which to do it. Masks came off at midnight. They needed to be gone by then. Nolan took a small step backwards and resheathed his knife.

She glanced pointedly at his sleeve where the knife had disappeared. 'Do you carry that thing with you everywhere?'

'Yes, he's quite the friend in tight spots.' Nolan smiled and put his mask on, signalling it was time to return to work.

'I think it's intriguing that you find yourself in so many tight spots to make such a "friend" worthwhile.' She lifted her own mask and fitted it to her face. Nolan stepped behind her and tied the ribbons. He allowed his hands to linger at her shoulders, his mouth to pause at her ear.

'I'm a gambler, a good one. Tight spots are an occupational hazard.'

She detected his innuendo. Her head bowed slightly, her own voice husky. 'I think tight spots might be an occupational hazard for reasons other than cards.'

'It's up to you now. Which way do we go?' Nolan whispered at her ear, knowing she'd hear that innuendo, too. They could abandon their quest and pursue another sort of quest in the alcove. But he knew, too, which one she would pick.

Gianna led him through the dark halls, up a staircase at the far end of one and into another wing of the *palazzo*. They could barely hear the party, only the occasional strain of music reached them. They were in dangerous territory now. No one would accidentally wander this far from the ballroom. Nolan slipped his knife into his hand. Would the count have guards posted? It wouldn't be uncommon with Carnevale going on. Carnevale was notorious for unexpected guests.

'It's here in the count's rooms,' Gianna whispered and Nolan swallowed hard. They were burgling the count's personal rooms? Of course it couldn't be in a study or library, or some kind of common room they could have claimed they stumbled into accidentally and then chosen to stay in it for an illicit rendezvous. Nolan tightened the grip on his knife. If they were caught in the count's chambers, there would be very little to explain.

He was starting to realise just how much trust he'd put in her, and for what reason? Why should he trust her beyond the fact that she swayed him with her beauty, and the rare glimpse she offered him into her truths? Truths he had not bothered to test. He'd believed her when she said the count was her enemy, that she'd lived here as a veritable prisoner, that the item they were after was really hers to claim.

A hundred 'what ifs' ran through his mind—it was what he got for being such a critical thinker, although the critical-thinking piece was making a rather late appearance. He should have thought of all this earlier. Was this an elaborate set up? Was she somehow in league with the count and trying to wreak some revenge for the losses at the tables?

Nolan was well aware that it might have been his idea to come here tonight, but it had been *her* idea to come at all. Were she and the count trying to frame him for a theft? Nolan had no particular desire to experience the Venetian prison system as part of his Grand Tour. She'd so expertly drawn him in with her story, he hadn't thought to ask these questions until now when it was too late. Mostly, because they were questions he didn't *want* to ask. He wanted Gianna to be the damsel in distress, not a femme fatale using him for her own purposes. He wanted to believe he was not that easily duped by a pretty face.

Gianna cracked the door to the count's rooms open and they slipped inside. A lamp had been left burn-

ing. 'I'll go to the safe. You watch the door.' Gianna
glided away from him, finding her way easily in the
dim room. Nolan took up a post to the side of the door.
If anyone came through it, they'd meet him and his
friend before they took two steps inside.

He could hear Gianna working on a lock in the
semi-dark. A moment later, he heard Gianna whisper
triumphantly, 'I have it.' There were the sounds of a
safe shutting, a picture sliding back into place, then
she was beside him, the case in her hands. 'Let's go.'

Nolan peered into the hall, it was dark and empty.
He started to relax. Maybe it would be just this easy.
Back they went through halls, down the staircase,
around the last corner. One more corridor to go. They
neared the ballroom. The light, the crowd, meant
safety, although the light would make it harder to
obscure the jewel case between them.

'No, this way.' Gianna put a hand on his sleeve and
nodded towards another hallway. 'It will take us out
to the docks without going through the ballroom.' It
should have been a good choice. They had met with
no one so far except partygoers now that they were
in range of the ballroom. They veered off down the
hall, strolling casually. Nolan put a hand around her
waist and drew her close, for authenticity and for protection. He wasn't sure it actually afforded her more
protection or him any more ability to provide it, but
it felt that way to have her against him.

They were nearly to the docks when he spied the
two hulking men coming towards them, dressed in
the count's livery. Not guests then, as he'd hoped. Gi-

anna tensed against him in confirmation. He needed her relaxed. Tension could be spotted. There were only two reasons someone would be in this part of the house tonight. One would raise suspicion—why not exit out the main entrance like everyone else? The other would be more appropriate for seeking out dark corners, although Gianna might disagree with his methods. Nolan bent his mouth to her ear. 'Kiss me hard, Gianna.'

Gianna gasped, her startled yelp stifled by the press of Nolan's mouth swallowing her surprise. He swung her against the wall, crushing the jewel box into invisibility between them. The corner of the case dug into her hip, but she hardly noticed. She was too busy trying to read the signals from Nolan's body, all of which said this needed to be a compelling seduction. His hips moved aggressively into hers, his hands ran up her ribcage to rest in the place below her breasts, his tongue, engaged in obvious labour at her mouth. 'Moan, dammit…' Nolan breathed into her mouth.

She did, coming to her senses and realising it would take both their efforts to make the scene compelling. It wasn't difficult to summon a response. His touch was arousing even when it was just meant for show, the effect making it difficult for her body to determine the difference; heat pooled, her blood warmed. His hand moved up her leg, pushing her skirt up in its wake.

He groaned against her mouth, making incoherent Italian love words. *'Mia cara, mia cara, voglio fare l'amore con te.'* Nolan's teeth took the soft flesh of her ear, biting, nibbling.

Gianna sighed, her lids lowered just enough to appear closed. Beneath them, she watched the two footmen pass, elbowing one another. One of them made a lewd comment, but they moved away, giving the lovers privacy such as it was in a hallway. It occurred to her that it would be her job to let Nolan know it was safe to move on, safe to end the impromptu seduction.

A very wicked part of her didn't want to end it, not yet. It was all pretend anyway and somehow that made it safe—far safer than what had happened in the gondola and far less real. But that knowledge didn't stop her response from being real. Gianna arched against the wall, her breath coming in hard pants as his hand skimmed the inside of her thigh close to her curls, conjuring echoes of what had been, of what she'd felt that afternoon.

'Are they gone?' Nolan's voice rasped against her ear.

'I—I think so,' Gianna managed, hoping it sounded convincing. She would die a thousand deaths if he guessed she'd prolonged this interlude on purpose.

He stepped back and gave her a moment to straighten her clothes. 'I'm sorry I could not be more circumspect,' Nolan offered as they continued down the hall, his arm about her.

'We needed to be compelling,' Gianna said rather matter-of-factly, but inside she was swallowing her disappointment. It had been a rather exciting, heated, gambit for her, but apparently not for him. All in a night's work. He probably ranked faking seductions in hallways right up there with always taking a knife to card games: *de rigueur*. Clearly, Nolan Gray's life was more exotic than hers.

Gianna pushed open a door and they stepped out into the night. Nolan had them in a gondola in short order. Plenty of them were moored alongside the pier awaiting partygoers. She sank back against the padded seats and let a moment's elation fill her, let the silly disappointment ebb away as the gondola left the dock. She should be celebrating. They were safe. The case was safe. She was one step closer to keeping Giovanni safe and being safe herself. She turned her smile on Nolan, hugging the case to her. 'We did it.'

Nolan smiled back, with his eyes, his mouth. His voice was low in the semi-darkness beneath the *felze*. 'So now I've done burglary.'

His hand came up to stroke her cheek. Her breath caught. She should be used to him touching her by now, but her body reacted to the slightest touch as if it was a gift. 'Tell me, Gianna, what's in there that's worth the risk?'

Their eyes held, searching one another for truth. This was a test, his test of her, and it suddenly seemed very important that she pass. He'd risked committing what looked to be on the surface a crime for her tonight. Now, he was asking her to take a risk of her own. What would she risk for him? He had walked into the count's *palazzo* blind, on her word alone. Would she give him this truth in exchange? The mental debate was short. What could it hurt? Maybe it could even help, although she knew giving him that answer would simply provoke more questions.

Gianna drew a deep breath, not daring to look away, wanting him to see that she gave him a whole truth. 'Everything is in here. My whole life.'

To his credit, Nolan did not ask for more in the gondola, although she might have preferred it. The conversation would start when the trip ended. She'd be able to give him the abbreviated version. Perhaps he'd guessed that, and perhaps, too, he'd guessed that the short trip between the count's *palazzo* and the hotel wouldn't be nearly long enough. Instead, he waited until they were behind the doors of his suite and even then he picked his moment carefully, waiting until they were settled, their masquerade garb put aside. *Then* he came to her with déshabillé and tea to tempt her secrets from her.

Chapter Fourteen

The soft clink of china on a tray alerted her. Gianna looked up from where she sat cross-legged on the big bed, her hands stilling on the lid of her mother's box. Nolan stood in the doorway dressed in his banyan and carrying a tea tray, dark-blond hair loose at his shoulders, grey eyes trained on her. 'Is it all there?'

'I don't know. I haven't got that far yet.' It was hard to look away from him even with the temptation of her mother's box on her lap.

A smile played at his mouth as if he were a concerned friend, nothing more, certainly not the man who had so expertly ravaged her in the dark hall of the *palazzo* or a man who might want to continue that ravishment here on the bed, more was the pity. She had mixed feelings about that, thanks to the afternoon. Pleasure was addictive, especially when she'd had a taste of it and there was more to be had.

Nolan set the tray down between them and matched her cross-legged position on the bed, careful not to overset the tray with his weight on the soft mattress. 'I thought tea might be in order.'

'No brandy?' Gianna teased, trying to ignore the flutter in her stomach, a flutter that always seemed to be there when he was present. She'd not bargained on feeling such attraction. The longer they were together, the harder it was to ignore. The attraction had begun to put down roots, to move beyond the physical. Sharing stories had been dangerous.

Nolan laughed, his eyes crinkling at the corners. 'You haven't learned your lesson? I thought we'd both be better off without brandy tonight.' He passed her a cup, and she curled her hands about it, appreciating its warmth. He sobered as he fixed his own cup. 'I also thought you might want company. If not me, then at least the tea. In my experience, memories and the night don't always make the best companions.'

His thoughtfulness was as seductive as his kiss, further proof those roots were digging in. Right then, she would have given up going through her mother's box to hear his experiences. What other memories haunted him, this man who seemed so self-assured, who always knew what to do next, what to be next? He anticipated her needs, read her thoughts as if he *knew* her. That was the danger. He wasn't her friend, not really. She was smart enough to know better. He wasn't the only one in the room who knew how people thought, how they worked in any given situation.

It was their circumstances that made them seem more intimate than they truly were. People who risked burglary together, people who'd found kinship in a fish market, who'd sought pleasure in an afternoon gondola and faked rather realistic sex against a wall, couldn't help but feel a false sense of closeness, a false sense that they knew each other or were somehow entitled to know each other. Throw in the fact that he'd saved her from drowning, had kissed her on more than one occasion, that she'd had her hand on his phallus and several more close occurrences of the dubious kind, including casting up her accounts in his presence, and it was easy to see where that illusion of closeness came from.

It was also easy to see why the illusion seemed so very real, especially now as they sat casually together in their nightclothes on a bed, as if they were a young honeymooning couple. Based on her body's response, that was quite the wrong comparison to make. A bolt of yearning shot through her. What would it be like to celebrate the start of a life together in a luxurious suite of rooms, every whim catered to?

The heat was from more than the wealth. What would it be like to be married to a man who would take care of her, but not hobble her in return? Marriage had always meant dependence to her. Was it even possible otherwise? *He's only catering to you so that you will leave. He has plans and they don't include you*, came the cold reminder. Better to focus on the task at hand and then the next task after that. There was no place here for romantic fancies. She'd had her afternoon—it was all she had promised herself and even that promise had been made on the condition that it be temporary.

Gianna lifted the lid and braced herself against the faint, familiar scent of lavender and cedar. After five years, the box still smelled like her mother. All of the count's plundering could not change that and in some ways the scent was worth more than the handful of jewels left inside: five rings, one necklace and two bracelets—a far cry from the days when the case had been populated to overflowing with expensive spangles and baubles.

Gianna felt the sting of tears in her eyes. She dug her nails into the palm of her fisted hand in a covert attempt to stop them. She was not going to cry in front of Nolan. It was bad enough she'd thrown up. She wasn't going to add this to her list of notorious accomplishments. She'd promised herself she'd be strong. She'd known the count had likely been pillaging. She should not be surprised. How else could he have afforded to keep Romano Lippi and his extravagant lifestyle?

This was business, this was the first step towards her new life with Giovanni, somewhere away from Venice and the past. The true monetary value of what was in this case didn't lie in its jewels.

'My mother smells of vanilla and roses,' Nolan said quietly, taking her mind off the jewels. 'I think smell is a highly underrated scent when it comes to memories. We rely so heavily on the visual instead.' He moved the tea tray to the floor and stretched out alongside her, his head propped in one hand.

'And yet, each one of these represents a story.' Gianna reached for an amethyst ring. 'She used to let me sort through the case when I was young. I'd try on all the jewels while she was getting ready for an evening out.' Gianna set the ring down and selected another piece, a bracelet of peridots interspersed with tiny diamonds. 'Her life, all the gifts, seemed glamorous at the time. She told me a man always gifted his truth. A woman could take a man's measure by the magnitude of his presents.'

Nolan gave a wry laugh. 'I suppose there is some truth in that. I suppose, too, it depends on what measure is being taken.'

'The measure that matters,' Gianna answered. The memories were starting to draw her in now. She could see herself in her mother's boudoir, sitting cross-legged on the bed, case on her lap—just as she was doing now. She hadn't realised she was doing it. She could see her mother at the mirror with her maid, her mother lecturing gaily about the nature of men. 'My mother said the measure of a man's loyalty, his respect and, at the end of an affair, his overall regard for a woman's well-being was reflected in his gifts. A courtesan's life is dependent on that most of all— the money that comes at the end of the affair to see her through until she can find another man who suits her, who is worthy of her so that she does not take just anyone. Desperate women are never as attractive.'

She glanced over at Nolan. 'On those nights, life seemed like one big party full of jewels, furs, gowns, sumptuous apartments and every man was a handsome one. But it wasn't always like that. Sometimes there were no men for a while and the apartments were less luxurious. My mother was very particular, it was part of her charm.' Gianna unfastened the bracelet and reached for a ring, turning it over in her hand. 'May I confess something? I secretly liked those times, too—having my mother at home to tuck me and my brother in even though I knew those times worried my mother the most. A ring or two would disappear from the case.'

'Why did she marry the count?' Nolan's question came quietly.

Gianna looked up and put the ring back. 'The same reason any mother does anything. For her children. She wanted respectability for us. I was fourteen and growing up fast. I think she feared what would happen if a gentleman took a fancy to me. Like most parents, she wanted more for my life than she had for hers. The count had a title and he was willing to give her the respectability of it in exchange for her small fortune. On the surface, it was an equitable bargain, the kind of happy ending many courtesans might dream of.'

'Her fortune?' Nolan's brows drew together. Of course, it wouldn't make sense as he stared into a near-empty jewel case and listened to her stories of leaner times.

Gianna gave him a patient smile. 'Her last protector was an older widowed man who was very rich and very taken with her. I always thought if she was to marry anyone, she would marry him. He was a merchant with grown children. But he died quite suddenly one day at his warehouse. He remembered her in his will, however.' Her mother had used that money in an attempt to buy respectability for her children. Only it hadn't worked out that way. Gianna gave a small shrug. 'I don't have to tell you the rest. You can reason it out. I imagine you've kept a mistress or two.'

'What a leading question!' Nolan scolded with a teasing tone, but she noticed he declined to answer. He reached over and picked up a ring set with a cushion-cut diamond. 'This one is beautiful.' He held it to the lamplight, letting its facets catch the light. 'Breathtaking. Tell me about it.'

It was a simple, forthright distraction, but it was a dangerous one. She shouldn't tell him any more tales. It only fed the illusion of intimacy between them. But he was looking at her, his eyes inviting her: *tell me, draw me in with your tales of growing up a courtesan's daughter, tell me anything.* He was right. The night and memories made difficult companions. She wanted to tell someone, n*eeded to tell* someone about her mother, a woman she'd loved and ultimately had never understood.

'The ring is from her first lover,' Gianna said softly. 'She loved to tell the story about it. He told her the perfection of the diamond reminded him of her, how she sparkled.' Gianna shrugged. 'I am sure the story has become embellished over time.'

'Maybe not.' Nolan's voice was low and private as he passed the ring back to her, his hand brushing over hers, sending a delicious tremor down her spine. 'One never forgets their first.' Was there innuendo in that? An invitation? He had earned every right to be her first at the card table and multiple times since then. But the invitation was gone as quickly as it was issued.

Gianna shut the lid, the enormity of what the count had stolen from her coming over her for the first time in its entirety. 'I wish there was more. I can't believe they're all gone.' She choked on the last word. Eight pieces were all that was left plus the pearl set. 'I've tried so hard not to be like her, not to be dependent on anyone, but that doesn't mean I didn't love her.' The tears were coming hard now. She couldn't stop them, she didn't want to. They were her rage, her sadness. She raised her face to Nolan's. 'There should be more to her life than eight pieces of jewellery, don't you think?'

Frankly, Nolan thought the count should be horse-whipped in Piazza San Marco. He moved to Gianna without hesitation and gathered her to him, muffling her sobs against his shoulder. He murmured soft, comforting words into her hair, into her ear while his mind contemplated murder and other torturous ways to die.

'It's silly to be upset about the jewellery,' Gianna mumbled, her sobs becoming hiccups. 'They're just things.'

'They were more than jewels to you, they were your memories. He had no right to take those from you.' On second thought death might be too kind for the count. Death could martyr even a bad man. But beggaring was a different story. Poverty would be a long, slow social death for a man like Minotti, just like each scandal of his in London was another nail in his father's pious coffin. He could do it, he could ruin the count. One night at the tables, one fabulous game…

No. This wasn't his fight. He had plans. She had plans. He didn't figure into hers any more than she figured into his. Their association was free to end now. And yet, the smell of her hair, all rosemary and sage, and the memory of her body in his hands were far more compelling arguments for ignoring those realities in exchange for what he could give her in this moment if she would let him.

Nolan pressed a kiss to her hair, to her cheeks where her tears dried, to her mouth where her lips parted for him, her body leaning into him. Her hands gripped the lapels of his banyan, fisted in the material with want and need. He wooed her with gentle kisses, slow kisses that gradually moved them away from sorrow and consolation and towards something hungrier, needier. He had her beneath him now, the work of a few quick manoeuvres to transfer her from his lap to her back, her hair tumbling across the pillows, her hazel eyes wide with desire.

Her hands were on him, slipping inside his robe, thumbs running across his nipples, hips pressing up against him, inviting the rise of his erection, answering his invitation. His own hands were sliding beneath the hem of her nightgown, sliding the garment up over thighs and hips so that his mouth met bare skin in its downward journey. This time, his body would have its way, it would finish what it had started against the chapel wall and in the gondola.

He kissed her navel, feeling her body tense in excitement at his touch. He kissed her mound, the scent of her, the heat of her surrounding him. 'Are you ready?' he breathed against her, his mouth finding her intimate cleft, his tongue sweeping the pearl nestled inside. He felt her gasp, then cry out with the discovery of pleasure. He drank of her, her essence, her joy. This was a heady delight indeed, her pleasure feeding his as she bucked beneath him. He could feel her body shake, could hear her give a hard cry as the pleasure overwhelmed her.

He trailed kisses up past her navel, to her breasts, her throat, feeling her body come down beneath his mouth from its fevered pitch. 'You are delicious,' he whispered against her mouth.

'You are wicked,' she murmured. Her knees bent, squeezing gently around him where he rested between her legs, her body's invitation clear. Her teeth nipped at his ear, her breath blowing against his lobe. It was the little things she did that drove him beyond good sense. If that didn't do it, her words did. 'Tonight, Nolan, I want you to make me forget.'

Sweet heavens, how he wanted to! It would be so easy. But how many nights had he thought as she did now? How many nights as he asked for the same in not so many words? 'Lady X, Lady Y, Miss This Night, Miss Last Night, make me forget.' It had never worked, not in the long term anyhow, not beyond the moment. He knew what he had to do, hard as it was.

Nolan placed a kiss to the side of her mouth. 'In the morning you will be disappointed.'

His body was in full protest by now, hardly believing what he was turning down. He'd been attracted to her from the first and now he had her asking, she was choosing him as he'd wanted. But not this way. She was at the mercy of a very emotional evening— the burglary, the near discovery in the hall, the pawing man in the ballroom, the depleted jewel case. Her body and her mind were responding accordingly. But she would regret it in the morning. More than that, she might regret *him*. That was unthinkable. Perhaps it was vain, but he didn't want to be one of her regrets.

She tugged at him, unwilling to admit defeat, her hands dropping to the waist of his robe. 'Please, Nolan.'

He covered her hands and stayed them. 'Trust me, sex will bring pleasure, it will not bring forgetfulness.' He dropped a kiss on her cheek and was gone. If he stayed any longer, he would be lost. She was far too tempting.

'Where are you going?' she called into the other room as he pulled on discarded clothes.

'Card game,' he mumbled. His least favourite game to play, solitaire, but what could he expect when he'd become St Nolan, protector of Venetian virgins?

Chapter Fifteen

He had to stop sleeping in club chairs or else rec-
ommend that the Danieli get more comfortable ones.
Better yet, have them invent some that converted into
sleepers for poor male victims of capricious women
everywhere. Nolan rolled his shoulders and his neck
experimentally, wincing when he felt a kink.

'Something wrong with your own room?' Brennan
Carr strode into the empty club room, dressed for the
day, making Nolan wonder how long he'd slept. Brennan was not the earliest of risers. He hadn't wanted to
sleep too late. There were things that needed doing.
He was supposed to meet with his man of business
in Venice, he had money issues to settle, Gianna's
clothes were arriving and there were things to settle
with Gianna as well, although he was hard-pressed
to define what those things were exactly.

Brennan took a chair next to him and stretched
into it, trying out a few different positions. 'Not the
best for sleeping, I'd imagine. You, by the way, look

terrible,' he said pointedly before sending one of the waiting *facchini* to bring coffee and breakfast.

'Thanks,' Nolan drawled, pushing a hand through his hair. 'What do you want?'

Brennan leaned forward, his blue eyes laughing, his face alight with mischief. He radiated envious amounts of energy. 'I want to know what's going on. I haven't seen you in three days. When a man's travelling companion disappears with the exception of a few moments at midnight to request a nightgown, one gets—'

'Jealous?' Nolan interrupted.

Brennan leaned back into the chair with a laugh. 'I was going to say curious.' The *facchino* came and laid out breakfast, English-style, the way Brennan liked it: shirred eggs, kippers, sausage, toast and a huge carafe of coffee. Nolan opted for toast and coffee in the Italian style, but Brennan fixed himself a towering plate of food.

'You eat like a horse.' Nolan shook his head at the pile of food in front of Brennan.

'I need it.' Brennan winked. 'You need it, too. You look like a stag at the end of the rut.' Brennan shovelled eggs into his mouth. Even with the finishing of Paris and now Italy, Brennan ate for fuel, the aesthetics of the meal lost on him as he fed his furnace. 'So? Who is she? Is she worth it?' he asked around a mouthful of eggs.

Normally, Nolan shared quite freely about his affairs with his friends, but he was hesitant this morning. 'It's not like that. This is different, complicated.'

He sipped his coffee, marvelling over Brennan's already half-empty plate.

Brennan snorted. 'Not that different. I heard her last night, and you, too, through the wall. Apparently, the nightgown is working out.'

'Yes and no.' Nolan set down his coffee cup and leaned forward, hands on his thighs. 'Can I ask you something seriously?' This would be new territory for the two of them. They usually confided in Archer or Haviland, but those two friends had married and were off on their own adventures. The group of four that had left England was just a pair now. It was an unlikely pair, too. They were the wild ones, the ones to whom everything was a lark, the two without any responsibility. Now, they just had each other.

Brennan managed to sober and stop eating. 'What is it?'

'Bren, have you ever met a woman you can't have sex with?'

There was a long pause and Brennan managed to look suitably appalled. His voice, however, was *unsuitably* loud. 'Oh, God, Nolan, are you impotent? How? When? Last week, I thought you and the countess had… And what about last night?'

Nolan waved a hand to hush him. The *facchini* were starting to look. 'Lower your voice, of course I'm not impotent,' Nolan said through gritted teeth.

'Then what?' Brennan's eyes grew round. 'Do you have syphilis?' He whispered the last, but it came out as a stage whisper. He might as well have shouted it to every *facchini* in the club room.

'No,' Nolan said evenly, starting to lose patience. 'I do *not* have syphilis, nor am I impotent. I am perfectly capable of pleasing a lady.' Brennan had a way of making him justify the most ridiculous things. He drew a deep breath and tried again. 'It's like this: I could have her, but it would ruin everything.'

Brennan was getting interested now. He hadn't touched his plate in the past two minutes. 'And last night? Didn't you already "have" her? Were those not the sounds of "having" that I heard through my wall?'

'Cunnilingus,' Nolan clarified.

Brennan considered him for a moment, head cocked. 'What do you mean by "ruin everything"? How much can you ruin in a one-night stand? Besides, didn't you win her in a card game? I thought ruining was a given.' Brennan paused, an idea starting to click in to place. 'You didn't ruin her. All this time I thought you'd been in that hotel room rutting like a stag and you haven't touched her. Why? Are you sure you don't have syphilis? I know someone who can help…'

'No, enough with the syphilis—you're starting to sound like your father,' Nolan said sharply.

Brennan's face went stony. It was a mean thing to say. Brennan's father was no better than his when it came to paternal instinct. This was the man who'd sent his son off on a Grand Tour not with loving words or a farewell hug, but with a packet of French letters and the stern admonition, 'Don't get syphilis.' Nolan had been standing there when he'd said it.

'I'm sorry, Bren.' At least Brennan's father had

said goodbye. 'Please, just listen to me. This is not about sex.'

'I might not be your man, Nolan. I'll try, though.' Brennan meant it, but they both knew Brennan's whole world was sex. He was the product of a father who had towed him to a brothel on his fifteenth birthday. Usually, it made Brennan interesting. This morning, it just made him limited. To be fair, this was new ground for Nolan, too. Gianna raised a host of uncomfortable reactions in him.

'If I take her to bed, all it proves is that I can seduce a woman into sex.' Which wasn't news. He'd been seducing women into bed with him for over a decade. 'In her eyes, it makes her just a wager, a prize I was simply entitled to.' It proved he was no better or different than the men she knew.

'But in your eyes? Don't tell me you have feelings for this winsome prize of yours,' Brennan prompted, picking up his plate and filling it for round two of breakfast.

'In my eyes, I think she's in trouble. She needs help.'

'I think she *is* trouble. She needs protection, is what you mean.' Brennan blew out a frustrated breath. He shook his head. 'You intend to be her knight in shining armour? Perhaps you might tell me why you think so?'

'She was wagered against her will as punishment for not accepting a marriage offer…' Nolan began. 'I offered to let her out of the deal.'

'Very wise man. You have your own plans,' Brennan said pointedly. 'But apparently your option didn't happen because she fell in the canal and suddenly she's ensconced in your luxurious rooms, you're borrowing nightgowns from your friend, sleeping in club chairs and she's still here three days later.' Brennan sighed. 'Can't you see it, Nol? She's played you like a harp, just stringing you along. She's got you buying her clothes, what else does she have you doing?' Brennan gave a chuckle. 'Here's the beauty of it, Nol. She's got you believing she's really a virgin and she hasn't even had to earn her keep on her back. You're a frigging holiday for her. She gets all of this for free while you're worried about what happens to her sensibilities if you sleep with her.'

'You're a cynical bastard when you put your mind to it. What happened to "What sort of trouble, Nol? How can I help"?' Nolan groused. Brennan was usually all energy and good humour. He supposed he'd expected Brennan to commiserate with him, hypothesise with him about the depth of Gianna's trouble and come up with a solution.

Brennan shrugged. 'I don't let my dark side come out to play much, but when I do, it's positively lethal.'

The problem was, Brennan's thoughts weren't far from his own. Nolan had thought the same thing, had even accused Gianna of the same thing. He'd got slapped for it. He understood that urge now. He wanted to do more than slap Brennan for it, too. 'Part of me wants to hit you for that,' Nolan confessed glumly.

'Have you asked yourself why?' Brennan was

being serious now. He reached for his coffee cup and drank, grimacing a little at the heat.

'I can't believe I'd be so blind to such ploys. She's *not* using me. I would know,' Nolan protested. 'I'm a master at reading people. I know when they're lying, I know what motivates them.'

'Maybe that's precisely why you can't see it. You *know* how it is; the master who can resist or detect the most complex of ploys is brought down by the simplest of manoeuvres,' Brennan warned, sipping carefully from the coffee cup.

'No, I'm certain of it. She's in trouble. Last night, we crashed the count's masquerade and retrieved her mother's jewel case—' He didn't get to finish.

Brennan choked on the hot coffee, spluttering and cursing as he coughed, coffee splashing a little too warmly on his thighs. 'Dammit! Dammit! Ouch! Get me a napkin!

'Whoa, stop right there. Did you hear what you said? You took a jewel case out of another's house without permission? That's not *retrieving*, Nolan, the English word for that is *stealing*. She has you *stealing* for her. How is that "not using" you?'

Nolan was regretting not keeping Brennan informed. There was so much to explain now and hearing it all at once did lend it a sense of the preposterous. 'The jewel case belongs to Gianna. It's not the count's and he has plundered it. There was hardly anything left. If anyone did the stealing, it was the count.' Nolan felt his anger rise in remembrance of Gianna's fallen face, the tears. 'Gianna was entirely undone when she saw it.'

'I'll bet she was. She was likely planning to live on those jewels until she could get another Englishman to hold up a few coaches for her.'

'You may play the cynic all you like. You don't know her like I do.' Nolan could hear the defensiveness in his tone and in his thoughts. But for good reason. Brennan hadn't fished her out of the canal, hadn't seen her fear when he'd pulled the knife to cut her laces, hadn't felt the honest abandon of her passion when he touched her, hadn't heard her cry out—well, not the last apparently.

In all fairness, it was easy for Brennan to doubt. He hadn't seen her, hadn't talked to her. He had no history with her. *And what do you have? Does three days qualify as history? Even so, is it three days of history or three days of lies woven by a skilful temptress? Her mother was a successful courtesan. How far did the apple really fall from the tree, after all?*

Whoa, that wasn't fair. That was like saying he was his father, the puritanical bastard who had beaten his brand of justice into Nolan until he was old enough to leave.

'I am sorry, old friend. I sense our conversation on the subject has reached an impasse.' Brennan spread his hands in a gesture of surrender. 'So what if she's using you? I mean, it can be fun that way, too, as long as you're not overly invested.' Nolan appreciated Brennan was trying to make him feel better.

'Just promise me you'll be careful, Nolan. I am

your friend and I am here for you, although I'd rather you avoid trouble altogether.' He offered a wry smile. 'Ursula von Hess was asking about you last night. The baroness seems *very* taken with you, something about your sharp tongue and its compatibility with a particular body part of hers.'

Nolan laughed for form's sake. But his heart wasn't in it. He knew what Brennan was suggesting: stick to the formula—sex for physical pleasure and women who understood that rule. Women like the baroness. Women like Gianna who were either virgins in honest peril or women playing a deeper game that went beyond a tumble in the sheets were trouble either way.

Brennan rose, tugging at his jacket. The club room was starting to fill with men coming in to read their newspapers and journals. 'I'm going to see the tailor. Perhaps you'd like to come? You can clean up there.'

Nolan shook his head. 'I think I'll finish my coffee and then I have appointments to keep.' He wanted a moment alone with his thoughts now that he was past the emotions of the night and the surprisingly hard cynicism of Brennan's comments. Something bothered him about the jewel case, the logic of it seemed flawed. But he had not been able to concentrate on why in the aftermath of opening the case.

That thread of logic was easier to trace this afternoon in the quiet of his mind. Had she really risked going back into a home that she feared for a case that she had to have known would have been plundered? Did the case hold something else? What did she see in it that he didn't? He felt confident in assuming there was something more valuable, something the count would overlook even after five years of plundering. That meant it was hidden.

All right, Gray, follow that line of thought, and he did, right to the conclusion that the case must have a secret compartment or drawer. Should that hold true, it also opened up another inescapable, less savoury conclusion: she hadn't trusted him with the real truth of the case. Instead, she'd distracted him with tales of jewels, and tears over plundering stepfathers, and he'd fallen for it. Unlike so much between them, this at least could be tested. Nolan rose from his chair. There was only one way to find out.

He was halfway up the stairs to his room when Signora Montefiori met him coming down. '*Signor*! There you are. I thought perhaps I misunderstood when to deliver the dresses. You were not in your room.'

Nolan flashed her a charming smile. 'Surely Signorina Minotti is there?'

'No, *signor*. I knocked on the door, but there was no answer.'

'Perhaps she is asleep. We had a late night.' Nolan kept his smile in place, but it was an effort not to race up the stairs as if he was worried.

He opened the room and called for Gianna, thinking she might be in the bathing room. Running water could obscure the sound of a knock. But a short search confirmed the dressmaker's original assessment. 'You may leave the dresses in here on the bed.' Nolan smiled. 'It appears she has gone out, shopping perhaps.' Or perhaps not. He didn't think for a moment she'd go shopping. His stomach was starting to knot as he followed the dressmaker out, thanking her for her haste in preparing the order.

Nolan shut the door and leaned against it. There was no good reason Gianna would leave this room. Had the count found her and forced her from the room? He doubted something like that would escape the notice of the concierge in the lobby, and the jewel case was still on the bureau.

Had she departed, upholding her end of the bargain? That, too, made little sense. They had not talked of leaving last night, and why would she leave with nothing to wear but a nightgown, a masquerade costume and two ready-made dresses, especially when new clothes were coming? If she waited a few hours, she'd have a whole wardrobe to take with her. It was possible she'd try to go out and pawn some pearls from her ruined dress, but a quick survey of the gown proved that moot. It was time to test the hypothesis of the jewel case.

Chapter Sixteen

Nolan lifted the lid to assure himself the paltry collection of jewellery was still there, further proof that she hadn't run. He felt guilty doing it. Doubt had motivated this. What he was doing now felt far more like burglary than breaking into the count's house. Perhaps because he'd believed the count deserved it and Gianna didn't. But that raised an uncomfortable question: What did he believe Gianna deserved and why?

Nolan ran his fingers along the bottom of the satin lining searching for a catch, an irregularity. Nothing. He ran his fingers along the seams of the lid, pressing it for telltale signs of something hidden behind the fabric. Still nothing. He picked up the case and shook it lightly, then a bit harder. The bottom gave, sprinkling folded papers on the floor, each one a secret of its own. What else did one keep in a hidden compartment but things that needed to be protected because knowledge of them in the wrong hands would be dangerous?

A suspicion began to unfurl in his mind, one he'd rather not face. It was easier to study the case, to note the fine construction of the false bottom that had kept the compartment concealed from a man who must have spent years looking. It was excellent craftsmanship. He might have missed it, if the bottom had closed properly. He could see now that the bottom had opened because the catching mechanism hadn't caught when it had been shut. One mystery solved, but several others awaited.

Nolan knelt on the floor and gathered up the folded papers. Whatever Gianna had been looking for was here, or had been here. It probably wasn't 'here' any longer but with her, wherever she was. The reality stung. She had trusted him with her memories, with the pleasure of her body, but not with this.

If he had been more of a gentleman, he wouldn't have looked, would have left the papers folded up in their worn creases, but his own self-preservation was on the line along with Gianna's privacy. In the wake of Brennan's comments, that was no small thing. What sort of woman was he dealing with? *Had* he been used? He had a right to know. If these papers could offer up some information, he *deserved* to know.

The first two were not helpful, just letters from people he didn't know. But the third was written to Gianna. He conducted a quick assessment, checking the signature at the bottom, the date and the salutation at the top: *Dearest Daughter*. It was from her mother and had been written a little over five years prior. The penmanship was shaky, indicating the effort creating the message had taken. Perhaps a final note? Last instructions to her daughter?

The little monster of his guilt roused itself from its nap. He was intruding. It was hard to keep reading. This was private. He was holding a dying woman's last words. The last paragraph was significant, considering the turn of events.

When you turn twenty-two, take the receipt you find here to the jewellery shop at the foot of the Rialto Bridge.

Nolan folded the note with careful reverence and put it back with the others, his earlier suspicion full blown now. There was no ignoring it. She'd needed the jewel case to take the next step, which wasn't, as she'd implied, leaving Venice to escape the stain of scandal. That was simply too neat. That scenario had a beginning and an end to it: girl gets jewel case, leaves city to live quietly happily ever after out from under the thumb of her ruthless guardian. But there was more here. Retrieving the jewel case hadn't been the end, but the beginning.

A hundred speculations rose in Nolan's mind. It was his punishment for being such a critical thinker. He twisted and turned stories, looking for different perspectives. The count had wanted to scare her into marriage. Why? For this case? To simply cover up the fact or control the fact he'd anticipated her dowry and sold her mother's jewels ahead of the wedding?

Or had he wanted to marry her for the secrets in this case? Was the receipt valuable enough to warrant marriage?

Her mother had obviously suspected the count of perfidy by the time of her death and had worried over her daughter's future. The particulars of what she'd hidden away were not terribly important, but the conclusion was. Gianna and the count were engaged in a private battle over control of money and jewels, enough to ensure that she could live independently if she chose, or enough to ensure she had a dowry. Neither was no small matter and both were worth fighting for—they represented an opportunity for freedom, an escape from oppression. Gianna had never said anything about life at the count's, but there'd been hints enough to safely assume life with the count had not been easy.

There was a war between the two of them and that speculation led to the second. How far would the count go to retrieve Gianna and the box's secrets? Even if he didn't discover the box was gone, Gianna was still in danger. His key to whatever her wealth was lay with possessing her more than it did with the box, and the clock was running. She'd been gone three days, out of the count's sphere of influence. The man had to start thinking she might not be coming back…unless there was something else the count held over her?

The third and final speculation was this: What was he going to do about it? He and Brennan were both right. Gianna was in trouble. Nolan didn't doubt his speculations were far from the truth. But she had used him most expertly, giving out bits of information like a trail of breadcrumbs, just enough to draw him forward inch by inch until he was here, in his room, sitting on the floor with his head in his hands, wondering if he should take the next step forward or if it was time to cut and run. He owed her nothing more.

Technically, he could walk away. Carnevale was ending, he had made enough money. Even now, that money was being transferred to his brother in England, the deed he'd dreamed of was being drawn up and signed. He could kiss Gianna and Venice goodbye and move on to the next European watering hole. Brennan had mentioned wanting to see Greece. There was Naples to consider, Turkey even, assuming the count let him leave. It might be rather naïve to think Gianna was the only one with a clock ticking. After all, he was the one who'd given her sanctuary, the one who had not compelled her to return. Perhaps he didn't have to decide. His actions had already made the decision for him, had already decided for him what came next—he had to go after her.

Nolan was up and dressing, grabbing a coat, tucking in his shirt and feeling for his knife in its familiar sheath. A knife might not be enough. He opened the bureau drawer and dug underneath his shirts for his pocket pistol, its size made for discretion. He slipped it into the pocket of his greatcoat and caught sight of himself in the mirror. Brennan was right. He looked like hell. He ought to shave, but there wasn't time.

Gianna was out in the city, alone. Her only hope of protection lay in the count not having started an effort to reclaim her.

'I want her back here with all haste.' Count Agostino Minotti paced behind his desk, delivering instructions to the two footmen. They were guards more than servants, men he'd hired to keep watch over Francesca at first and then over Gianna. Not because he had wanted them protected, but because he thought the mother and the daughter plotted against him. 'It has been three days. If we wait any longer, she could leave the city and then it will be much harder to find her.' It was more than that and it was too embarrassing. He'd been able to pass the blame on to the guards who'd been on duty last night, but it didn't quite erase the sting.

'Start with the Englishman,' Romano Lippi offered from his slouched position in a corner chair where he'd been watching the proceedings with interest. 'She'll either be with him or he'll know where she went.'

'*Signor?*' one of the footmen enquired, turning back to Agostino. 'What if he is protecting her?' It was what the count feared most, that somehow Gianna had persuaded the Englishman to be her ally. Being alone made her vulnerable, and he was betting on that. Alone, with nowhere to go, made it far easier to find her.

The count gave a cold grin and took a seat behind his desk. 'I think you'll find he'll be more interested in protecting himself if you put it to him in the right manner. You have your knives, yes?'

The two men grinned back. 'Just making sure we understood the parameters of our power. We'll start with the hotels.'

'The nice ones. The Englishman has money.' Romano rose from his seat, unfolding elegant, long limbs and crossing the room, his eyes hot. It was time to send the footmen away.

'You don't still think she's a virgin?' Romano drawled, standing behind him, hands resting on his shoulders.

'I don't care if she is or isn't,' the count snapped. 'I care that she's nearly twenty-two and free to claim her inheritance.'

Romano gave a dry laugh as he began to massage the tight muscles. 'Why do you care so much? You've spent most of it anyway. The jewel box is nearly empty.'

Agostino sighed. Romano was a handsome man with dark hair and soulful dark eyes that belied a streak of cruelty that ran as deep as his own, but while some nuances came naturally to him, some did not. Romano only saw the money on the surface, not the larger fortune. 'That's not the point. The point is, she was *here* in this very house last night and she slipped through our fingers *with* the jewel case. Nearly empty or not, it's the principle of the matter. The audacious bitch was here, dammit!'

Agostino brought his fist down on the desk, barely able to contain his temper as he thought about it again; how he'd walked into his bedroom and seen the picture slightly askew, how his hands had fumbled with the lock after a night of heavy drinking, only to discover the safe was empty. It had proven what he'd long suspected. There was more to the case than jewels, only he'd been unable to discover what that might be.

'Still, it's just a case,' Romano soothed. But that wasn't good enough. It was time Romano knew the truth.

'There is more than just the jewel case.' Agostino sank his head into his hands.

Romano's hands stilled. He had Romano's attention now, money always did. Romano loved the flash and glitter of Venice. He'd been a gondolier when Agostino had met him. Now, he was a man of leisure who accompanied Agostino almost everywhere, doing odd jobs for him. He had made Romano, fashioned him out of his wife Francesca's money, given him access to the most debauched circles of Venetian society where men and women alike flocked to him for their sordid pleasures. Agostino wondered, would Romano leave him if the money dried up? What if he failed to find Gianna before her birthday and lost the rest of Francesca's money?

'May we speak plainly, Agoste?' Romano's hands starting working again on his shoulders with firm, kneading strokes. He could feel the tension of the past days give a little.

'Always.' Agostino sighed into relaxation.

'It may be time to consider more drastic measures

for dealing with Gianna.' Romano's hand moved to his neck, pressing away the knots of worry.

'You're talking about murder,' Agostino said wearily. This wasn't the first time Romano had suggested such measures. 'My answer is still the same. Marrying her is more direct. As her husband, I take immediate control of her inheritance. This works for us. Even if I have to marry her after her twenty-second birthday, I would regain control of anything in her possession.' He reached a hand up to cover Romano's where it rested on his shoulder. 'Marriage won't change what there is between us, it is just a business arrangement. But you and I, that is something beyond business, no?' He needed to hear the words, the commitment from Romano.

Romano bent to his ear, his voice soft. 'How much money is involved?'

'Twenty thousand lire plus the diamonds, if they still exist. Only she knows where they are, which is another good reason for keeping her alive.'

Romano's hand drifted across his neck, raising a delightful shiver. 'Twenty thousand alone justifies murder. Perhaps we can forgo the diamonds if we must. We find her and do her before she turns twenty-two and it's all yours, all ours.'

It was tempting, truly. It would solve his problems and it wasn't as if he hadn't done murder before. Still, it was hard to compromise and give up the wealth of the diamonds. 'Not before she tells us where the diamonds are, Romano. Murder is final. We have to make sure we know everything beforehand. Murder didn't exactly work out for me the last time.'

He'd thought he'd known where Francesca had put the diamonds, thought he'd known how her will had been put together. He'd been wrong on both accounts and had only discovered it when it was too late to correct it. As a result, he'd been reduced to pillaging a dead woman's jewel case for funds these past five years, waiting for her daughter to come of age.

'It wasn't murder. It was death by slow poisoning,' Romano corrected. '*Murder* is such a base word. Murder is what thugs in alleys do. But we are masters and to us it is a craft. Besides, Agoste, this time we'll be sure everything is in order. It will be swift, not like poor Francesca's "lingering illness". All that time, and she never suspected a thing.' Romano gave a hard laugh.

Agostino didn't bother to argue the point. In the intervening years, he'd come to think Francesca might have known more than he realised. He'd certainly been surprised to see how her will had changed, the protections in place that she must have paid dearly for to ensure her money went to Gianna. The best he'd been able to do was to be named the girl's guardian and even that didn't give him permanent access to everything, only permission to oversee it.

Romano's breath feathered his ear. 'Leave it to me. I'll do it for you, for us. There will be no mistakes this time.'

'You are an angel,' Agostino whispered. It would be easy to lay that burden at Romano's feet. Sometimes he thought Romano was absolutely insane, a brilliant genius of the macabre. Who else could talk of murder while rousing his body? 'But it might not be enough. Giovanni is her protection. It all goes to him unless she marries, then it goes to her husband.' He all but spat the name. Giovanni, the unlikely knight in this chess game. He'd hated Giovanni for ever, a useless boy except for the fact that Giovanni was always in his way, almost as much as Gianna.

Romano whispered his evil promise. 'Then I'll do them both. That poor boy will never see me coming.' Then he laughed at his poor joke.

Chapter Seventeen

The problem with covert activity was that it made one feel as if everyone was watching. In reality she knew better. Everyone was consumed with their own errands, except the count and that was what had her nerves on edge as she see waited for the jeweller in the tiny shop off the Rialto.

If Minotti hadn't come for her yet, he would soon. His circumstances demanded he couldn't let her remain at large much longer and it had to be clear to him by now Nolan wasn't sending her back. Of course, he had to find her first. She didn't think it would be terribly hard to find out. Englishmen of means in the city had certain preferences when it came to lodgings.

Gianna fought the urge to tap her foot in impatience. Once she had the necklace, she could be gone, perhaps even before nightfall if she could manage it. It would mean eluding Nolan if he was in the room. If the jeweller would just hurry, she might not have to worry about encountering him again, which would be for the best. They'd formed certain…habits…when they were together, habits which made it hard to leave, habits which were hard to resist. Last night was proof enough of that. But it wasn't only the physical pleasures that tempted her.

Coward. You can't bear telling him goodbye to his face. It wasn't cowardice, it was protection. If she saw him, she would crumple. He would not want her to leave, he would want to help, and she feared very much that she would let him.

How had she fallen so far, so fast? She was in grave danger of becoming the one thing she wanted to avoid: dependent on a man. She'd been careful, plotting her every move, weighing every decision, seeing each of his generous actions with a cynic's eye and it still hadn't been enough. Nolan Gray had dismantled her defences with the relentless advance of a master who knew what he wanted and knew how to get it. Now, all she could do was slip out the proverbial back door.

Most certainly, the option to waiting until morning tempted fate on all fronts. Staying offered another night with Nolan, another chance to experience the bright, hot flood of passion that rose when they were together. Both times, that passion had threatened to overrun its banks. Another night meant another opportunity for it to do just that.

Staying also increased the chances the count would find her. He could not be far behind, she felt it in her bones with frightening assurance. The consequences would not be pleasant, they might even be deadly—

in fact, they most likely would be. She was under no illusion what her resistance to his marriage proposal had done to her cause. Time was running out for the count.

The situation between them had become a zero-sum game. The hidden location of the diamonds had protected her this long. The count couldn't harm her without losing his access point to the diamonds, but once they were in her possession and he found her, there would be nothing stopping him.

If she could just get the jewellery, she could go. Leaving was the best way to protect herself and protect Nolan. If the count found her, it would be because he'd found Nolan, too. Staying any longer put Nolan in danger, and that was unfair. He was a bystander in this drama, sucked in as the result of a 'lucky' hand of cards.

The jeweller returned at last from the back room with a triumphant smile, and Gianna breathed a sigh of relief. 'I have the box here. It was hiding. I apologise for the delay. It's been in storage for a very long time. Shall we take a look, *signorina*?' He blew a layer of dust off the brown-velvet lid of the long slim box. 'So much dust, I'll be just a moment, let me get a rag.'

'No, that will not be necessary,' Gianna said quickly. She had no more time to spare. Some sixth sense had her neck prickling. She needed to get back to the sanctuary of the hotel. It had been beyond dangerous to come out into the city alone.

He looked at her queerly and lifted the lid. 'We'll

just take a look inside and make sure this is what should be in there before you sign the receipt.'

Gianna smiled at the jeweller to hide her impatience. He was simply doing his job, but even this little courtesy to vouch for the contents was too much. What if he was stalling on purpose? What if he'd sent a messenger to the count? But that was foolishness. The count didn't even know the jewels were here or he would have been here long ago and she would have been dead, the count no longer having need of her knowledge.

The jeweller lifted the lid and pulled back the pink wool protecting the gems. Finally a piece of luck! The stones were all there. The necklace was intact. Tears stung at her eyes as Gianna reached out a hand to search beneath the padding for the provenance, a square thick card. It was there. She didn't need to read it. She knew it by rote, had been required, in fact, to memorise it.

For a day just like today. In spite of her fear, her heart sang.

The Marchetti Diamonds: a necklace of eight perfect cushion-cut diamonds, originally from the mines of Kashmir, brought to the Venetian republic in the seventeenth century.

A gift to her mother from her besotted merchant lover in the days before her mother's mad bid to be 'respectable' and her daughter came of age.

'Yes, this is all correct. Everything is here. Where

can I sign?' Gianna took possession of the box. She slid it into the folds of her cloak as the jeweller's eyes moved to a point over her shoulder. The bell above the door jingled and she tensed. She'd been so close to leaving.

'*Buongiorno, signor*, please look around the shop. I will be with you in just a moment.' The jeweller was all obsequious courtesy.

'No need, I've already found what I'm looking for,' the voice behind her drawled, arrogant and confident. 'Gianna, you've been very reckless.' Nolan. She swallowed, relief making her knees weak. She'd heard the anger beneath his words, but she didn't care. If anyone was going to find her, Nolan was a far better choice. She felt him come up behind her, his presence reassuring even in his displeasure. 'If you're done here, I've come to walk you home. I trust you got what you came for?' He gave her a thin smile.

He waited until her business was concluded and they were outside to scold, his grip firm on her arm. 'What in blazes did you think you were doing, traipsing around the city alone? The count could have had you at any point.' His eyes narrowed. 'Unless any danger he poses is merely a figment of your imagination?'

Gianna tugged her arm free. Calling her a liar about the count was beyond the pale. 'He *is* dangerous. You have no idea. That's why I had to come today.' She hissed, 'If I wait any longer, it will be too late.'

Nolan took her arm again, this time to manoeuvre her through the crowd on the bridge, and she let him.

She felt safer in the crowd, knowing he was close. 'Too late for what?'

She spied a place on the other side of the bridge where they might stand in some privacy. When they reached it, she faced him, her answer ready. 'Too late to leave, Nolan.' Too late to live, too late to save Giovanni, too late for everything. 'I am trying to hold up my end of the bargain, here. I promised to leave once you helped me retrieve the jewel case. You've done that and more. Let me do my part.'

He should take the deal. The gambler in Nolan knew this was a good offer. Little Miss Trouble was actually leaving and that meant he was free to pursue his project, free to continue with his Grand Tour. But looking at Gianna's earnest face, her eyes begging him to agree with her, he simply couldn't. She wanted this too badly. That alerted him, awoke his moral conscience. Up to this point, she'd been so intent on pulling him in to get what she wanted, now she was intent on pushing him away. One reason suggested itself for such an about-turn, but he wanted to hear her say it, admit to it.

He gave her a cynical smile. 'Do you think it's that easy, Gianna? You've got what you wanted from me and now you can just cast me off?'

'No!' Her green eyes flashed in indignation. In that single word, he had the truth he wanted.

'No, it's not. I agree. You're in danger and you're trying to protect me by simply disappearing. If you really want to protect me, tell me what's going on.

Let me help you.' He ushered her back into the flow of the crowd. 'We have to keep moving. If anyone is looking for us, we'll be harder to spot.'

'If anyone is looking for *me*,' she corrected.

'Us.' Nolan let his hand rest possessively at her back. 'Don't think I can escape involvement at this late date. You have implicated me by association.' He'd guilt her into talking if he had to.

Nolan led her into a quieter side street of San Polo, the water of the canal lapping sluggishly against the brick banks. There was a church up ahead he knew from his many walks through the city. This was one of his favourite neighbourhoods with its fish markets and smells, but today he was only concerned about sanctuary for her. He'd been worried sick for her as he'd made his way to the jeweller's, his mind reeling with all types of gruesome scenarios in which he arrived too late to divert disaster. But there'd been no disaster, not yet. There'd just been her standing in the shop, admiring a box of jewels as if she had all the time in the world.

The church was empty and would be until vespers. They stopped in front of a series of paintings— Tintoretto's, Nolan thought vaguely. 'You were going to leave without saying goodbye.' It had occurred to him that while he was racing across the city to her aid, *she* had been thinking of leaving. It didn't speak highly of her impression of what had passed between them last night or on other occasions.

'I was going back to the hotel.' She didn't look at him, he noted. Her gaze never left the painting.

'In the hopes I wouldn't be there, perhaps?' Nolan supplied. 'Your dresses came. They look lovely.' What would she say if he told her he was looking forward to seeing her in them?

'You found the hidden compartment and read my mother's notes.' It was her turn to level an accusation.

'I was worried. I couldn't just sit there and wait for you to return. If you had waited, I would have come with you. How much trouble are you in, Gianna? You might as well tell me. I've already figured out the jewel case wasn't the end of anything, but the beginning.' He'd also come to the conclusion that all this garnering of jewels and protecting of wealth wasn't an end in itself either, but for something larger, for *someone*. 'For all that you've told me, there is still quite a lot you're hiding.'

Then again, he'd made himself an easy mark. He'd demanded to know very little. He'd been content to see this scenario as nothing more than a young woman wrongfully oppressed by her guardian. But the longer he was with her, the more clear it became this situation ran far deeper than a man with a gambling debt who'd wagered his ward's virginity to cover it. He couldn't possibly leave her now. His conscience demanded it.

Even if his conscience hadn't, other parts of him would. In a short time, she'd become more than just someone in need of help, more than a potential *affaire*. He never wanted to feel again the way he felt when he'd entered the bedroom and known she was gone. Not only because she'd put herself in danger, but because he was not ready to be without her.

Gianna took a seat on a nearby pew, hesitating for a moment, holding an internal debate with herself. Nolan waited, letting her decide. Eventually, she drew out the box hidden beneath her cloak. 'This is what the count is really after.' She lifted the lid, and Nolan let out a low whistle of appreciation.

He'd seen diamonds before, he'd *bought* diamonds before, but nothing like this. Eight large princess-cut diamonds made up the centre while the rest of the necklace was strung with tiny, perfectly cut miniature versions. 'Not quite a king's ransom, but close,' Nolan complimented. 'These will ensure your security for life.' Or not. They might also sign her death warrant. Had she thought of that? Now that he'd seen them, Nolan doubted the count would rest until he found her. Where would the freedom be in that; always looking over her shoulder, always on the move?

Gianna replaced the lid. 'My mother willed them to me. They are mine, but until I am twenty-two, the count is considered my guardian. All my mother left me is under his purview. He can't stop me from redeeming these diamonds, but he can control what I do with them. I can't sell them without his permission. He doesn't even know where they were hidden, only that they're mine.'

'An insurance policy, then,' Nolan said grimly. If the count decided to do away with Gianna, he would lose any link he had to the diamonds.

'Yes,' Gianna admitted matter-of-factly, her weary

tone giving evidence that this was a chess game she'd played for years. His admiration for her rose. It was no wonder she did not trust easily.

Gianna continued. 'The count took her jewel case and hid it away after her death before I even thought to take it. He might have taken it before then, I don't know. My mother was desperately ill, and I was too focused on other things in those days to pay attention to what the count did. We were stalemated. I could not run without the diamonds, and he could not do away with me and claim the prize for himself. I was his prisoner, but he was mine, too, in a way.'

Gianna looked at her hands. 'It didn't mean I didn't try to leave. Once he'd sent Giovanni away, I was more willing to take my chances without the diamonds than he was.' Her voice trailed off, and Nolan waited. Silence was often a more powerful prompt than a question.

'He caught me. A girl of seventeen can't get very far on her own, especially when she lives on an island.' She tried to slough it off with a laugh, but Nolan wasn't fooled. There had been consequences. 'I didn't try again.'

'That bad?' Nolan asked quietly.

Gianna shrugged. 'It wasn't so much what he did to me that mattered. It was what he did to Giovanni because of me.' She looked at her hands. 'I was naïve. Giovanni had already been sent away by then. I thought it was the worst the count could do, but I was wrong. The count locked me in my room without any clothes and a diet of bread and water for a week. But I still wouldn't promise not to run again. I was too proud. It wasn't until he sent word to where Giovanni was held that he should be punished, too, that I broke down.' She gave a shrug. 'As you can see, my life is something of a mess. You should walk away right now. The count is a monster and Romano Lippi encourages the worst in him.'

'Lippi?' Nolan hadn't heard that name before.

'The count's paramour.' Gianna cringed as she said it. 'I know what you're thinking, everything just gets weirder and me with it. You were right to want to set me aside that first night.' He heard her voice catch. 'Who would want me, Nolan? The daughter of a once-popular courtesan who married a corrupt count? That alone is an enormous mark against me. I tried so hard to stay apart from it, to not let my life become a pattern card of hers. The glamour and the drama suited her, but I didn't want that for me. I just wanted normality and I ended so far from it.'

Nolan closed his hand over hers, feeling her pain. It was eerily close to the pain he'd once grappled with. 'We all want normality. We don't all get it. You're wrong about one thing, though. *I* want you. I am glad you didn't go.' How he wanted her! He wanted her safe, in his bed, in his arms, in his life.

He had to tread carefully. Like last night, he suspected she would come, she would take that offering because she was alone, scared, desperate. He didn't want her that way. He didn't want to be a temporary escape from her fears. She would regret coming to him on those terms. She would see her choice as weakness. He could only have her when she was safe and able to make the decision on her own. So he would see to it that she was. He would see her safe. His mind started to plan. He would take her to England. He could protect her there…

'We'll go back to the hotel, pack our things and go,' Nolan said out loud, unwilling to disclose the entirety of his thoughts for fear that Gianna would balk. She was not used to taking help. She'd have to be led along in small steps. In his mind, he kept a running checklist of things that needed doing. He'd have to tell Brennan, perhaps even encourage Brennan to come with them in case the count learned he had a travelling companion.

'We can go to Siena. I have friends there.' He thought of Archer's villa in the countryside, of Archer's uncle's home in the city. There would be plenty of protection there, and Archer's new wife, Elisabeta, would welcome Gianna openly, would understand even what Gianna had been through.

'No.' She gripped his arm with no small amount of alarm. 'We can't go south. We have to go to Padua.'

'Padua? As in Shakespeare's *Taming of the Shrew*?' It took him a moment before he remembered. Giovanni. Of course she wouldn't leave without him. The jewel case, the diamonds, they were not the most valuable things she needed to collect before she could flee the count entirely. 'Is that where your brother is? Then by all means, we'll go to Padua.'

'Tonight? We'll still leave tonight?' Worry flickered in her eyes. 'We have to get there ahead of the count. Giovanni will never see trouble coming.' She bit her lip, and Nolan yearned to run his finger along her mouth and erase the worry marks left by her teeth, yearned to kiss away her fears.

'How old is he?' Was Giovanni a young child? He couldn't be younger than seven or he'd be the count's own son.

'He's seventeen.' Gianna shook her head. 'It's not that he's unaware. He knows very well the treachery of the count. It's that he literally won't see the count coming. Giovanni is blind.'

Nolan blew out a breath. The surprises just kept coming. He was to elude the count while guiding Gianna, her blind brother *and* a fortune in diamonds across Europe. Gianna smiled. 'What? What's so funny?'

She laughed, some of her anxiety leaving her for the moment. 'You are. The look on your face. I finally surprised you. You've known so much, guessed so much about me that it's eerie. But you didn't bargain on this.'

'As I tell my friends, I am a student of human nature. It does not make me psychic.' Nolan grinned. The task might seem impossible, but he'd take it one obstacle at a time. For now, he should celebrate the fact that she'd accepted his help. He knew what a big step that was for her. 'Let's get to the hotel and then let's go to Padua.'

Gianna put a hand on his arm. 'You're a good man to go get my brother. I won't forget this.' The brother was nothing. Padua was nothing. He'd go to hell and back for her, to see her safe and free. No one should be bound to another by the chains the count had imposed. Wasn't this the very reason he had sent the money to his brother, bought the deed to the property? So that people like him, like his brother, like Gianna, children in untenable situations, had somewhere to go?

He squeezed her hand. 'I have a younger brother, too, remember. I know a little something about how important they are.'

'Well, anyway, th—'

Nolan pressed a finger to her lips. 'Don't thank me, it's bad luck for us. You should know better by now.'

'Then let me kiss you,' Gianna whispered softly, stretching up to reach him, twining her hands about his neck. He let himself be drawn close.

Brennan would have a fit over him leaving Venice with a questionable woman. To hell with what Brennan thought. Right now, Nolan didn't care. He grinned. 'Now *that*, I can allow.'

Chapter Eighteen

⁓⁓⁓⁓⁓

This was the kiss that changed everything. Gianna drew him to her, letting her mouth linger on his, savouring this moment suspended in time. For her, time would be divided into 'life until this kiss' and 'life after this kiss'.

Nolan hadn't thrown her aside, hadn't been disgusted with her life, with her. Instead, he'd offered his help. He'd offered his help before, but that had been with the express purpose of getting *rid* of her. The want made it different. It made *her* different. He'd offered to help in order to keep her with him. He didn't *want* to let her go. This wasn't about what he needed to do or what she needed to do, it wasn't about dependence, about not having the choice to accept help. It was about choosing to accept the help offered. The knowledge of that thought made her heart beat faster.

Her tongue caressed the inside of his mouth, lazily duelling with his. She liked the feel of his hands, strong and warm at her back. A little moan escaped her. What she didn't know about him didn't matter, only what she did know: he'd saved her, protected her, provided for her, pleasured her and never once pushed his advantage.

Nolan's mouth moved to her earlobe, and she knew a moment's regret as she issued the words, 'We have to go.'

He whispered one word before giving her up to reality, a sinful smile on his lips. 'Later.'

'I like the sound of that.' Later was a promise, a future and in the immediate bliss of the moment, she was willing to contemplate that possibility.

Dusk had arrived when they exited the church. Even in winter, Venice was beautiful this time of night. It would be a while before she'd see the city again like this. Gianna felt a lump rise in her throat, reality hitting her hard now that the decision was made. She was leaving the only city she'd ever known. In the frustration of having her original plans thwarted, of having to readjust her strategies, the rush to redeem the diamonds and the jewel case, she'd not allowed herself to think about what this all meant, perhaps because she could do nothing about it. As long as the count was here, Venice wasn't safe. Gianna hesitated for a short moment, looking up at the Rialto Bridge as they passed.

'You'll be back some day. The count can't live for ever.' Nolan's voice was at her ear, his arm about her, drawing her close. 'Fresh starts often require fresh places. It will be all right, Gianna.' But she made mental pictures of the places they passed anyway as they made their way to the hotel: the Doge's Palace, Piazza San Marco with its cafés, the gondolas bobbing at the lagoon pier.

At the hotel, Nolan paused outside the entrance, uncharacteristically hesitant. 'Why don't we just leave now? Forget everything inside. My friend can pack our things and bring them later.'

'The case,' Gianna protested. 'I couldn't leave it behind.'

Nolan's jaw set. His right arm gave a slight twitch, feeling the comforting presence of the hidden blade, as he scanned the steps of the hotel. 'I'll go up. You stay in the lobby.'

A wave of fear gripped her belly at his caution. She tried to brush it aside. 'The count isn't here.' But saying it didn't make it true.

Nolan shrugged and stood his ground. There would be no arguing him out of this. 'I don't want you upstairs where you could be trapped in a small space, where there's no one to witness anything.' She understood his reasoning. In the lobby, she'd have room to run, she could scream. She'd have resources.

'I'll arrange a boat to the mainland.' She had to be useful or she'd go crazy waiting for him, imagining enemies everywhere.

This was crazy, madness at its finest. Nolan took the stairs with quick strides, his mind already racing through the room. He'd grab the case, a change of clothes, his stash of winnings. He would give himself no more than three minutes. He hadn't wanted to come in—intuition had warned him against this, but he couldn't deny Gianna her request. The count had taken so much from her already.

Nolan cautiously opened the door to the room, half expecting the room to have been burgled, half expecting to be attacked by a lurking intruder. The count couldn't be far behind them. He had to know Gianna wasn't coming back. He would also know where to look for her. The room was untouched, however. Good, they were still ahead of the bastard. He'd feel better once they were on a boat and Venice was behind them. Not that it solved anything. The count would know they were headed to Padua, to her brother.

He heard the scream before he reached the bedroom. Nolan raced back to the hall and peered over the railing, taking in the scene below him in the lobby. The count had Gianna about the waist and was forcefully, awkwardly, attempting to drag her from the lobby. It was an ignoble scramble, Gianna fighting him for every inch, kicking, screaming, clawing at him.

Nolan raced for the stairs, his knife flashing in one hand, his pocket pistol in the other. He should have listened to his gut—they should not have come in. Why was no one helping her? Did Venetians not recognise an abduction when they saw one? Everyone in the lobby had withdrawn to the corners, some racing for the exit.

Nolan scanned the area from the vantage of the stairs, the height giving him a full view. Ah, someone had tried to help. There was the prone, bleeding figure of a man by the concierge's desk. The count had brought help, then. His wicked paramour, Romano Lippi, perhaps? Nolan saw him now, a dark-haired man with a blade holding the desk clerk at knifepoint to ensure no more interference, as if the bleeding body wasn't deterrent enough.

A cold, calculated calm settled over Nolan. He would take the dark-haired man first, use him as leverage against the count. He would use his pistol on the dark-haired man. He'd save his knife for the count. 'Let her go, or I do your man!' Nolan let his voice carry through the lobby, forceful and loud. Volume intimidated, unstoppable movement intimidated. Pistol raised, he advanced on the count's accomplice.

'I'll have the desk-clerk's throat slit before I die,' the dark-haired man countered with a snarl.

Time to bluff. 'I don't care. I am interested in the girl,' Nolan replied in bloodless tones. It wasn't true. He'd rather not have anyone else harmed. He had three shots, the small pistol sporting a secret third chamber. He fired the first one, narrowly missing the man, letting the bullet embed in the thick wood of the counter. The man went pale.

Nolan advanced, gun still held high in active position. 'It's easy to throw around such braggadocio about your willingness to die, but in the end it's not so easy to actually do it. Is this how you want to go? Shot down in a hotel lobby?'

The man was wavering. Nolan had no doubt the man was malicious, had a cruel, torturous streak, but that didn't make him any braver than the next man. That bravery was being tested now. Nolan could see it in his eyes. At his core, this man was no different than the card sharp in Dover.

'Don't worry, Romano, he hasn't got another shot.' The count was edging closer, dragging Gianna with him, still struggling. Nolan grinned. This was what he wanted; the count and Gianna closer to him, farther from the door. The risk had been that the count might be selfish enough to let his paramour die while he escaped with Gianna.

'I do have a second shot.' Nolan clicked the second chamber.

'You're bluffing.' The count scowled. 'He's bluffing, Romano.' But Nolan noted Romano didn't look convinced.

'I'd be hesitant to make that wager, Minotti,' Nolan said in cold tones. 'You didn't do so well the last time you wagered a person. You lost her as I recall. Let her go.' It was time to end this. He didn't like bloodshed, wasn't proud that he'd partaken in it on more than one occasion, but sometimes blood was what it took to be understood. 'I will count to three. You let her go or I'll shoot and we can test your two-bullet theory.'

The flash of a look passed between Romano and the count. 'One…' Nolan began. 'Two…' He readied himself. He did expect the count to relent. He did not, however, expect the count to play fair.

'Agoste!' Romano Lippi's voice held a desperate edge.

'All right!' the count growled. He shoved Gianna

forward, straight into Nolan. It was meant to catch him off balance, but Nolan was ready. He sidestepped and charged the count, showing no quarter. The goal now was to gain the entrance and go. He didn't want to be here when the watch, or whatever they called it in Venice, showed up.

Nolan took a swipe with his knife, catching the count across the cheek with a vicious slash, sending the man reeling backwards, his hand clutching his torn face. 'Go, Gianna!' he yelled. Romano looked uncertain, his gaze darting between their fleeing prey and the wounded, screaming count. Nolan backed towards the door, making the decision for him. He fired his second shot, catching Romano in the shoulder. Only then, with both of Gianna's attackers disabled, did he pocket the gun and grab her hand. He wanted to get out before anyone in the lobby decided he was the guilty party.

Nolan raced down the pier, hailing a boat. He didn't wait for the boatman to reply. He grabbed Gianna about the waist and swung her on board. 'Take us to the mainland as fast as you can.' Nolan reached in his pocket and drew out a wad of bills. He stuffed them into the stunned man's hand. It didn't matter how much was there, only that the man take them. 'Go!' He made wild a gesture with his hand towards the open water. The man glanced at the money in his hand, then at Nolan.

'No questions and there's more when we arrive,' Nolan promised. He assumed a positive response and strode to the rail. It would be harder for the boatman to disagree now and he didn't. The boatman threw off the moorings and steered them out into the lagoon.

'Are you all right?' It seemed he'd spent an inordinate amount of time asking that question since he met Gianna. He wanted never to have to ask it again. He wanted to know that she *was* all right, always.

'I'm sorry.' She drew her cloak around her against the wind off the water or perhaps against the post-rescue shock that was sure to come. 'We have nothing. How will we get to Padua now?'

Nolan laughed into the wind. 'That's the easy part. I'll find a card game.'

His confidence made her smile. 'Do you ever lose?'

'No, only when I want to. Sometimes losing can be more beneficial.' He felt her relax beside him, her mind wanting to concentrate on something other than the gory moments of blood at the hotel.

'How do you do it? How can you manage to win so often?' She leaned on her elbows at the rail, letting the wind take her hood and push it back from her hair, the rising moon catching the profile of her face in its light. She looked like Tintoretto's Madonna: strong, and yet there was kindness behind that strength along with fierceness.

Nolan covered her hand with his, their fingers interlacing. She had him spinning, as Brennan liked to say. She had him fleeing cities, stealing jewel cases, going after blind brothers, and he hadn't even slept with her. Now, she had him telling her his secrets—more of them. The first had been to ease her way in sharing her own. But these were secrets he was sharing without provocation.

'I can see the cards. Not literally. I can see them in my mind. Once they've been played, I remember them.' He'd told his father about it once when he was eleven in an attempt to win his father's favour. That had been a mistake.

'That's incredible.' Gianna breathed her awe. 'How much can you remember? How many cards?'

'Four or five decks. I usually don't have to remember that many except for *vingt-et-un*.' He'd not told her to impress her, he'd just wanted to take her mind off other things.

'That's quite a gift.'

Nolan snorted. 'My father didn't think so. Growing up, I thought it was a gift from God. I thought he'd be impressed—my father, that is, not God. But he thought it was the devil's curse instead.' He paused, looking out over the water. He hadn't meant to tell her that. Now that he had, he might as well tell her all of it. 'My father decided to beat it out of me and when that didn't work he decided to starve it out of me. I never mentioned I could count cards after that.' He turned his head sideways to take in her reaction. 'You're not the only one who wanted normality and didn't get it. You got the count and I got saddled with a puritanical father who was obsessed with his religion.'

Gianna's only answer was to squeeze his hand and curled her fingers around his even tighter. Sometimes silence spoke louder than words. This was one of those times.

Nolan paid the boatman and found them a carriage and driver willing to take them a little farther down the road at night. He'd had to pay dearly for it, though, using up most of his cash, but the distance would be worth it even if the inn they arrived at shortly before midnight wasn't. He'd thought he'd put rough Italian inns behind him when he'd arrived at the Danieli—apparently not. It made no sense to continue—accommodations were not likely to get better the farther they got from Venice, and Gianna was tired. This was probably the best they could hope for. There was a room available, and Nolan took it, too weary to barter the exorbitant price.

'It's not the Danieli,' he said wryly, showing Gianna into their new quarters. He shrugged out of his greatcoat and jacket. 'But you'll be safe here tonight. There's a bar for the door.' From the looks of the customers downstairs, that bar probably saw a fair amount of use. He wished he had somewhere better for her, for himself. There was only the one room and he wasn't looking forward to bedding down in the common room. He was getting soft. The Danieli had spoiled him.

'It's enough.' Gianna tested the bed with a hand. 'The bed will do. We may be a little cramped, but we'll manage.' She furrowed her brow at his hesitation. 'What?'

'I'll sleep downstairs. You'll have plenty of room. I probably won't sleep much anyway. Maybe I can get a card game together, make some money.' He gave her a 'don't-worry-about-me-I'll-be-fine' smile, but she wasn't having it.

'That's ridiculous. You're as tired as I am. You are not going to sleep downstairs where we both know you'll have to sleep with at least one eye open most of the night. Besides, those people down there didn't seem like the card-playing types.' Gianna threw back the covers to check the condition of the bed linens. 'These are surprisingly fresh. It would be a shame to let them go to waste.'

Dear Lord, she would tempt a saint and he was miles from that. Did he have to spell it out for her? Did she understand just how dangerous it was for them to spend a night together in *that* bed? It was smaller than his positively kingly bed at the Danieli and they both knew how that had ended; with his head between her legs, the two of them panting their pleasure through the walls. It was time to remind her. 'Gianna, what exactly do you think would happen if I stayed?'

The question changed the room, the powerful something that existed between them surging to life. Gianna stood from her inspection of the bed, eyes locking on his in hazel solemnity. 'What should have happened a long time ago.' She raised both hands to her hair in a provocative gesture that threw her breasts into relief against the tight bodice of her gown. She pulled the pins, letting her hair fall in a dark cascade, Godiva and Eve rolled into one intoxicating woman. 'It's past time. Take me to bed, Nolan Gray.'

Chapter Nineteen

Gianna moved into him, her arms about his neck before he could refuse. Truth was, he didn't want to refuse. She was right, this *should* have happened already, but the circumstances of their acquaintance had prevented it. Now, Nolan no longer cared about circumstance and motives. They had moved past that, moved beyond being two strangers who had been thrown together. They were more now, although what that 'more' was had yet to be defined: friends, lovers, sensual co-conspirators…

Her mouth moved over his, and he did not protest the press of her lips. He loved her mouth—every taste he'd had of it left him wanting more, wanting it back where it might have been that first night if he'd allowed it.

'Let me undress you,' Gianna murmured, her hands already working free his cravat, the buttons of his waistcoat. 'Tonight, I am your valet.'

'I thought *I* was taking *you* to bed,' Nolan quipped,

enjoying her feminine attentions too much to truly complain.

She gave him a sly glance. 'You are, but first there is this.' *This* happened to be a very erotic shirt removal. No tailor or valet had ever undressed him like this; nails trailing an arousing, barely there touch over his nipples; her fingers drew feather-light lines down his breastbone, across his ribs, coming to rest on the waistband of his trousers. 'You're beautiful, all planes and hard ridges,' she whispered at his ear.

Her hand dropped to the hardest ridge of them all, cupping him through his trousers, the bowl of her hand lifting him, shaping him to her fingers. Her mouth nipped his earlobe, eliciting a groan, her hand around the hard, aroused contours of his cock elicited more than that. This was exquisite pain, exquisite pleasure wrapped into one. 'You will have me beyond the point of self-control in a moment.'

He hoped she wouldn't test the truth of that statement. It was probably a lie. He thought he was already beyond that point. He couldn't recall the last time a woman had made the effort to prime him for sex. It was usually the other way around, a given that he was ready. That Gianna did not want to take that for granted was a potent aphrodisiac in itself. He did not exist to serve her pleasure solely. They were to be partners in this. 'Be careful you do this for the right reasons, Gianna.' When had she decided she wanted this? Last night? Was this no more than misguided emotions from the harrowing afternoon? Men wanted, even needed, the outlet of sex after battle.

Was this merely her rendition of post-battle coitus or something more?

Gianna looked at him, her hand still on him. 'This is for me, for us. This is not about owing.' She released him and took a step back, her eyes moving over him in slow, raking perusal. 'Take your trousers off. I want to see you, all of you.'

He'd been right. She was willing and able to take charge of her pleasure and of his. This promised to be a most wicked night. Nolan let his lips curve into a wolfish half-smile full of sexual promise. 'As you wish.'

She was going to pay for that in glorious pleasure, he would see to it. He didn't merely take off his trousers, he made it into a tantalising taste of masculinity the way a good appetiser sets the stage for the main course. He held her eyes, his fingers flicking open the buttons of his trousers one by one with languid dexterity. He was purposely in no rush. He watched her for the minutest of reactions, his own eyes darkening in response to the rising desire he saw in her. She made no attempt to hide it, didn't want to. Good. Lies and obscured truths had no place between them. Tonight was not about those sorts of games. Tonight, sex would be honest.

Nolan pushed his trousers over lean hips, registering the catch of her breath as they fell. Her eyes locked unabashedly on his cock and then on his eyes, full of awe. 'Good lord, Nolan, you're a Greek god in disguise.'

'I am just a man.' But there was an unmistakable

rush of heat to his groin at her words, at knowing she found him pleasing to look upon. This was a promising start. Tonight, he wanted her to own every ounce of her pleasure for what it was.

He moved towards her, his hands working the laces of her gown free. 'It's time to level the playing field,' he murmured, pushing the dress from her shoulders. It gave no further resistance, neither did Gianna. She was as eager to be undressed as he was to do it. She raised her arms, and he slid her chemise over her head, her undergarments over her hips, until she was naked against him, her skin pressed to his, the rise of his phallus against the soft swell of her stomach. If he wasn't careful he would spend right now. In an effort to restore his control, Nolan swept her up in his arms and carried her back to the bed. The straw of the mattress crackled as he lay her down, as it took his weight beside her.

'Tell me you want me.' He kissed the sweep of her jaw, trailing a line of tiny kisses along it.

'I want you, Nolan. You know I do.' Her answer was a delightful hitching gasp as he drew a slow line down her breastbone. She was glorious aroused: her eyes emerald dark, her pulse strong at her neck, her sensitive skin responding to the slightest of touches.

'Tell me where you want me. *Show* me. Own your pleasure, Gianna, with your words, your touch,' Nolan cajoled, his mouth at her throat. 'Here? Do you want me here? How about here?' He bent to take the pink tip of a breast in his mouth, teasing it with his tongue, feeling it pebble and strain where his tongue passed.

'Where else, Gianna? Where else do you want me to be?'

Everywhere. She wanted him everywhere, with everything at his disposal, his mouth, his tongue, his fingers, his hands, his cock—that magnificent rigid staff that had pressed too briefly against her. He made her into a wanton. She'd thought to control this, thought she could keep her desire on a leash, that she could somehow enjoy this without committing to it body and soul. If that had ever been a possibility, it was gone now. Now that she'd committed to this, there was no withholding. Nolan's next words obliterated the prospect entirely. 'Show me, Gianna. Show me where you want me.'

His words called her to wickedness and she did not flinch from the invitation. Tonight she could afford to be decadent. Tonight she was safe. For a few hours she could set aside her agenda. She could indulge. When would she get another chance?

Gianna drew her fingers down to her navel, issuing husky commands. 'Kiss me here.' He did, with the soft press of his lips, his hands bracketing her hips with gentle kneading. Her hand went lower still to the place between her legs where Nolan had wrought such pleasure once before. She touched her cleft. 'I want your mouth here, where my nest is damp for you already.'

These were shocking words she uttered, and she could not be embarrassed about what she said, what she did, what she asked for, not with Nolan. She recognised in her boldness another sort of security. He would not let her be ashamed of her desire, of her wanton requests. He *wanted* her to give them free rein with her words, with her body.

He answered them with his fingers at her fold, parting, making her ready for his mouth and then he was there, finding the centre of her pleasure with lips, with the graze of teeth. She arched into him at the first contact, her hips lifting, her urgency rising in response to the lick and lave of his tongue. The more he gave, the more she wanted.

She was going to burst, *wanted* to burst. She cried out against the ache he built in her, until the throbbing ache simply couldn't be borne. Only then, with her hands wrapped in his hair, her body pulsing, did he let her burst. And that made it worse. It was enough, and not enough, not tonight. Tonight, that little explosion of relief was merely a primer that drove her to the edge of a wildness not yet fulfilled.

Nolan lifted his head, his hair loose and tangled about his shoulders, his eyes dark. He was hungry, too. This had been an appetiser for them both. Gianna drew him to her, bringing him up over her body length to length, her legs parting to accommodate him, his hips hard against hers, his arms bracing his body above her, his cock pressing its invitation at the cradle of her thighs.

'Gianna.' His voice was strained, hoarse with the effort of holding his desire in check. 'Are you sure? I don't know if I can be gentle.'

She smoothed the hair back from his face, framing him with her hands. 'Yes, I am sure.' She was sure, too, that he could not be gentle. As a lover, it simply wasn't in him: he was assertive, confident, driven. He'd not been gentle in the church, or on the Danieli's big bed. Gentle would not do them any justice. This was not a mild passion.

Yet he found the right balance between the wildness that drove them and the reality—he was going to enter her for the first time. Nolan came into her with confident steadiness, moving inexorably deeper into her channel, halting his progress to let her body stretch around him, withdrawing a little to press forward once more.

Her own body picked up the thrusting rhythm of his, hips lifting once more, mouths meeting as their bodies claimed the cadence of lovemaking together. Her legs gripped his waist, her arms encircled him, nails digging into his back as the rhythm rose, speeding them towards some cataclysm. She could feel his body clench, his breath coming in hard pants, words degenerating into nothing more than grunts. This act was beyond words. Knowing his body this way, feeling his body join with hers, was an expression of intimacy far beyond any words she possessed. When the end came, brilliant and explosive, the feel of his release mingled with hers carried with it an alarming profundity.

This could never happen again. It was the first thought to surface once the bliss had passed. Not because it seemed unlikely something so extraordinary could be repeated, although Gianna did wonder, but because she couldn't stand it. Or, more accurately, she couldn't *withstand* it. This pleasure of his would bind her to him. It would be impossible to leave. This was an imprisonment far more compelling than any method of force the count had ever used. Worst of all, she'd asked for it. *Take me to bed, Nolan Gray.* He'd done more than that. He'd taken her to the edge of pleasure and beyond.

Gianna ran an idle hand down Nolan's chest. He was oblivious, sleeping hard. She smiled in the dark, but it wasn't entirely with pleasure. She was laughing at herself. She'd been so bold, never imagining she'd be the author of her own downfall. Well, that might be premature. She could control this if she set her mind to it and that control started with remembering her goals: get to Giovanni before the count; whisk herself and Giovanni off to somewhere safe, somewhere anonymous out of the count's reach; start a new life where she wasn't a courtesan's daughter or a sadistic, greed-driven count's stepdaughter.

'Stop thinking.' Nolan's voice was slurred with sleepiness, but he was awake.

'How can you tell? It's dark and you're barely awake.' Gianna rolled away from him and propped herself up on an elbow.

'Barely awake means not quite asleep.' Nolan gave a low chuckle. 'Your hand stopped moving on my chest, a sure sign your brain had found something else to occupy its time.'

Gianna gave his shoulder a playful punch. 'How did you get so good at that? You know how to read people.'

'A gambler has to.' He played with a strand of her hair, twisting it around one finger. The question made him self-conscious, she realised. He didn't like talking about himself.

'Is that how you see yourself? A gambler?' It was appalling how little she knew of him considering what they'd been through. She was hungry for any little titbit. What was his life like back in England? What were these plans he mentioned? She'd settle for anything.

He made a wry smile. 'Does that disappoint you? Did you hope I might be a nobleman in disguise? Prince Charming, perhaps?'

She felt defensive now. The comment was somehow demeaning although she couldn't quite work through how. 'No, I never thought that, nor wanted it.' Her own tone was brisk. 'I just wanted to know something about you.'

His eyes softened. His hand stilled at her hair. 'I'm a gambler. That's all. I've gambled my way across Europe. Gambling keeps my pockets full. I have nothing to my name except what's in my travelling trunks. No land, no secret estates to retire to when I'm tired of wandering.'

Now, thanks to her, he didn't even have that. All of his worldly possessions were back at the Danieli. She really was bad for him. 'I'm sorry, that's my fault.' Pretty soon he was going to figure out how awful it was to be with her and she wouldn't have to worry about how to leave him. He would leave her. She just hoped it would be after they had Giovanni.

Nolan merely shrugged, raising one of his beautifully sculpted shoulders. He traced her collarbone with a long finger that sent a delicious shiver down her spine. 'I am always up for an adventure. Brennan will bring my trunks and your case. I'll send word to him once we reach our destination.' He gave her an expectant glance, his eyes asking her to fill in the details. What was their destination? Padua was only a stop to collect Giovanni.

He gave her a penetrating stare. 'You don't know where you're going after Padua, do you?'

'I'm sure something will present itself.' Gianna hoped she sounded more confident than she felt. She didn't know exactly where they'd go. 'It only needs to be a place where we can have a new start.' But part of her was starting to recognise how elusive that might be. Freedom meant running. To stay free meant being able to outwit the count. The diamonds were worth following, revenge was worth pursuing. The count would not rest and neither could she. A woman with her looks, independent means, and a blind brother would not be allowed to fade into the background of any village.

Someone would always want to know more. She would always be on the move, there would always be Giovanni to care for, which meant there would never be a husband for her, never a family of her own to settle down with because there would never *be* any settling down. But there could be tonight. The count and Romano Lippi were delayed in Venice, nursing their wounds. She and Nolan would have at least a half-day head start on them. Tonight she was safe. She wasn't going to waste it, wasn't going to let Nolan see how empty her hope was.

Gianna swung a leg over Nolan's thighs and levered herself astride, dropping a full-mouthed kiss on his lips. 'Enough talk, Nolan Gray. Tonight isn't for plans, it's for passion.' She slipped a hand between his legs and cupped the tender sac behind his phallus. She was rewarded with a moan. 'It's my turn to take *you* to bed.' She might be too sore to take him inside again so soon, but there were other ways to pleasure him and herself.

She slid up his body, palms running up the smooth expanse of his chest over the atlas of his muscles. 'You're in good shape for a gambler who sits at a card table all night,' she said between kisses.

'I ride. I fence. I box. I shoot and throw.' He managed to get the words out, and she laughed against his chest, emboldened by the knowledge that her touch affected him. She sucked on the tiny points of his nipples, letting her tongue run over him as he had her.

'All that?' She let her hair brush his skin as she moved her attentions down his chest with a delicate caress of lips until she reached his hip bones. She looked up at him, a coy smile on her lips. 'Shall I?'

His tongue flicked across dry lips, his response more of a groan than a word. 'Please.'

She flashed him a wicked look and sank between his legs, her hand sliding the length of him, readying him for her mouth. He was hard and heavy in her grip, her thumb working the tender tip and its moisture. He arched ever so slightly into her hand, and she knew it was time for more. Her mouth came down on him, tasting salt and male essence. Above her, Nolan moaned, his body starting to shudder, giving up control, giving over to unleashed desire, and it drove her on. She wanted him to feel the unbearable throb of his body, pulsing with pleasure as it neared its release.

'Gianna!' His hoarse cry was both warning and accolade. His body tightened and then bucked in masculine relief. The sight of Nolan in climax was beautiful, private and...*vulnerable*. In those moments of relief, he was entirely helpless, this man who had slashed the count, who had saved her more than once, whose talents of mind and body made him seem nearly impregnable.

Yet, right now, he was without control, and therein lay the intimacy. It was in the allowing—that he had allowed her to see him at his most vulnerable, that he had allowed himself to *be* at his most vulnerable, a Samson without his hair. She would not allow him to be alone. She held him as he came, feeling his cock jerk in her hand full of life, feeling the warmth of his seed fill the cupped bowl of her palm.

She met his eyes, his hand reaching out to gently stroke her hair in these quiet moments. Her earlier fear returned, tinged with sadness this time. She had to leave him before she could love him. It would be too easy to stay, to easy to love him. But she would not drag him down with her. Two days, she promised herself. Enough time to get to Padua and to say goodbye before he would regret having ever met her.

Chapter Twenty

What happens next? It was the question Nolan had fallen asleep to and the one to which he awoke. It was the one that occupied his thoughts in the carriage on the road to Padua. Likely, it was the one that occupied Gianna's thoughts, too, but perhaps for different reasons. Nolan stole a glance over the edges of his borrowed book acquired from the inn's common area. He'd made a circumspect show of turning pages approximately every minute to create the illusion of reading, but he hadn't read a word of his book and neither had she. Mid-morning had passed in silence, afternoon was headed the same direction.

'Are you a slow reader?' Nolan enquired in deceptively mild tones.

Gianna looked up, her expression defensive. 'No, why would you think that?'

Nolan gave a nod towards her book. 'You haven't turned a page in forty-five minutes. Maybe you are too busy regretting last night to focus properly on the story?'

She blushed gamely and very honestly met his eyes. 'I don't have any regrets about last night.'

'Then perhaps you are thinking about seeing your brother? Or maybe you are thinking about where you'll go? Coming up with ideas where you might settle?' Nolan pressed in benign tones. He'd done some thinking of his own last night after Gianna had fallen asleep against him. Alone, her future didn't look promising. Had she also realised that? Was that why she didn't know where to go next? He had some solutions, however, and he might not get a better chance to share them.

Nolan set aside his book. 'Why don't you and your brother come to England with me?' He'd not planned on going home, but why not? He could see the property he'd deeded to his brother, could help his brother get their project off the ground.

Gianna gave him a sceptical stare. 'I thought you didn't have any property?'

'Technically, I don't. It's my brother's.' Nolan paused. He'd never shared this project with anyone before, not even his friends. He leaned forward and took one of Gianna's hands, worrying it with his thumb. 'It's a safe house and there would be a place for you, a need for you, actually. It's a house in the country, far from a city. It's a house for boys who come from broken homes. Maybe girls, too, but we thought we'd start with boys.'

Because he and Edward knew about broken boys, how they thought, how they saw the world, how they blamed themselves when mothers went away or died too early, how they tried to protect others with puny fists even at the expense of themselves when their fathers lashed out, how eventually they would give up trying and run away, hoping to just be lost, hoping the world would leave them alone.

Gianna gave him a considering look. 'Where will you be while your brother and I run this home?'

'In London, maybe Paris. I liked Paris quite a lot last spring. Wherever there are card games to be had, that's where I will be. Boys don't feed and clothe themselves. It will cost money to keep the place open. Money's my job.'

'You lied last night. You're far more than a gambler, Nolan,' she said softly. 'You're a brother, a landowner, a rescuer, a runner.' The last was said sharply with a hint of condemnation.

'Maybe that's why I understand you so well,' Nolan shot back, the atmosphere in the carriage becoming charged as they got too close to unsettled issues between them. *What next?* 'What sort of existence will you have here on the Continent? Surely you've figured out the count will not give up if there's a chance to reach you? You will do nothing more than move from place to place, living in hiding, living under assumed identities.'

'I know,' Gianna answered solemnly. 'But I have to try.'

'Have you thought about turning the diamonds over to the count and the money, too? Then he'd have no reason to pursue you.' It was an abhorrent idea as soon as he voiced it. But if it meant safety and freedom, if it meant an end to living in fear, perhaps it would be tolerable. Sometimes principles were too expensive to uphold.

Gianna gave him a hard look, finding the idea as repulsive as he did. 'Aside from the ethical consideration of letting evil triumph, what would I live on? How would I support Giovanni? Even a cottage of our own would be beyond us.' Her eyes met his. 'I do not wish to be a courtesan like my mother.'

'I could support you, give you an allowance,' Nolan said hastily. He'd not meant to imply she take up prostitution to support herself.

She shook her head. 'As you would a mistress? I don't think so, Nolan. I do not want to owe any man. It wouldn't be freedom, not truly.' They hit a rut in a road, and she put up a hand to grasp the leather handle and glanced outside. 'We're nearly there.' She gave Nolan an apologetic smile as if to say she was sorry the conversation had to give way to other concerns.

'This is not over,' Nolan said firmly. 'We will discuss this later.' Perhaps when she had her brother and was faced with the reality of what no options meant, his options would look more appealing. Sometimes the hardest thing to do was to save someone from themselves. He needed to be patient.

The place was outside the city, a sprawling old manor, run down and falling into decay, not exactly the most hospitable of environments. Its appearance did not improve once Nolan got out of the carriage. Nolan squinted up at the windows, noting the iron bars. Was it so bad the blind would actually try to escape that way? And go where? There was nothing but empty countryside unless they managed to miraculously walk the five miles to town. 'It looks like a prison.'

'It *is* a prison, a prison for the mentally and physically disabled,' Gianna said shortly, taking his hand and climbing down from the carriage. He noticed she did not let go.

'We'll get him out,' Nolan said tersely. 'What needs to be done?' He made a mental calculation of the remaining cash in his coat pocket. It was enough, maybe, for small bribes if guards needed to be cajoled. He'd spent most of it on the carriage and the room.

'We have to sign his papers of release.' Gianna was all brisk authority now. Whatever fear she'd felt upon seeing the asylum had been effectively hidden away.

There would probably be fees, too, some legitimate, others less legitimate to expedite the process. Nolan thought about what was in his pockets, his person: his gold watch, his gold money clip, the onyx ring on his finger. Would it look odd if he offered items to cover the fees instead of cash? Would they care? The people who ran these institutions were often as morally depraved as some of the inmates. 'Will they release him to you?' On second thought, the whole 'not caring as long as there was enough money on the table' would probably work best for them. Fewer questions, more silence.

'Not to me. Not for three more weeks and two days when I'm twenty-two.' Gianna whipped off her cloak and began tugging at the bodice of her gown until it showed off a fair expanse of bosom. 'But they will release him to you, if you're the count.' She looked up at him through dark lashes, her eyes suddenly soft. Good Lord, did she think she could flirt him into this?

He'd thought the bosom exposure was for the guards and anyone else inside who might be persuaded by more feminine charms, not for him. Now, he wasn't so sure. Nolan raised an eyebrow. Was that bosom and those flirty eyes supposed to make up for committing fraud? 'You want me to impersonate the count?' This made burgling the *palazzo* look like child's play—besides that, it was impossible. 'Have they ever met the count? We don't look anything alike beyond being tall.'

'It's been years.' Gianna brushed the shoulders of his greatcoat and adjusted his cravat as if he'd already said yes. 'I doubt the same warden is even here. It's not exactly a post anyone wants for life.'

Nolan grabbed her hands and held them against his chest. 'Gianna, I'm English. My clothes, my accent, will give me away.' He took risks, but they were calculated risks and this was downright foolish. 'Gianna, it has to be you. I'll be the count's man, his secretary perhaps, his proxy.' He winked at her. 'It seems the count has become an anglophile.'

Inside was dark and damp. Nolan stood to the side, letting Gianna make the initial case. She was brilliant with her businesslike tone, bending ever so slightly over the desk as she told the clerk she'd come to claim Giovanni Angelico, that she was his sister. It was the first time Nolan had heard her use her true last name, the first time he even knew what it was. Perhaps he should be alarmed by that, a reminder of how little he knew of her, how short a time he'd known her.

'I am here as the count's representative,' she said smoothly when the clerk at the desk pulled out the papers and noted the guardianship. She smiled and played with the pearl at her throat. Nolan knew just how distracting that particular gesture could be. The clerk was not immune.

'Let me get the warden.' He hurried away and Nolan stepped up to the desk.

'What cell is he in?' Nolan scanned the documents quickly. 'Cell thirty-four. That might be useful. Possession is nine-tenths of the law. Can you handle the warden?'

Gianna paled. 'What are you planning? Aren't you coming with me?'

'You go flirt with the warden. I need twenty minutes. I am going in after Giovanni. Do you have a pocket in your dress?' He pressed the small pistol into her hand. He felt less guilty about leaving her if she was armed. The door to the warden's office opened. 'If you can't flirt with him, you can always shoot him,' Nolan murmured and stepped back, only half joking.

'Signorina!'

The warden came out, a corpulent, unclean fellow whom Nolan could smell at a distance. Both hands were extended in welcome, his eyes immediately drawn to Gianna's bosom. Nolan hated him on sight. If it weren't part of the play Nolan would show the leering bastard what happened to men who ogled his woman—they lost a few teeth. Only this fellow looked to have lost a few already and definitely all of his white ones. He was rethinking the wisdom of leaving Gianna alone.

But Gianna didn't hesitate. She took the warden's hands and beamed as if he were the most attractive man in Italy. '*Signor*, I am here for my brother. The count could not come and now...' Her voice trailed off the way it had that night in the gondola when she'd stuck her hand in his pocket. She gave the warden a delicate glance, all helplessness and femininity. 'Now, it seems there is some problem with the paperwork. We've come all this way for nothing and after the trouble we've had getting here...'

She was good. She'd have tears rolling in a minute. Gianna sniffed, and the warden was undone, no match for the threat of a woman's tears or the promise of her bosom.

'Why don't you come into my office? There's tea and we can sort this out. I'm sure we can come to an arrangement.' There was another not-so-subtle look at her bosom, and Nolan didn't need an imagination to know what type of arrangement the warden might be angling for.

Nolan turned to the clerk. 'While we wait, perhaps you could give me a tour of the facilities? I'd like to take back a report to the count.' He was careful not to sound too businesslike or too smart. It was best if they thought Gianna was the brains.

'Yes, do take him,' the warden agreed a little too enthusiastically as Nolan had known he would. It would be far easier to 'negotiate' with the lady without the presence of a secretary looming outside the door.

The clerk pulled a large iron ring of keys out from behind the desk and unlocked the thick wooden door. Nolan gave a subtle flex of his arm, feeling the reassurance of his 'friend' in its sheath.

'Is there anything you'd like to see in particular?' the clerk asked, clearly thinking it was an odd request. No one wanted to see the inside of an asylum. Nolan grinned and swung an arm around the man.

'There certainly is, I'd like to see the C wing.' Then he laughed like a hyena. 'Did you get the joke? See and C?' He took out a handkerchief and wiped his eyes. 'I suppose it is only funny in English, since the Italian word for see is *vedere*.'

The clerk looked at him as if he should be the next candidate for admittance. Good. No one feared a silly man. The less dangerous the clerk thought he was, the better. He wanted the element of surprise on his side when he pulled out his little friend.

Gianna would have laughed if circumstances hadn't been so dire or the stakes so high. Nolan was hysterical as the not-so-bright secretary. Part of her was thrilled. Nolan was going in after Giovanni. Giovanni would be free. It was a testament to the amount of trust she'd come to put in Nolan that she assumed he'd be successful. All she had to do was keep the warden entertained in a manner that didn't involve taking off her clothes, which was proving rather more difficult than one might imagine.

'The tea is delicious, very restorative.' She smiled over the rim of the chipped tea cup.

The warden spread Giovanni's papers out in front of him. 'Now, tell me what the problem is?'

'I am here to get my brother. The count would like to bring him home for a while.' Gianna leaned over the tea tray purposely, reaching for the sugar bowl.

The warden's eyes followed her motion. 'It would be no trouble if it wasn't for the unpaid fees. We can't release anyone whose bill is in arrears.' He met her eyes, his own gaze glinting with greed and lust. 'You understand how easy it might be for someone to be released and never come back. We'd have no way to collect the bill.'

She smiled sympathetically as if she understood completely how the institution used their patients as collateral for extorting extravagant sums from their families. Although, she doubted families that actually cared for their family members would ever consign them to this place. 'What is the amount, sir?' Best not to show any shock over the bill.

That caught him off guard. He'd expected her to protest on the count's behalf. Probably a lot of his clients didn't simply agree to his fee. She smiled patiently. He didn't know what to charge her. She could see his thoughts whirring behind his beady eyes. Too little and it would be a wasted opportunity. Too much and she might grow suspicious, or refuse outright, or worse, she might summon the count, which would take her out of the equation entirely. That was not what he wanted. He wanted her. She could see that, too.

'Three hundred lire,' he said at last.

She managed to look anxious, her hand worrying the pearl at her throat. 'That seems reasonable, but I don't travel with that sort of cash on me. It's not safe, I'm sure you'd agree.' She wet her lips. Just a few more minutes. Nolan would be out with Giovanni. And if he wasn't? What if the clerk proved problematic? Then she'd need to play her part in earnest. She hoped it wouldn't come to that. 'Perhaps we might arrange some form of payment? I have this necklace. It was my mother's.'

'Oh, now, I don't want to deprive you of your mother's baubles.' He heaved his bulk out of his chair and came around her chair, his hand going to the nape of her neck in a rough caress. 'I might be able to do you a favour, if you do me one. It wouldn't be much.' His hand dropped to his trousers, undoing his flies.

'I don't know. The count might not approve.' Gianna rose, feeling more in control on her feet. She smiled, fighting the urge to cringe at the smell of him, of the idea of touching him *there*. She backed towards the door. The warden was faster than his size seemed to indicate.

He grabbed her arm, dragging her close, no longer full of his earlier leering bonhomie. This man was big, strong and determined. 'On the few occasions I've met the count he didn't strike me as a man who minded sharing. Now, kneel. It won't hurt you to be friendly for your brother's sake.' He pushed her to her knees. A wave of terror-sprinkled revulsion swept Gianna. She knew this feeling, had felt it time and again in the count's home. How quickly she'd forgotten it after a week with Nolan. Gianna's hand closed over the gun in her pocket.

A commotion sounded in the hallway. The warden turned his head towards the sound and she took her chance, coming to her feet, drawing her weapon. 'Stay where you are.' She backed towards the door, Nolan's little gun trained on him.

'You little bitch!' The warden lunged for her, but this time she was ready for his speed. She raced for the door, flinging it open, calling for Nolan.

He was there in the foyer, a dirty, ragged Giovanni with him, her brother's sightless eyes wild, his thin body coiled, ready to make his bid for freedom in the confusion. 'Nolan!' she cried, taking refuge behind his broad shoulders as the warden lurched from the office, trousers undone, genitals exposed.

'What is going on here?' The warden glanced from her to Nolan to Giovanni. 'You, you devil's spawn, shouldn't be out!'

'Neither should that.' Nolan's gaze dropped to the man's exposed privates, his hand flexed around the hilt of his knife, and Gianna felt a moment's vindication. The warden was going to be sorry. 'Now, if you'll excuse us, we'll be leaving.'

'You can't leave, you can't take him, there's a bill

Chapter Twenty-One

'What do you mean he's gone?' Agostino Minotti was going to strangle someone if Romano didn't stab them first. They'd been up since dawn making all haste to cover the twenty-six miles to Padua, only to be met with ineptitude. 'Giovanni Angelico is a blind man out in the middle of nowhere and locked in a room to boot. How is he simply gone?' Agostino raged in the entrance hall of the home.

'It was your ward.' The clerk shot a nervous look at the warden. 'She said you had sent her to bring him home for a visit.'

'And you believed her?' Agostino rounded on the trembling clerk and then thought better of it. '*You* believed her, too?' He pointed a finger at the warden. Ultimately this was his fault, he was the man in charge.

'She had a man with her claiming to be your secretary.' The warden was defensive, and Agostino could smell a lie among other odours rolling off him.

There was more at work here than a mere paperwork mix-up.

'An Englishman?' Agostino snarled. Not that he expected the warden to notice, not when Gianna had been in the room. 'An Englishman with a knife, perhaps?' Agostino turned his cheek to reveal the jagged scar running down his jaw. 'That Englishman is no secretary. He is helping her steal from me: jewels, people, money. They will stop at nothing. He did this to me.' It hurt like the devil, too, even after Romano had done his best to stitch the wound. He'd carry a scar for the rest of his days. That was reason enough to hunt the Englishman down. Between the Englishman's knife and Gianna's diamonds, they would both pay when he found them.

Romano came up beside him, a calming hand on his arm. 'What is done is done. What is important now is where they went. The longer we stand here berating these two idiots, the farther away she gets.'

Agostino nodded. Of course. Romano was right. Catching Gianna mattered more than explanations. 'Where were they headed?'

'West' was all the warden had to offer. Well, yes, west. East would have been back to Venice, back into the lion's den, and that could hardly be what Gianna wanted.

Romano grimaced. 'They're three hours ahead of us and there's only the one road. We'll catch up to them tomorrow. They'll have to stop tonight wherever there's an inn. Giovanni will need looking after and they'll need a new driver. I doubt any coachman they picked up along the way will want to keep going after the contretemps today.'

They were going to need transport, preferably private. And clothes. More immediately, they needed hot food, rooms and a bath. Most of all, they needed to press on. Gianna hated the idea of stopping with an hour of daylight left. An hour meant four, maybe five more miles between them and the count. But there was no guarantee of an inn when darkness fell or of safety. Italian roads were notorious for their poor conditions and their highwaymen. Besides, Giovanni was in no shape to travel farther.

Gianna stared at her brother sitting rigidly across from her in the coach as they waited for Nolan to make arrangements. He was here, really here, with her at last after four years apart. But, oh, what a mess he was! The smell of him filled the carriage, another reason they couldn't go any farther. That could be fixed with a hot bath. A body could be washed. Hair could be cut, a beard could be shaved, but he was so thin. That would be the work of months to see his body restored. He would need nourishing food—a lot of it.

Where was she to find that food on the road on the run when her first priority was staying ahead of the count? How was she to protect him? Would he ever be able to truly protect himself without his sight? The enormity of what she'd taken on, of what she faced, swamped her.

'I know, it's awful. I'm awful.' Giovanni managed

to get the words out, as if he was remembering how to speak. She'd been so caught up in his physical appearance she hadn't thought about the rest. What of his mind? He'd been locked away for years. No one emerged unscathed from such an experience.

Gianna reached out a hand, grasping his filthy one. 'No, you are not awful. Nolan is in there right now arranging rooms. We'll get you cleaned up and you will feel better.' Now that the thrill of reunion had ebbed, she felt the full thrust of her guilt. 'I should have come sooner.'

'How, Gia? You were no less guarded than I, just in a different place. I should have protected us better.'

'How?' she asked, mirroring his words. 'You were fourteen.' It was ridiculous to think he could have done more. He'd done all he could.

The whisper of a smile played on his cracked lips. 'Exactly. You were barely seventeen, a girl with no resources, no power. What more could *you* have done?'

'I have power now, Giovanni. I have the diamonds and in a few weeks I'll have the money.' Although she had no idea how she would ever access it without giving away her location to the count. If she ever tried to draw a draft on it, he would be able to track her, but that was the least of her worries right now. 'I can take care of us, we can live somewhere together, the two of us. We'll be safe, I promise.' It was a promise she wasn't sure she could keep.

'The two of us? What about Signor Gray? He risked much to come for me. I doubt he did it out of charity. What is he to you?'

'Some time you'll have to tell me what happened in there. How did Nolan convince the clerk to open your room?'

Giovanni was not fooled by the redirection. 'I think the clerk found Signor Gray's knife quite compelling. But you did not answer my question. Who is he to you?'

The carriage door opened and Nolan put his head in, his tone cheerful as if this were a grand holiday. 'Everything's arranged. I've got rooms. They're getting a bath ready right now. Giovanni, give me your hand. I'll help you down. Careful, there's mud to your right. This inn yard is one big meadow of muck. I am sorry for it. Your feet just have to go a little farther, though, and they can be clean. I'll find you some shoes.' He turned to her. 'Stay here, Gianna. I'll be back for you.'

She watched them go, the image of the two of them together stinging her eyes—Nolan with his hand on her brother's arm, leading him with gentleness, with consideration that preserved whatever might be left of a young man's pride.

Nolan slogged back through the mud and reached for her. 'Are you ready?' He swung her into his arms. 'I can carry you, at least, and spare your dress the damage.'

'Nolan, wait just a moment.' She laid a hand against his cheek and pressed a kiss to his lips. 'Thank you for what you did today, for what you're doing now. I had no right to ask for any of this. I can't possibly thank you enough.'

His response was gruff as he carried her over the mud. 'I didn't do it to be thanked. You should know that by now.' It was tempting to ask why he did it, but she wasn't sure she wanted to hear the answer. It wouldn't change anything in the end. She would still have to leave him behind. Now that she had Giovanni, there were no more excuses. It was time to set Nolan free. It was time to begin her life on the road. Funny that when she'd imagined her freedom she'd never equated it with running.

Nolan took the inn stairs two at a time. Things were looking up. What a difference a few hours could make, even a day. Luck had been with them. They'd actually found a decent inn, something he'd doubted existed in Italy. There had been hot stew for dinner and he'd been able to trade his silk-patterned waistcoat for some clothes and shoes for Giovanni. The innkeeper had been thrilled to own such a finely tailored garment in exchange for a few items that had once belonged to his grown son.

After that, the innkeeper had been keen to barter. Nolan had also been able to trade his pocket watch for a wagon and horse. It wasn't a glamorous carriage and they'd be out in the elements as they travelled, but it was the best they'd find in these parts. If his Grand Tour had shown him anything it was that the English had a far superior coaching-inn system than anywhere else in Europe. Better roads, too—two things he'd never thought to appreciate before. Best of all, there'd been cards. Nothing rich, just farmers and a few travellers. Nolan had played carefully, not wanting to incur the local wrath, but it had been enough to put some coins in his pocket. They would be able to buy lunch and other food supplies tomorrow.

At the top of the stairs, he opened the door to his room and stopped, his breath catching. His night was just about to get even better. Gianna sat before the fire in her shift, combing out her hair. Something swift and visceral struck, a *coup de foudre*, perhaps, as the French called it. This was all he needed: a warm room, a warm bed, an even warmer woman and a few coins in his pocket to get to the next adventure.

Gianna looked up and smiled when she saw him. 'How was cards? Did you win?' She asked it the way Nolan imagined a woman might ask her man how was work. *Her man.* Did Gianna look at him like that? As more than a lover, more than someone who could be of use? Was that what he wanted?

'Yes.' Nolan jingled his pocket in demonstration. 'I've managed a wagon, too.'

She rose, the firelight outlining the curves of her body beneath the thin linen as she came to him, wrapping her arms about his neck. 'I knew you would.' She helped him of his coat, commenting on the lack of the waistcoat and laughing when he told her its fate. 'It has done us a good service, then.' She untied his cravat and he thought he could get used to these little rituals: Gianna undressing him, laughing with him, waiting for him.

'Is Giovanni settled for the night?' Nolan nipped at her ear, letting her slip his arms from his sleeves.

It had been ages since a woman had done for him. It was as compelling as more direct means of seduction. He'd been hard for her the moment her hands had touched him, perhaps even before that. It had started the moment he'd walked in the room.

'Yes, he's sleeping next door.' Her hands stilled on the waistband of his trousers. 'He looks much better. Thank you for the bath, for helping him, for the clothes.' She paused and looked up at him. 'I could not have managed it on my own.'

'You would have come up with something,' Nolan offered, but he knew how much the admission cost her. It was an admission not so much of her own limitations but of the truth; she could not do this alone. She'd seen her limits first-hand today. He'd seen them, too. It had strengthened his resolve to see her safe whether she wanted his help or not. It had terrified him to see the warden, tiny as his cock was, lunging after her. She had done her job too well.

Nolan took her cheek in his hand and turned her face to his, capturing her mouth in a slow kiss. It was time to persuade her she needn't fear accepting assistance, that his plan was viable without threatening her autonomy. 'You don't have to go this alone. You have options. You have me, Gianna. We can go to England.' He pressed his argument from this morning. When better to make his case than when he had her in his arms, his lips on her body, reminding her of all he could do for her? 'We can head north tomorrow to Turin and up into Germany after that.' He could see the route in his head the way he saw the playing cards. They could sail from Ostend or cut across to the west and stop in Paris.

She had her hands in his hair, fingers fanned against his temples, eyes locked on his. He could smell the sage and rosemary of her. 'Not tonight. Can we just make love? Please?' Her hand slipped inside his trousers. 'I need this. I need *you.*'

He should resist. There were likely red flags galore. They had issues that needed addressing, mainly the nature of their future together. They could not go much farther without discussing it, discussing what they meant to one another. But Nolan had never been good at resisting temptation, only in joining it. It would be a shame to start now when Gianna needed him, when she needed him to be his most persuasive if he stood a chance of seeing her safe in England. The stakes of this seduction had suddenly got higher. Thank goodness he knew exactly what she wanted.

She wanted to forget the demons of the day; wanted to forget seeing the conditions her brother was kept in, the condition he'd been found in, the escape, holding the warden at gunpoint, and even after all that, the fear wasn't quite behind them. The count was still out there, on the road. Or not. The count was a twisted bastard. He would know the real fear lay in the not knowing. She had to always assume she was being chased. It was a lot to forget, but Nolan was up to the challenge.

No walls tonight, no beds, at least not to start. He scanned the room and found what he wanted; the waist-high bureau with the washing basin and cracked mirror. He led her to it, stood her in front of him and whispered against her ear, 'Look. Look at that beautiful woman.' He kissed the tender hidden place between her ear and her neck where a pulse beat ever so softly. 'I love her hair, how it falls over my hands, how it smells of rosemary and sage, the smell of a summer herb garden.'

He closed his own eyes, breathing deeply of her as he nuzzled her neck, placed kisses on her throat, his hands cupping her breasts, moulding them through the fabric of her shift before tugging the string at the low neck loose, before giving it a push from her shoulders and letting it shimmy to the floor. 'She is too lovely not to be seen,' he murmured, his hands returning to those beautiful breasts, lifting them, kneading them with a gentle caress. He ran his thumbs over the peaks of her nipples, feeling her arch into him as the pleasure started to spread.

She wanted to close her eyes, but he wouldn't let her. 'Watch this woman, watch her come alive,' he commanded in low, stern tones. He needed to forget, too. He needed to know he was the one she saw when the pleasure took her, that there was no room for memories of anything else but him. He needed to prove she was his, that the warden and the count had no place here. There was only them, the couple in the mirror; a man about to roughly pleasure a woman and a woman about to take pleasure.

He nipped at her neck, his love words becoming coarser, a prelude, perhaps a caution that what was to come would not be delicate. She answered with a moan, her arm reaching back to encircle his neck, her body pressing into his, feeling the power of his erection against her bottom.

He bent her forward, her arms taking her weight against the bureau. He whispered a harsh command at her ear. 'Watch, your warrior would make you his sheath.' He thrust into her then, his cock meeting the upturned buttocks, one hand filled with her breast, the other anchored on her mons, pressing against the hidden nub, stroking it in rhythm with his cock, driving her wild, driving himself wild. This was rough coupling at its finest, fast and obliterating.

He watched her in the mirror, feeling himself drown in the sight of her, her hair about her, her eyes dark with desire, *his* desire. *He* did this to her. She moaned and gasped, she gave her body over to him, lost to his touch, his stroke. His own body was off its leash, any attempt at finesse lost when the final pleasure took them. He no longer knew who was at whose mercy. They were gloriously lost together. When had he ever so thoroughly lost control?

Nolan held her tight against him, her buttocks against his stomach, his cock still entrenched, but calm now that the storm had passed. He felt her breathing start to slow. He watched her come back to earth in the mirror. Her eyes rested on their reflection, a moment's yearning in her expression. 'I don't deserve this, I don't deserve you, but thank you. You took my mind off it for a little while.' It wasn't exactly what a man dreamed of hearing after mind-blowing sex in front of a mirror, but it would have to do. For now.

Chapter Twenty-Two

Nolan got them to the bed and stretched beside her. At least now she was relaxed and might talk about some of the things she kept pent up inside her. Touch helped. He was a big believer in the idea that people responded better to you if you touched them. He drew figures on the flat of her stomach, idle designs to match his languid mood. 'Did you know about the place?' He wasn't even sure what to call the home they'd found Giovanni in. It was part hospital, part prison. It was in no way a nurturing, wholesome environment.

'I suspected. The count told me it was a school. He told me Giovanni had gone to a special boarding school for boys with infirmities. He would get special attention there.' Gianna shook her head. 'But I knew it wouldn't be a good kind of special.' Her voice broke, and Nolan looked up from his designs. 'He was sent there because of me. It was my fault he was there at all.'

Gianna sat up in a rush, her words angry. 'The count sent him away to punish me and I could do nothing to get him back until today.' She bunched her hands in the sheets in frustration self-loathing. 'I let him suffer. I should have stood up to the count no matter what. I should have found another way to run. I should have tried again and again until I succeeded.'

Nolan's hands closed forcefully around hers, stilling them. 'It's not your fault. The count would have found a way to remove Giovanni no matter what. Together, you and Giovanni were a threat to him. You supported each other, and he couldn't overcome that. Separated, he stood a better chance of using each of you as leverage against the other.' He blew out a breath. 'I know, Gianna. I used to think the same thing.' He gathered her to him, rocking her. 'It was the same for my brother and me. You can't change it. You can just go forward.'

And make damn sure it didn't happen again. It was what he and his brother were doing with the safe house in England. They couldn't undo their childhoods, but they could help other boys regain theirs, boys like Giovanni. Giovanni would love the house in England. He would be a mentor to the younger boys. Nolan had to stop himself. He was putting the cart before the horse. Gianna hadn't agreed to come. But Nolan had thought of nothing else while he'd helped Giovanni bathe away the grime. There was so much they could do for him in England. Blind or not, Nolan could give Giovanni a new life there. He wished he had as much to offer Gianna, wished he could take away the fear she had to live with.

There was one way to do it. It had come to him in Venice the day he'd found the secret bottom to the jewel case. It was admittedly risky not because she might reject it, but because of what that rejection might reveal—things he didn't want to face.

'Gianna, I've been thinking…' Nolan began, his mouth in its familiar place at her ear, her body warm against his, his arms wrapped around her in the dark. 'If you could be free of the count's harassment and not have to give up the diamonds, would you do it?'

'Yes, I'd do anything.' She sounded defeated, as if she were tired of this futile exercise.

'Then marry me. Let me give you the protection of my name. It would put your diamonds out of his reach.' Nolan breathed his request in the dark and then he waited. How had it suddenly become so important that she say yes? Last week, she'd been an obstacle to his plans and now she *was* the plan.

'So the count can kill you instead? So I can be a widow?' she snapped, pulling out of his arms. 'That's a *fabulous* idea. It will solve everything.' She made her sarcasm obvious. 'How does that solve anything, Nolan? It only transfers the count's attention.' She saw him wince, and she felt a twinge of guilt. Even the urbane Nolan Gray who effortlessly rescued damsels in distress *and* their brothers had feelings. He'd just proposed and she'd thrown it back in his face. Better to be angry, though, than to be moved by his offer.

She softened her tone. 'It's a generous offer, but

it's not practical. When you stop and think about it, you will see I'm right.'

'I'm offended *you* think *I* haven't thought about it, that this is some spontaneous post-coital offering. I assure you it is not,' Nolan retorted, making her feel even worse. Great, now both of them had managed to turn the supposed most romantic moment of a girl's life—a marriage proposal—into something awkward and quarrelsome. Apparently, proposals weren't destined to be her thing.

'Nolan, be reasonable.' She waved a hand at the bed. 'Just look at us. We're sitting here naked in a rented room, running from a madman, and suddenly marriage is a good idea? Our very situation defies the logic of that.'

Nolan leaned back on the pillows, arms behind his head, his body on glorious display in the firelight. 'I am being logical. The count doesn't want you, he wants what you possess, ergo, if you divest yourself of those items, he will stop chasing you. Whether you like to admit it or not, marriage is the best legal route by which to control a woman's assets.' He rolled to his side and bent his knee. It was a position that showed off the elegant muscles of his thighs, the heavy fall of his phallus, gorgeously masculine. He was like a prone version of the *David*.

'I know. It's why I'm running in the first place,' Gianna ground out. 'And you can stop doing that.'

'Doing what?'

'Lying like that. You know very well you're carved from the very moulds of Olympus.' The offer of marriage was more compelling than she let on, even if it was for the wrong reasons. Well, really just *one* wrong reason. She could have this, have *him* every night she chose.

Nolan grinned. 'So, you like my body. That's a start. I like yours.'

'One should not get married for sex alone.' She sounded like a prim spinster, not like the woman who had watched herself come in the cracked mirror of an inn room, mounted like a mare by a veritable stallion of a man.

'Why not? It seems like a better reason than most. I'd choose mutual pleasure over mutual respect any day from a wife.' Nolan was making this difficult with his ridiculous arguments, as if they were actually debating this seriously. He got up from the bed and stretched. He strode to the fire and picked up a poker to arrange the logs, bending and flexing in masculine beauty. He was making it hard on her, even when she knew better.

Sex wasn't enough. The life of a courtesan was a cautionary tale that proved it. Every night a man spent with her mother was a night he hadn't spent with his wife, a night he spent in physical betrayal of her and his vows. It would be terrible when Nolan strayed. And he would stray. Most men did, and Nolan was far handsomer, far more charismatic. Women would flock to him and there would be plenty of temptations to pick from when he tired of being her knight in shining armour. What was she doing? Sex wasn't even the real issue here.

'Sex is a just a red herring, so you can put down the poker and give up the buttock-flexing. Nice as it is, there are other arguments, too, for not marrying you—more practical ones like your personal safety. The count is not your problem.'

He came back to the bed, hands on hips. 'But you are. You became my problem the moment I won you.' He grinned down at her, boyish and vital and alive, as if this was a lark, as if nothing serious rested on this decision. When he looked at her like that, she wanted nothing more than to say yes. But 'yes' was rash and dangerous.

'Look what it's got you,' Gianna pressed. 'You've had to pull me out of the canal, you've had to vacate your hotel, you've had to defend yourself at knife-point on not one, but two occasions, you've broken into an asylum and a *palazzo*. You've stolen a patient and a jewel case. You've had to leave your worldly possessions behind. You've traded your clothes for a wagon and an old horse.'

Nolan's grin spread wider. He flopped on the bed, making her bounce with the impact. 'Yes, I have and I've had the time of my life. This is the best adventure I've had in a while. I'm in no hurry to end it.' He stared at her with laughing eyes. 'That rather takes the wind out of your argumentative sails, doesn't it?' He looked altogether too pleased with himself.

'How about this, then? People don't get married

on a one-week acquaintance. You had barely met me this time last week.'

'Correction. *Normal* people don't get married on a week-long recommendation.' Nolan was insufferable. 'We established some time ago, you and I aren't normal. Ergo, we shouldn't feel bound by the constraints of normal courtship.'

'Enough with your *ergo*! You can't just throw a Latin word in there and make it all better.' She was losing this battle hard. The situation was degenerating quickly. Who was she fooling, it had already degenerated. Gianna grabbed a pillow and swung it at him.

'Oof!' Nolan scrambled up. 'That does it. I am done talking about this. I am just going to make love to you until you agree.' He grabbed her about the waist, and she went down under him with a squeal of pseudo-indignation. He pinned her wrists above her head, but there was nothing intimidating here, just good fun and pleasure, one more addictive facet of Nolan Gray.

She climaxed fast with him, her eyes fixed on his face as release took him, that smile, those laughing eyes that drank up the joy in every minute. And yet, he could be fierce in bed and out. She was in so much trouble. It would be too easy to say yes, to lay her burdens at his feet. It would be far harder to say no, but no would have to be her answer, for his sake. Some day he would understand that. She had tonight. In the morning she and Giovanni would be gone because sometimes the only way to win an argument was to simply leave.

Chapter Twenty-Three

Nolan's arm reached out across the bed, his body searching for Gianna before he was even awake, already anticipating the feel of her warm curves against him, the swell of her breast in his hand as he drew her to him. He found paper, dry, thin, crinkled paper. His eyes opened, every instinct screaming something was wrong. The fact that there was enough daylight to read by and that was wrong, too.

He held the paper up to the window light. There were only two words on the torn half-sheet. 'Thank you.' They were not two words that usually struck terror into the heart of a man who gambled with a knife up his sleeve and gun in his pocket but they did now. Dammit! What had she gone and done?

'Gianna!' he called out in the hope she was nearby, perhaps next door with Giovanni. Nolan gathered up his clothes from the floor, hastily pulling on trousers and a shirt. He tried to think beyond the panic. Panic was irrational. He had to be logical. If she wasn't next door, perhaps she was downstairs having breakfast. But the panic in him knew better, the panic knew exactly what she meant with her two words.

Nolan swung his greatcoat about his shoulders and looked about the room for any left-behind items out of habit. How late was it? He didn't know. He'd traded his pocket watch for a wagon and horse, neither of which could tell the time and—Lucifer's balls!—were most likely gone. That sent him pounding down the stairs and out into the yard.

'Buongiorno!' The ostler ran over, looking harried. 'It's been a busy morning. What can I do for you?'

'The woman with the dark hair and the blind brother, when did she leave?'

'Right after sunrise. She took the wagon.' The ostler looked at him slyly, suspecting he was on the cusp of a juicy story. Beautiful women didn't drive off in wagons without cause. 'Did she steal from you, too? Not that I would mind, a thief that pretty can have whatever she liked from me.'

'Too?' Nolan interrupted abruptly.

'There were two men on horseback who came through here around eight this morning, riding hard. They were looking for her, had her description down perfectly and the boy.'

'What time is it now?' A cold pit settled in Nolan's stomach. Gianna had left him, had *wanted* to leave him, and now she was out on the open road with no protection and the count behind her. The count would catch her. He and Lippi would travel far faster on horseback than she could by slow wagon, assuming she even knew how to drive a wagon with any skill.

'I would guess it's just after nine.' The ostler shrugged.

Nolan pulled out a coin from last night's winnings. 'I need a horse.' He shaded his eyes and looked down the road. There was only one direction for them to have gone and that was towards Verona.

The ostler took the money but shook his head. 'I haven't got much to offer you. The two gentlemen switched horses and took our fresh ones. The horses have only had an hour's rest, but they're fed and watered.'

They were strong, too. Nolan checked their hooves and ran a hand over their flanks, their coats cool. They weren't too winded, then. 'I'll take this one.' He chose the powerful-chested black and dug in his pocket for more coin. Within minutes he was off, cutting across country to make up time and riding as fast he dared to push the horse. He had to reach Gianna in time—no, that was heroic thinking. She was nearly three hours ahead of him. But the count was only an hour ahead. Nolan readjusted his thinking. He needed to reach the count before the count reached Gianna.

Brennan would be saying, 'I told you so' and laughing his head off at the irony of him, the student of human nature, taken in so completely by a woman. He would say Gianna had used him and left him when the using was over. She'd got him to break into a *palazzo* and abduct a patient from an asylum, and then left him cold.

There, Brennan would be wrong. She hadn't left him cold. She'd left him hot and that was all Nolan needed to know. The real irony was that if she was using him, she would have stayed. She would have recognised the need for him—he had value as an armed man who would fight for her, who would make arrangements for them, who had the ability to see them sheltered and fed. Instead, she'd left him out of a misguided notion of protecting him. She was giving him his freedom, his life. Quite likely at the expense of hers.

Nolan pulled on to the road, giving the horse a chance to walk and breathe. What did she think would happen when the count caught her? Had he not spelled that scenario out for her clearly enough last night? The count would not do it quickly either.

Luck was with him. The roads were not too muddy, but every ounce of speed the roads gave him, they'd already given to the count. He urged the horse into a trot, thinking positively. *When* he caught up to the count, what resources did he have at his disposal? His knife in his sleeve stood ready, but his little gun was empty; the shots were used back at the hotel in Venice during their getaway. There had been no opportunity to reload. All of his remaining bullets, specially made for the secret second barrel, were back at the Danieli. Even so, the list was not impressive. These were weapons for a quick defence of his person. They were not weapons designed for launching an offensive assault.

A large object loomed ahead in the road, dark

against the grey winter sky. Nolan suddenly felt very alone. He slipped his knife from its sheath. The last thing he needed was Italian bandits. Was there an ambush up ahead? Was it the count? He was missing Haviland and Archer, and even Brennan. They would have his back. If they'd been here, they would never have let him ride off alone no matter what their outlook on Gianna might be.

Nolan slowed the horse and swore. Bandits would have been preferable to this. The object pulled to the side of the road was the wagon and it was empty, no horse in sight. Nolan swung to the ground, investigating the wagon and telling himself not to panic. There was no need to jump to conclusions. Wagons were abandoned for all sorts of reasons: a broken axle, a wheel that had come off. But there was no sign of mechanical difficulty. Perhaps they had ridden off, although it seemed an odd choice. The horse wouldn't get far carrying two.

Nolan came around the wagon side and halted, his hand going reflexively to his mouth. The horse lay on its side, shot through the head, dead. Flies had begun to gather. He hadn't been able to see it from where he'd dismounted. It was an entirely senseless act. The horse could do nothing to the count. But Nolan knew why the count had done it: to intimidate Gianna. Nolan closed his eyes, trying to dispel images of Gianna stranded here, faced with the two men, trying to protect her brother, standing between Giovanni and the count. Had the count threatened Giovanni, too, to gain her compliance?

Nolan didn't want to do it, but he had to know. How long ago did this happen? He stooped and touched a hand to the horse's body, dipped a fingertip in the pool of blood. There were still traces of warmth. An hour maybe. He would catch up to them by evening. He hoped Gianna would last that long, but he couldn't guarantee it. The count might tire of his games and take the more expedient route to her fortune.

Nolan threw his head back to the sky with a sharp howl. 'Damn!' At least she wasn't lying dead on the side of the road with the horse. While he was glad for it, it did puzzle him. They were out in the middle of nowhere with no witnesses. Why hadn't the count simply taken the diamonds and killed them both? It would be expedient and Lippi wasn't beyond such direct measures. It made Nolan's gut go cold to think of the reasons it hadn't happened. The count was after revenge as well as diamonds. Perhaps he intended to make Gianna pay in other ways. Whatever the reason, Nolan should be glad there was still time.

Nolan kicked the ground with his boot and strode out onto the verge. He ran a hand through his hair. He needed to think before he got back on the horse. Rushing off hot wouldn't serve Gianna when he caught up to her. He needed a calm perspective. He nearly stepped on a long, slim, brown-velvet box not far from the road. Nolan's breath caught. He knew this box! He flipped open the lid to confirm the contents. Gianna's diamonds. Had she tried to run? Had she thrown them on purpose in the moments before the count caught her?

Nolan picked them up and put the box inside his greatcoat. Smart girl. Losing the diamonds would keep her and Giovanni alive a little longer. Once the count realised she didn't have them on her, he would also realise she was the only one who knew where they were, the only one who could help him retrieve them. It wouldn't solve her problems, but it would buy her some time.

Nolan returned to the horse and swung up. 'We've farther to go, my friend.' Gianna was waiting for him. The future was waiting for him on the road to Verona. He would not hesitate to bargain the diamonds for her. No fortune was worth her life. Nolan kicked the horse forward. He would not fail her.

Gianna sat rigidly in front of the count on his great beast. She kept her body aloof from his, hardly able to tolerate the iron band of his arm about her for balance. She would have fallen without it. A broken arm or a sprained ankle was not what she needed right now. If there was a chance to run, she'd need all of her parts functioning. But the press of his thighs, the heat of his groin, were intimacies she could do without, especially with memories of Nolan and last night still fresh in her mind.

She let her thoughts wander a now-familiar path. Had Nolan found the necklace? Was he even on the road or had he decided to let her go? Perhaps he had woken this morning, seen her note and said 'good riddance'. Maybe even now, he was on the road back to Venice and his luxurious hotel room. It was what any normal man would do, but Nolan had proved to be far from normal. He'd proved to be extraordinary, in fact. Not just in bed or in looks, but in his person.

If she were a selfless person she would be hoping he didn't come after her, that he'd take all that extraordinariness of his and flee the mess of her life. But she wasn't selfless. She'd spent her selfless quotient that morning. It had taken all her willpower to leave Nolan's warm bed knowing she meant to leave it permanently. Now, she was merely selfish and the selfish person in her was hoping against hope that he'd come after her. But until that happened, she had an obligation to rescue herself and Giovanni.

She glanced over at Giovanni, riding behind Romano Lippi. She did not regret leaving this morning, however, even knowing how that had turned out. It was the noble thing to do. Nolan had proposed marriage last night. She couldn't allow him to throw his life away just to keep her safe. If she loved him, if she truly cared for him, leaving was the best gift she could give him. Giovanni had protested, of course. He'd not liked being awakened before dawn and he had not liked the idea of leaving Nolan. Already, Nolan had impressed Giovanni with his kindness.

She'd had to listen to Giovanni enumerate Nolan's praises the whole first hour on the road. It hadn't made leaving any easier. She couldn't argue with Giovanni because he was right, except about maybe the last thing. 'He cares for you deeply,' Giovanni had concluded his arguments. 'I can hear it in his words, in his tone when he speaks to you. I think you like him, too. You should stay and let him help us.' But she had not turned back. An hour later, the count and Lippi had run them off the road at gunpoint.

Those had been horrific moments. Instinctively, she and Giovanni had tried to get off the wagon box and run, but the two of them were no match for armed men on horseback. Still, the effort had bought her time enough to hide the diamonds in the grass. Having the diamonds on her was an immediate death sentence. She'd hid them not a moment too soon. Lippi had turned his gun on Giovanni while the count conducted a rather thorough and aggressive search of her person. Her cheek still stung from the force of his hand across her face when he'd realised they weren't on her.

'Where are they?' he'd demanded.

'Where do you think?' she'd shot back, forgetting their danger for a moment as her temper soared.

'If I knew, do you think I'd have followed you? I would have simply taken them,' the count had growled. 'Romano, the pistol!'

The hammer had clicked behind her, not for her, but for Giovanni and she'd remembered their danger. She had not needed to act horrified as she choked out her lie. 'Venice, they are still in Venice.'

It had satisfied the count. It was plain that he would not kill her until he had the diamonds in his hand. She had a little power left. They would return to Venice. But she'd only bought them some time, a day and half at most. When they got to Venice and the diamonds weren't there, what then? She hoped they wouldn't make it to Venice. She hoped Nolan would see the wagon, find the diamonds and come after her long before that. It was admittedly a lot to hope for, especially since the man most likely to help her was also the man she'd sent away. 'Do you know what happens to you if you're lying?' The count had twisted her arm up behind her back in a cruel grip. That was when the count had shot the horse, making it clear that no defiance on her part would be tolerated. She had screamed, the count had laughed.

But it got worse. They didn't turn back towards Venice. They kept going forward. 'I want to see who comes down that road, don't you, Romano?' He'd laughed wickedly. 'I'm surprised we've only got two of our birds in our net.' His hand had run over her breast. 'Or have you chased off our Englishman? I rather thought he'd be with you. I am told he was with you yesterday.'

The count called over to Romano, 'Let's stop at the next inn and make it easy on our Englishman. I bet he's here by afternoon, just in time for tea, as those British say.

'Are you excited to see your lover again, Gianna, one last time before I dispatch you both to your reward?' The count's voice drawled at her ear. 'Of course, I've been thinking I might spare you if you married me even after I have the diamonds and you can tell me how Englishmen fare against a real lover.'

'He's not coming,' Gianna answered stoically. It was too bad. If she ever saw Nolan again, she'd tell him more than thank you. She'd tell him she loved him because he was too extraordinary not to love.

The count's hand hefted a breast as if he were testing a fruit for ripeness. She stiffened at the intimate contact.

'After he's had this, Gianna? Oh, he's coming, all right.'

Chapter Twenty-Four

If he hadn't seen the horses, Nolan would have ridden straight through. There was a stone-and-brick building that advertised as an inn and a few other smaller stone homes that stood guardian over the fields. The place hardly qualified as a village, but the count was here, Nolan would bet on it. No one else would have such fine animals in such a remote place. He slid off his horse and felt in his pocket for his dwindling supply of coins, calling to a boy idling in front of the building, 'Who owns those two horses?'

The boy puffed up with importance. 'Two fine men from Venice. One them says he's a count.' The boy looked Nolan up and down. 'Are you a count, too?'

Nolan laughed. 'Hardly.' He offered the boy a coin. 'Take care of my mount and have him at the ready. When I come out, I'm going to need him fast. You might want to have one of those other two ready as well.' He hoped Gianna could ride. He would have to take Giovanni up behind him. Another thought occurred to Nolan. 'Did the count take a private parlour or a room?' He wanted to know what he was walking into, it would determine how he entered the room. Would he be face-to-face with the count immediately?

'A private parlour, *signor.* He had a lady with him.' The boy held his hand out for another coin. At this rate, he was going to be broke. Nolan paid him, then stepped into the inn. He nodded to the innkeeper behind the bar, letting his eyes adjust to the dim interior. The taproom was empty and the innkeeper raised an eyebrow.

Nolan nodded. 'I'm here for the woman.'

The innkeeper jerked his head, indicating the direction of the parlour. Nolan flipped him a coin. 'By chance, is there a deck of cards in there?'

'In the drawer of the sideboard.' The innkeeper looked at him sceptically. Nolan kept walking. It was better not to give the man a chance to ask questions. If he was lucky he'd be out of there before an explanation would be worth the effort. Besides, how did he explain this anyway? He tried it out in his mind: *a covetous count has kidnapped a woman I met only a week ago. I am madly in love with her, but the count wants her diamonds.* Ah, no. He wasn't going to be explaining that to anyone any time soon. He could already see Brennan rolling his eyes.

He was just outside the parlour door when he heard Gianna scream. There were sounds of a struggle. 'You take your hands off me!'

Knife in his right hand, gun in the left, Nolan kicked the door open, his eyes rapidly scanning the room. Gianna was forced against the table, the count wrestling violently with her skirts. On his periphery, a form moved, agile and fast. Lippi thought to take him unawares. Nolan turned with lightning reflexes. He didn't think, he just threw. The knife took Romano Lippi in the throat.

Now he had the count's attention. 'Romano!' the count cried, but he was too cagey to let Gianna go. He pulled her in front of him. 'You've killed him!' he snarled, his own blade at Gianna's throat.

'You took something of mine. I've taken something of yours. Quid pro quo, I believe. We're even,' Nolan said with a coolness he didn't feel. The odds were even now, sort of. It was one on one, but the count had a weapon that worked. He trained the empty gun on the count, scanning the room for Giovanni. Nolan spotted him, tied to a chair by the fireplace.

'I'm here, Giovanni,' Nolan called out, his gaze now fixed on the count. 'I'm over by the door. I have a gun on the count. I'll come to you when I can.'

'Do you really think so, Englishman?' the count snarled.

'Yes, I do.' Time for the bluff of the century. 'We can either stand here at an impasse or until I shoot you. I am a crack shot, by the way. You aren't going to harm her, not without the diamonds.' Nolan watched the count's eyes flicker in surprise. He grinned. 'I know about them, so you see, I know you're bluffing with the knife. I'd say I have you at a disadvantage. You can't win this showdown. But perhaps there is a showdown you can win.'

'She's my ward. You do not set the grounds for negotiation,' Minotti countered, but Nolan could see the interest growing in his eyes. Nolan had to reel him in carefully now, get him to take the bait.

'She's mine. I won her in a card game,' Nolan replied casually. 'You lost her. I'd much rather give you a chance to win her back than shoot you.' *Bite, damn you. Take the bait.* 'You're a fair gambler. You simply had a run of bad luck.'

'What do you propose?'

'We settle this like gentlemen. I have no interest in shooting you. I just want Gianna.' He passed a long look over her form. He had to make the count believe whatever lay between he and Gianna was purely lust. If the count suspected there was any sentiment between them, Nolan would lose his slim edge. 'She's a treat in bed.' He saw Gianna stiffen. He was going to pay for that when they got out of here. But he'd pay any price, whatever it took, to free her from the count. He could not look at her too long, could not show any but the most carnal of interests in her. He stared at the count. 'Cards. Best two out of three. You once asked me for a chance to win her back—here it is.'

Good Lord! He couldn't be serious! Gianna watched in appalled amazement as the table was set for cards, a deck produced from the sideboard drawer. Nolan barely paid her any attention. She was going to kill him for the comment about bed. The only sign it was an act was the slightest lingering of his hand at her elbow as he encouraged her to sit at the table between him and the count. After all this, her fate was going to come down to three hands of cards, much as it had begun.

'*Vingt-et-un,*' Nolan said, shuffling the deck with elegant competence and fanning it out on the table face up for inspection. 'The highest hand without going over twenty-one wins.' He paused. 'I want the boy to deal. He's blind. He can't possibly do anything questionable to the deck.'

Gianna untied her brother and brought him to the table. Now, Giovanni would be free, it would make an escape possible.

She wanted to focus on Nolan, but she didn't dare to stare. She wished she could look at his eyes and see reassurance in them. As it was, all she could do was look at his hands as he studied the cards, one card face down to each of them. Nolan appeared so relaxed, so in control as if it were just another game, one in which her life was not at stake. Surely Nolan realised the count had no intention of letting her go. Once he had the diamonds he would have no more use for her.

The count showed a ten. Nolan showed a nine. The count did not ask for another card. Nolan took one more and grimaced. Real or feigned? she wondered. Nolan flipped over his cards—a three and a queen. Twenty-two. His hand was bust. The count grinned confidently, showing a king with the ten for twenty.

Nolan merely smiled and swept the cards aside. He slid the deck across the table to Giovanni. To the count he said, 'You're up one. One more hand and she's all yours.' He tapped his fingers on the table, irritatingly nonchalant. 'How about we throw the boy in for good measure? After all, I did go to a lot of effort getting him out and the odds are in your favour, I think. I've to win it all now and you only have to have half of the remaining hands.'

Oh, he was good. He had Giovanni free of the chair and now he had the count exactly where he apparently wanted him. Gianna watched the count's ego fairly inflate right in front of her. But it was one thing to stroke the man's ego, it was another to win. Had Nolan lost the first hand on purpose? What had he said? That losing could be beneficial? She hoped that was the case here, but she had no way of knowing.

Giovanni dealt. Nolan showed an eight. The count showed a six. The count's brow furrowed. Nolan's face was expressionless. The count called for another card and then another. He shook his head. Nolan didn't take another. Nolan turned his over. 'Eighteen.'

'Fifteen.' The count shoved the cards away with disgust, and Gianna breathed easier until she realised the next hand decided everything. Giovanni dealt carefully. Fourteen cards gone. She couldn't necessarily name them, but Nolan could. Behind those grey eyes, he was counting. Although it occurred to her as Giovanni dealt the last hand, that counting didn't ensure you won, it only gave you more control over your chances. That control grew the deeper into the deck you got. Were they deep enough to minimise another's luck?

'Last hand, everything up?' Nolan asked. The count agreed, his hand tapping nervously on the table.

Giovanni dealt. A two to the count and a king for an ominous twelve. A four and a three to Nolan. Neither hand was strong. Both of them would have to draw cards. If the count chose not to draw, all Nolan had to do was a draw five or better. Even she could see that his chances of doing so were high. Already, several small cards had been played. But the count could go bust. A face card or a ten would destroy him.

'One card,' the count asked. Giovanni slipped him a card and Gianna's heart sank. A four. Sixteen. Not very good, but enough.

'Another?' Nolan suggested.

The count thought for a moment. 'No, I stand with this.' Gianna tensed. It was up to Nolan now.

Nolan took a card, a three. The count swore. 'I should have taken it. I would have nineteen.'

'I have ten. I will take another.' Gianna prayed for a six or higher. Giovanni slid the card to Nolan and Nolan turned it over. A seven. Gianna slumped with relief. It was over.

It was not over. The count lunged for Nolan from across the table. Gianna ran for Giovanni, dragging him out of the way. She'd been foolish to think the count would have abided by the rules. But Nolan was ready for him, a right hook taking him across the jaw. She saw the count's neck snap back, saw his big body stagger. He went down, his head catching on the brick hearth of the fireplace behind them with a thud.

'Dammit!' Nolan raced to his fallen form, checking for the damage. He rocked back on his heels, his shoulders relaxing. 'He's alive. But he's going to have a hell of a headache when he wakes up.'

'Let's go, then.' She wanted to forget this place with the dead man in the corner, the count unconscious, the horrid card game. But Nolan seemed in no hurry. 'Please, let's go. He's going to be angry.' She wanted to be miles away when that happened.

Nolan grinned. 'It will be a while before he wakes up. We have time. No more getaways. For once, I just want to walk out of a place.' He stopped and patted his coat pocket. 'I have something for you.' He handed her a brown velvet box, and her heart raced. 'I believe you dropped these.'

'You found them,' she said quietly, reverently. 'Giovanni, he found he diamonds. We won't have to live in poverty.' But they would have to live on the run. Today had shown her that and it had shown her how inadequate she was for the task. It had shown her something else, too. She had a treasure worth more than diamonds standing in front of her.

'You left my bed. I didn't like it,' Nolan said tersely.

'To keep you safe,' she answered. 'You see how it will be. You saved us today, but it doesn't solve anything. The count will recover and he'll come after us. Is that marriage proposal still on the table or have you rethought it?' She wouldn't blame him.

Nolan's eyes went dark. 'It's still on the table.' He was trying to guess where this was headed. 'I'll take you to England.'

'Will you want me without the diamonds? If I am empty-handed? I think that's the only way I can come to you.' She didn't want the diamonds between them. She moved into him, a hand going to his cheek. 'I don't want you to ever doubt the reasons I am marrying you. I want to make it clear that I am marrying you not for safety or out of desperation.'

A smile played on his mouth. 'Then why?' He was going to make her say it.

'Because I love you and I will still love you even when there isn't anyone chasing us, even when our lives are, dare I say, normal?' She dropped the box on the floor with a thud. For once, Nolan looked amazed. A week ago, she would have been amazed, too. 'I've spent five years protecting that treasure. I want to spend the rest of my life protecting the one I've found with you.'

'Are you sure?'

'Let me show you.' Gianna reached up, arms about his neck, feeling his hands go about her waist as she kissed him. 'I was so afraid I wouldn't get to do that again, when they found us on the road…' Nolan's finger pressed against her lips.

'Don't think about it. You will never be in danger again. Not as long as I am with you.'

'I know.' She kissed him again.

Giovanni coughed. 'I am still here. I know I can't see, but I get the general gist of what's going on.'

Gianna moved to her brother's side, and Nolan held open the door. If the innkeeper had comments to make about what had happened in that room, he wisely kept it to himself. Outside, the horses were waiting. Nolan had been anticipating a quick departure. So had she. She'd never dreamed she'd be departing in such a leisurely fashion, or even if she'd be departing. She knew very well she could have died in that room and no one would have been the wiser.

'I do have one question,' she said as they turned out on to the road, Giovanni safely riding behind Nolan. 'Why didn't you just shoot him?'

Nolan laughed. 'You're a bloodthirsty wench at heart, Gianna.'

'Seriously, if you thought the count wouldn't abide by the rules, why play him at all?' She looked over at Nolan, surprised to see his expression sober.

'Because my gun was empty. I have no bullets to reload it with.'

'You threatened the count with an empty gun?' She tightened her grip on the reins, the enormity of what he'd done sweeping over her. 'You came after me with only your knife? The count could have killed you.' He'd been essentially unarmed after he'd taken Romano Lippi. 'Why would you do that?'

Nolan laughed. 'Do you really not know? Because everything I love was in that room, Gianna.'

'And everything I love is on the back of that horse.' She tossed him a coy smile. Tonight she was going to show him just how much, and then again tomorrow night and the night after that. She tossed her head, letting her happiness swamp her. She was just starting to realise how free she was. Love didn't make her dependent, it made her happy. It made her complete. In her stubbornness, she'd nearly missed it. The life she'd been dreaming of was beginning right now and it was off to a good start. She had the clothes on her back and Nolan Gray beside her. What else did she need? The answer was nothing.

Epilogue

❦

Verona

'Do you have the ring?' Nolan nervously asked Brennan, shifting from foot to foot in front of the church. San Lorenzo, he thought was its name. There were a lot of churches in Verona. It didn't matter. Any church would do. What mattered was the woman coming slowly down the long aisle towards him on her brother's arm in a gown of soft lavender chiffon, a bouquet of tiny white flowers in her hands.

'Yes, this is the tenth time you've asked.' Brennan was surly. 'What? Am I four? Do you think I'm going to lose it between the inn and here? I managed to get *all* of your luggage here from Venice. I can handle getting one tiny ring three streets.'

Nolan had to give Brennan credit. When he had written a week ago, Brennan had wasted no time packing up the hotel room and meeting him in Verona.

He and Gianna and Giovanni had taken rooms in

town and waited. They'd waited for a lot of things in the past week. They'd waited for Bren to arrive with their things, they'd waited for the marriage licence to be approved. The priest hadn't been entirely pleased. Nolan wasn't Catholic and Lent began tomorrow. The priest had been eager to point out no one married during Lent. But Nolan was absolutely *not* waiting forty days more to marry her. He was quick to make a large donation to the bell tower fund. It seemed to have done the trick.

The week had been a holiday of sorts, Gianna experiencing true freedom for the first time, but also there'd been worry to dispel. He knew Gianna felt it was too good to be true, that something would happen to burst the bubble of their happiness. It had taken a week for her to be convinced the count hadn't and wouldn't follow them. The count had the diamonds, but Nolan was convinced he'd got the better end of the deal.

'Our weddings seem to get smaller and smaller.' Brennan whispered as Gianna approached. There was no one here, just a witness the priest had cornered at the last minute, a young woman who worked at the inn.

'The people who matter are here.' Nolan stepped forward and took Gianna's hand from Giovanni. He supposed he, too, was worried the dream would end. When he'd set out from Dover last year, he'd not imagined his Grand Tour ending with a wife, or even ending. He'd been the one with nothing but time.

He lifted her lacy veil. 'You are beautiful,' he whispered, kissing Gianna on the cheek.

She laughed up at him, sliding a sideways glance at the priest. 'That comes later. You're upsetting the priest.'

Nolan arched an eyebrow. 'For what I paid him, he can marry us naked.' But he did sober when the priest starting speaking. He was only getting married once, he wanted to remember every moment of it. And he did; he committed to his formidable memory the way she looked in her gown, the way her dark hair caught the sunlight, the way her pearl necklace lay against her throat, the smell of her flowers, the tremor in her voice when she said her vows, the way her hand trembled when he slid the slim gold band on it, the way her body, her mouth, leaned into his as if they truly had become one. The priest pronounced them man and wife and it was over. Brennan clapped him on the back. 'Let's get some food before you go.'

Back at the inn a wedding breakfast waited for them, but Nolan was already wondering if they could just skip straight to the wedding night. He wanted his bride naked beneath him. But that would have to wait. They were leaving that day, eager to get on the road. They would spend their wedding night in an inn and several more nights after that.

'Are you sure you don't want to come?' Nolan asked Brennan after champagne toasts had been drunk. He felt bad leaving Brennan behind.

'On *your* honeymoon?' Brennan raised his auburn brows in mock incredulity. 'I should think not.'

Nolan shrugged and played a straight face. 'Why not?' he joked. 'Giovanni is coming.'

Brennan chuckled. 'No, thanks. I'm not ready to leave. Tell Haviland and Alyssandra hello from me.' Nolan and Gianna had decided to go home overland via Paris. With the threat of the count gone, they could take their time, perhaps stop in the Alps and revisit Nolan's favourite spots from the summer before. The clean alpine air would be good for Giovanni and there was no rush. They would stop in Paris before heading home.

Nolan looked at his bride. 'I never thought it would be me going home first. But I'm glad it is.' He knocked his glass against hers. 'If I was a betting man, which I am, I would have wagered on Archer or Haviland. It's a bet I am glad to lose.' Sometimes there were better things to count than cards, like his blessings. He was leaving Europe and it was a grand getaway indeed.

* * * * *

REQUEST YOUR FREE BOOKS!

♦HARLEQUIN®

ℋISTORICAL

Where love is timeless

2 FREE NOVELS PLUS 2 **FREE GIFTS!**

YES! Please send me 2 FREE Harlequin® Historical novels and my 2 FREE gifts (gifts are worth about $10). After receiving them, if I don't wish to receive any more books, I can return the shipping statement marked "cancel." If I don't cancel, I will receive 6 brand-new novels every month and be billed just $5.69 per book in the U.S. or $5.99 per book in Canada. That's a savings of at least 12% off the cover price! It's quite a bargain! Shipping and handling is just 50¢ per book in the U.S. and 75¢ per book in Canada.* I understand that accepting the 2 free books and gifts places me under no obligation to buy anything. I can always return a shipment and cancel at any time. Even if I never buy another book, the two free books and gifts are mine to keep forever.

246/349 HDN GH2Z

Name _____ (PLEASE PRINT)

Address _____ Apt. #

City _____ State/Prov. _____ Zip/Postal Code

Signature (if under 18, a parent or guardian must sign)

Mail to the **Reader Service:**
IN U.S.A.: P.O. Box 1867, Buffalo, NY 14240-1867
IN CANADA: P.O. Box 609, Fort Erie, Ontario L2A 5X3

Want to try two free books from another line?
Call 1-800-873-8635 or visit www.ReaderService.com.

* Terms and prices subject to change without notice. Prices do not include applicable taxes. Sales tax applicable in N.Y. Canadian residents will be charged applicable taxes. Offer not valid in Quebec. This offer is limited to one order per household. Not valid for current subscribers to Harlequin Historical books. All orders subject to credit approval. Credit or debit balances in a customer's account(s) may be offset by any other outstanding balance owed by or to the customer. Please allow 4 to 6 weeks for delivery. Offer available while quantities last.

Your Privacy—The Reader Service is committed to protecting your privacy. Our Privacy Policy is available online at www.ReaderService.com or upon request from the Reader Service.

We make a portion of our mailing list available to reputable third parties that offer products we believe may interest you. If you prefer that we not exchange your name with third parties, or if you wish to clarify or modify your communication preferences, please visit us at www.ReaderService.com/consumerchoice or write to us at Reader Service Preference Service, P.O. Box 9062, Buffalo, NY 14240-9062. Include your complete name and address.

HH15

She laughed and he thought he should like to hear he
do it more, her throaty humour catching. Tomorrow he
would be gone, away from Spain, away from these night
of talk and quiet closeness.

"Being happy suits you, Alejandra Fernandez y
Santo Domingo." Lucien would have liked to add that he
name suited her, too, with its soft syllables and music
Her left wrist with the sleeve of the jacket pulled back wa
dainty, a silver band he had not noticed before encircling
the thinness.

"There has been little cause for joy here, Capitán. You
said you survived as a soldier by living in the momen
and not thinking about tomorrow or yesterday?" She
waited as he nodded, the question hanging there.

"There is a certain lure to that. For a woman, you
understand."

"Lure?" Were the connotations of the word in Spanish
different from what they were in English?

"Addiction. Compulsion even. The art of throwing caution to the wind and taking what you desire because the consequences are distant."

Her dark eyes held his without any sense of embarrassment; a woman who was well aware of her worth and her attraction to the opposite sex.

Lucien felt the stirring in his groin, rushing past the sickness and the lethargy into a fully formed hard ache of want.

Was she saying what he thought she was, here on their last night together? Was she asking him to bed her?

"I will be gone in the morning." He tried for logic.

"Which is a great part of your attraction. I am practical, Capitán, and a realist. We only know each other in small ways, but…it would be enough for me. It isn't commitment I am after and I certainly do not expect promises."

"What is it you do want, then?"

She breathed out and her eyes in the moonlight were sultry.

"I want to survive, Capitán. You said you did this best by not thinking about the past or the future. I want the same. Just this moment. Only now."

Don't miss
MARRIAGE MADE IN REBELLION
by Sophia James, available February 2016 wherever
Harlequin® Historical books and ebooks are sold.

www.Harlequin.com